### Murder on the streets. But who was the target?

Sam Leroy and his team are called to a hit and run, which has left two dead and more injured.

It soon becomes a murder investigation when street cameras show the vehicle was driven deliberately onto the sidewalk.

Leroy looks at the case from two angles, one being to identify the vehicle and its driver, the other being the victims themselves, and who is most likely to be a target for murder.

One victim stands out from the rest: his personal and professional lives suggest he is the most likely target, but when Leroy and his team begin to delve into the man's background, they find themselves in the murky world of politics, deception, and secrets.

Philip Cox was born and raised in the UK seaside town of Southend on Sea, which lies forty miles east of London. After graduating from High School, he began a career in UK Banking and Financial Services, and spent the next decades working his way through the ranks, finally becoming a Branch Manager of a major UK bank.

Philip left banking after the birth of his first child to be a stay-at-home father, and it was during this time that, in between changing diapers/nappies, he began to write his first novel, 'After the Rain'.

Now having written fourteen books, he is based in Hertfordshire, some twenty miles north of London, with his wife, two daughters, and three cats.

During his spare time (what spare time there is between school runs and writing!), Philip enjoys indulging his interest in Model Railroading/Railways.

He is tall and slim, has a few grey hairs, and wishes he could get to the gym more often.

www.booksbyphilipcox.com
twitter @philipcoxbooks
www.instagram.com/philipcoxbooks
www.facebook.com/philipcoxbooks

## Also by Philip Cox

### *Detective Sam Leroy*
Last to Die
Wrong Time to Die
No Place to Die
Another Way to Die
Ready to Die

### *Jack Richardson*
The Value of Nothing
The Angel
The Coyote
The Trail

### *Standalone thrillers*
After the Rain
Dark Eyes of London
She's Not Coming Home
Should Have Looked Away

# NO REASON TO DIE

## PHILIP COX

This book is copyright material and must not be copied, reproduced, transferred, distributed, leased, licensed or publicly performed or used in any way except as specifically permitted in writing, as allowed under the terms and conditions under which it was purchased or as strictly permitted by applicable copyright law. Any unauthorized distribution or use of this text may be a direct infringement of the author's rights and those responsible may be liable in law accordingly.

Copyright © Philip Cox 2023

Philip Cox has asserted his right under the Copyright, Designs and Patents Act 1988 to be identified as the author of this work.

This book is a work of fiction. Names and characters are the product of the author's imagination and any resemblance to actual persons, living or dead, is entirely coincidental.

www.booksbyphilipcox.com

ISBN 979-8375077369

FOR ALISON, ELLA AND IONA

*Here's to the next visit*

## ACKNOWLEDGEMENTS

All I did was write the book! Other people helped in the process. I want to thank Anne Poole and Sagar Chauhan; also the Ford Motor Company, and the guys at the LAPD and LAX. In these books, most of the locations visited are genuine (I've been there!), so a big shoutout to The Laugh Factory on West Sunset; Du-pars on Third and Fairfax; La Tostaderia at the Grand Central Market; Musso and Frank and Cheetahs on Hollywood Boulevard; The Treehouse on Ord Street, and finally the many street food trucks which have provided Sam with so much sustenance (and salsa!) over the years.

Cover photograph by John Sequeira

The author is British, but the story takes place in the United States, and most of the characters are American. So: British English or American English? The narrative is in British English, and the dialogue is mostly American English. So: US readers please note that some words may be spelt differently, such as *tyres* for tires, *centre* for center, *armour* for armor.

## CHAPTER ONE

ONE MORE TIME, Rosa Delgado checked herself in the bathroom mirror.

She would never use much make-up; her swarthy skin colour made that superfluous. Just a dab of foundation, and a little lipstick. She checked her hair: jet black, tightly curled. Yes, all neat and in order.

She checked her watch. It was six twenty in the morning. Time to leave for work. Rosa finished in the bathroom, bumping into her five-year-old son in the hall.

'Are you getting ready for school, Pedro?' she asked the boy, moving out of the way so one of the other house occupants could get into the bathroom.

He was still dressed in a pair of Dr Strange pyjamas. 'Tia Isabella is making me breakfast first.'

'Okay,' said Rosa, ruffling his hair, and leading him into the kitchen, where his *Tia Isabella* was making him some eggs. Isabella was not a real aunt; just a close friend of Rosa's who lived in the same house.

'Here you are, Pedro,' Isabella called out. 'Your eggs are ready.'

Isabella spoke to Pedro in Spanish. Rosa shook her head.

'No, no, Isabella. In English. He needs to learn English here.'

Isabella shook her head and tutted, as she passed Rosa another plate of eggs. In Spanish, she said, 'You don't need to speak English to live here.' Isabella had lived in Los Angeles for nearly ten years. She could speak English to a degree. Not fluently, but she could get by. However, she stubbornly insisted on using her mother tongue as much and as often as possible.

'But I want him to do more than live here, more than just get by here,' said Rosa. 'I want him to get on.'

Isabella pulled a face and began washing the skillet. That was a sure sign the conversation was over, and it was an argument she and Rosa had had many times. Always good naturedly; deep down, Isabella knew Rosa was right. It was just so hard to let go of some things.

Six forty-five. Rosa stood and kissed Pedro on the top of his head.

'I have to go now. Be a good boy for Tia Isabella.'

'He always is,' Isabella said in Spanish. 'We're going to the market later, so I can make tamales for dinner.'

'I can call in at the store on the way home and pick some up,' Rosa replied in English.

Isabella pulled a face. She spoke in Spanish.

'He's not going to eat frozen tamales, heated up in the microwave. Not good for him.'

'All right,' said Rosa, reverting to Spanish. 'Thank you.' She embraced Isabella and kissed Pedro one more time.

'Bye, mama,' he said.

Rosa, Isabella, and Pedro lived in a large house in East Los Angeles, which they shared with two other Mexican families. For the last six months, Rosa had worked in a factory in LA's Fashion District. This necessitated a short walk down to Whittier Boulevard, where she would catch the 66 bus Downtown. She would alight at the stop at Ninth and Maple, then walk for five minutes to reach her place of work.

Rosa would work either on the sewing machines, or on the machines which would cut the cloth to the numerous templates they had, for tee shirts of different sizes and styles. She worked as a member of a group of thirty, all women, all non-indigenous. She preferred working on the cutting machine, as it was more interesting and less boring than the sewing machines. However, it did require more care, as making an error meant wasting material, the cost of which was deducted from the worker's pay.

She hoped that one day she would be moved to work on the printing machines. She would never be able to do what the two men did, and create the logos and pictures which adorned the fronts of the shirts, but she envied the three women who operated the printing machines.

Printed on the tee shirts she had sewn together would be a variety of images. Maybe a phrase, sometimes obscene; maybe a picture. Maybe just a logo or a word or two. Generally, they would be LA-centric, Southern California perhaps. Never any places such as Disneyland or any of the studios. The risk to her employer of being taken to court for copyright infringement was too great, and they would not pay the massive fee for a licence. She had heard the men talk about getting tee shirts done in preparation for the 2028 Olympic Games.

The shirts would then be moved to one of the many stores down below, intended primarily for the many tourists who scoured the one hundred blocks of the Fashion District.

Rosa had worked there since her arrival in the city with Pedro, after a long and difficult, sometimes dangerous, journey. Only now she was beginning to get settled. She hoped it would be permanent.

She got off the bus at the stop on East Twenty-third and

South San Pedro Streets, further away than normal, but she wanted to pick something up at one of the many stores for her lunch. She purchased a *carne asada* burrito, slipped the food, hot, but wrapped in foil, into her backpack, and carried on along Twenty-third. She was at the back of a group of six people, probably all headed to work.

Rosa turned as she heard a mix of sounds: a vehicle engine, some shouting…

## CHAPTER TWO

SAM LEROY SLID into his seat.

Right at the end, next to the aisle, second row. Right at the end so he could see the main players.

He adjusted his clothing, just to get more comfortable. He was wearing a grey jacket, white shirt, and dark green tie. A collar and tie were not his preferred or normal mode of dress, but he was in court. He double checked that his cell was on silent.

He leaned slightly to his right to get a better view of the prosecution table. The District Attorney's office was represented by Assistant Head Deputy Stacy Chen, a very able, early thirties, prosecutor. She had done very well in this case. Leroy had seen her on her feet a few times, and was impressed. She also smelt fragrant.

Today, she was wearing a black jacket, looking appropriately sombre and serious, over what looked to be a white collared blouse. She must have felt Leroy's gaze, as she turned round and saw him. She smiled and nodded. He returned the nod, but without the smile. Maybe a slight movement of the lips.

Leroy looked over to his right, to the defence table. There sat the defendant. Lionel Lynch was a forty-something, overweight scumbag.

He was also a serial killer.

For three months he had preyed on a specific type of victim: single women under the age of thirty. The FBI definition of a serial killer is the unlawful killing of at least two victims in separate events. Lynch had doubled that score, and was about to reach number five.

The media had dubbed him 'The Foothills Killer', or alternatively 'The 210 Killer', named after the eponymous freeway running from Sylmar to Redlands.

The police, however, referred to him as 'The 'Bater'.

After his arrest, however, Leroy and Quinn learned that his MO was slightly different to what they had figured. He would cruise the Gold Line between Highland Park and Sierra Madre Villa stations, where the Metro tracks shadow the 210 Freeway. Once he had identified a potential victim, he would follow her off the train, and to where she lived. After a few days' observation to make sure she really did live alone, and to learn her daily routine, he would break into the woman's home, and wait for her to return. Then he would overpower her, and strangle her. In the case of the first victim, there was no sign of any sexual assault; on the second, there were signs of attempted rape; the third and fourth had both been penetrated by a beer bottle. Then, Lynch would masturbate over the bodies, giving rise to the name, which was restricted to law enforcement circles. That detail was never passed to the media. Unfortunately for the investigation, and the subsequent victims, Lynch had no prior convictions, and so no database had a record of his DNA. On his arrest, he was easily linked to the victims, in spite of his denials.

Lynch was caught when Leroy and Quinn had a lucky

break. A woman in a third floor apartment off East Walnut noticed a figure walking around the side and back of the neighbouring property. She called 911, and by good fortune, a black and white was two blocks away. The two uniformed officers cuffed Lynch and held him for Leroy and Quinn to arrive.

Lynch pled the Fifth in every interrogation, but the DNA evidence was overwhelming. Early on in the case, Leroy had reluctantly, but on Lieutenant Perez's insistence, called in help from the FBI, who gave them a likely profile of the killer.

The profile fitted Lynch like a glove.

During the trial, the defence attorney tried to argue that the fact that Lynch's semen was all over the victims didn't mean that he killed them, but throughout the submissions, there was an air of desperation.

In the face of the overwhelming evidence against him, Lynch sat at the table, his folded arms resting on his belly. His grey hair was slicked back, tied in a small ponytail. He sported a matching goatee. He had a smug look on his face, which Leroy was praying would be wiped off once the jury had delivered their verdict.

Leroy looked over and Lynch turned and returned the stare. As their eyes locked, Leroy could feel Lynch's eyes burning into his. Leroy fixed his gaze onto Lynch, trying to look into this scumbag's soul. Now they were matching each other, seeing who would blink first.

It was not Leroy.

Sitting at the defence table to Lynch's left, was his attorney, another lowlife, by the name of Harvey Fisher. Leroy and Fisher had encountered each other many time before. Leroy could tolerate defence lawyers appointed for a defendant; after all, that was a legal entitlement, and Leroy accepted that was a defendant's right; but Fisher was not appointed by the court – Lynch had engaged him. For an unemployed creep, Leroy wondered how Lynch could afford somebody like Fisher, who had made millions by defending those whom Leroy had tried to remove from society.

Eventually Leroy turned away. He looked around the room. Everything was ready. All the players were in place. The defendant, the attorneys, the jury, who had just filed in. Judge Maria Abrahams was sitting at the front of the courtroom.

Leroy closed his eyes as the verdict was read out. There should have been no doubt, really; but sometimes, in the face of the evidence, something didn't quite click. Today, however, he was satisfied with the verdict.

Sentence was passed, and the court adjourned. Everybody stood to leave, and Chen walked over to Leroy.

'All over, Sam,' she said.

Leroy watched as Lynch was escorted out of the court. Fisher gathered up his papers with an *I don't give a shit, I'm being paid anyway* expression on his face. He turned back to Stacy.

'Yes, well done. Congratulations.'

'It's a verdict I'm happy with.'

'The verdict, yes,' Leroy said as he and Stacy left the courtroom.

'Meaning?' she asked.

'Thirty to life? That's what? Seven years six months for each vic.'

'It's thirty to *life,* Sam. He's shown no remorse. There's no way he's going to be outside of jail until he's well into his eighties.'

Leroy grunted.

They walked together to the wide glass doors leading out onto North Grand Avenue.

'Where are you parked?' she asked. 'The garage here?'

'No, I left my car at Police Headquarters and walked up.'

'Really?'

'Why not? Just habit. I needed to call in there for something, and it's easier to take the ten minute walk up to here, rather than negotiating a heap of traffic.'

'I've an idea,' she said, as they paused by the crossing.

'Let me buy you lunch to celebrate. It was a good verdict, and you put in a lot of work on it.'

Leroy opened his mouth, but hesitated.

'Come on, Sam; you know you want to. Edison's is only two blocks away.'

'Okay,' he nodded.

As they walked down First, Stacy asked, 'Where was your partner today? Ray...?'

'Ray Quinn. Oh, he and my other partner are working on a previous case, tying up some loose ends. It didn't need three of us to be here.'

'You have two partners?'

'Not exactly. It's just that another detective has been assigned to work with us, so we're a team of three. She's new to the detective team.'

'A boot?' Stacy asked.

'A boot?' Leroy laughed. 'No, she's not a boot. She's relatively new to being a detective. The phrase *boot* is used with uniformed rookies, straight out of boot camp at the Academy. Pamela has spent a few years on the street.'

'How do you feel about having two others to work with?'

'I'm fine with that. I'm a Detective Three, which means that I'm a supervisor. I don't get to do much supervising, only Ray, unless there's something like an officer involved shooting and I'm in the vicinity. It's good to stretch myself once in a while.'

'Here we are,' she said, as they arrived at Edison's Bar, 'and it's only one block to your car.'

'Cool,' he nodded, taking off his sunglasses as they went inside.

Just as they stepped over the threshold, his phone rang.

'Shit,' he muttered, putting the phone to his ear. He listened, nodding, then said, 'Okay. I'm on my way. Text me the location. I'll call the others.' He ended the call, and shook his head. 'Sorry,' he said to Stacy.

'Such is life,' Stacy said resignedly. 'Rain check?'

'Sure,' Leroy said as he turned to walk to his car. 'Rain

check.'

## CHAPTER THREE

LEROY EASED HIS black Taurus next to the police tape closing off East Twenty-Third Street. As he got out, a black Honda Civic parked across the street. Detective Pamela Velasquez got out and walked across to him.

Velasquez was the third member of Leroy's team. A few weeks back, Lieutenant Perez, Leroy's supervisor, felt that Leroy and Quinn could use some assistance in the Foothill Murders enquiry. There were making steady progress, but the case was becoming politically sensitive, and was maybe too much for two detectives working on their own. Velasquez's own partner had decided to retire from the Department, and she needed placing somewhere. Leroy and Quinn seemed ideal, and so, in spite of Leroy's initial protests, she joined them. Lionel Lynch was eventually arrested and charged. Off the streets. There was still no other Detective III looking for a partner, so Perez decided to keep her with Leroy and Quinn for now.

It seemed to be working well.

'Where's Ray?' Leroy asked, noticing that she was on her own.

She shook her head.

'I left a message for him to meet us here.'

'So did I,' said Leroy. 'Weren't you both working at the station together?'

'We were, but he had to go out. Left around ten. Said he had to take some personal time. Said he cleared it with you.'

Leroy frowned.

'No, he didn't clear it with me.' He took out his phone and dialled Quinn's number. Got voicemail. 'Ray, where are you? Pamela and I are already at the scene.' He ended the call. 'Come on, let's make a start.' He held up the tape to let her under, then followed her. She paused so Leroy could lead her to the centre of activity.

There were three black and whites parked at varying angles over the street, two other vehicles, one of which he recognised as the one used by the Medical Examiner's office, and his old friend ME Russell Hobson. Four uniformed officers were milling around talking to members of the public. As they walked to the corner, an ambulance slowly pulled away, its lights flashing. Two white vans from the Field Investigations Unit were also parked, and a handful of investigators were around the scene, measuring and taking photographs.

At the corner of the intersection with San Pedro Street, two bodies lay, already in black body bags. They were positioned neatly next to each other.

'Two fatalities,' Leroy muttered. He looked around and recognised Hobson sitting in one of the unmarked vehicles, in the driver's seat, sitting at an angle, working on an iPad. Leroy turned back to the bodies. He would talk to Hobson later. Velasquez was standing by the bodies. As Leroy approached, she pointed over his shoulder.

'There's Ray now.'

'About time,' said Leroy. He glanced over his shoulder,

and back to the victims. Quinn parked next to Velasquez's Civic, ducked under the tape, and hurried over to his partner.

'Sorry I'm late, Sam,' he said breathlessly.

Leroy replied, still looking at the body bags.

'Forget it. You're here now.'

Quinn stepped closer.

'Two vics?'

'Yeah,' Leroy said quietly. He paused, sniffed. Looking over at Velasquez, he said, 'You want to stay here, Pamela? We'll just be a second.' He took Quinn by the arm and led him back to the scene perimeter, next to the tape. He looked around to make sure nobody was in earshot. 'What the fuck's going on, Ray?'

Quinn looked puzzled.

'What do you mean?'

'You know what I mean. I can smell it on your breath, that's what I mean.'

Quinn looked around, his head jerking in the different directions.

'I've just had one drink, that's all.'

'One? Give me a break. Even one is too much. It's fucking unprofessional, for one thing. You're on duty, for Christ's sake. You need to leave the scene, right now.'

'I'll be okay.'

'You're fucking DUI. It's not okay. I don't know what's going on, but I don't give a shit right now. I want you out of here. Get an Uber home; I'll get one of the uniforms to drive yours back to the station.'

'What about my own car?'

'That'll have to wait. You need to get away from my crime scene, now, and hope that nobody else has noticed. Give me your keys.' He held out his hand. Quinn pulled his keys out and slammed them onto Leroy's palm. Then, saying nothing, he turned, ducked under the tape, and walked away, past his own city car.

Leroy swore under his breath, and walked back to where the victims lay. He knew Velasquez had been watching.

'Everything okay?' she asked.

Theatrically, Leroy looked back in Quinn's direction.

'I think he's sick. I noticed he was sweating; I think he has a high temperature. I told him to go home and get tested. He might need to isolate.'

'His car's still there.'

'He gave me his keys. He said he felt faint, so I said not to drive. That's a city car, so I'll ask one of the uniforms to drive it back.'

Velasquez said nothing.

Leroy crouched down to look at the bodies. He unzipped the top of the first bag. It was a man, early middle age, white. He was wearing a dark suit jacket over a white shirt, top two buttons undone. Already there was bruising to one side of the face. His hair was matted with blood. He felt inside the man's coat and pulled out a wallet. He checked inside and found his driver's licence. In a side pocket was a key ring, with a car key and door key.

'Scott Dempsey,' he read out from the licence, then handed the wallet to Velasquez, who had an evidence bag ready. Then he did the same with Dempsey's cell phone. Leroy looked up at Velasquez and back to the man. Then zipped up the bag. He then moved to the side of the other bag and did the same. This time it was a woman, around the same age as the man. From her face, Leroy guessed she was Latina. She wore a white tee shirt, with some kind of logo on the front. The side of her face was badly grazed and bruised: consistent, he felt, with high impact against the sidewalk. The back and side of her head were also badly matted with blood, a livid wound stretching from beneath her hair to her chin. Her ear was almost gone.

'Jesus,' he hissed. He took out the shoulder bag and passed it up to Velasquez, who checked through it.

'Not much in here,' she said. 'A pocket book with twenty-five dollars, a TAP Card, and a make-up bag. One cell phone. Door key, with a wooden key ring, carved in the shape of a Mexican dancer. No ID.'

Leroy took a face picture of each victim, then said, 'Okay, let's bag it all up.' Zipping up the bag, Leroy stood and said to Velasquez, 'I'm going to have a word with the ME. Can you find out who took the call, and was first on the scene?'

'You got it.' While she stepped over to the group of uniforms, Leroy joined Hobson.

Hobson looked up from his iPad when Leroy approached.

'Hey, Sam. You pulled this one, then?'

'Yeah,' Leroy sighed and leaned on the side of Hobson's car.

'Well,' Hobson said as he put down the iPad, 'you'll get the full report in time, but the gist is, both are victims of a hit and run.'

Leroy nodded.

'It was called in as a four-eighty.'

'And,' Hobson continued, 'both of the deceaseds have injuries consistent with being struck by a fast moving vehicle.'

'Can you tell what type?'

Hobson shook his head.

'Only that it was doing at least fifty, that's my guess.'

Leroy sighed loudly and pushed himself off the car. He saw Velasquez talking to two uniformed officers, a man and a woman, so walked over to them. Just as he was about to join in the conversation, he was stopped by an overalled driver from the Coroner's Office.

'Are you done with the bodies, Detective?'

Leroy stopped and looked the driver in the face.

'Yes, you can take the victims now,' he said, barely hiding his disdain.

'All righty,' the driver said, and signalled for his colleague to help load the van.

'Someone's happy in their work,' Velasquez said as Leroy got up to her.

Leroy shook his head.

'Maybe that's how they deal with what they get to see.'

## CHAPTER FOUR

LEROY TURNED TO the two uniformed officers who were talking to Velasquez. She introduced them to Leroy as Officers Culp and Johnson. Culp was a white man in his thirties, and Johnson a black woman at least ten years younger.

'They were telling me what it was like when they arrived on the scene.'

Leroy looked at Culp.

'How soon after the call did you get here?' he asked.

'About five minutes, I guess. We were only nine, ten blocks away. We arrived in the aftermath of the incident. People were screaming, wandering about, and some were lying here on the sidewalk.'

'There are two fatalities,' Leroy said, nodding his head down at the victims, 'so far. I saw an ambulance leave. How many have been hospitalised?'

Culp looked at Johnson.

'Five,' she replied. 'Three women, two men. That's right, isn't it?' She looked to Culp for confirmation; Culp nodded his agreement.

'Seriously injured?' Velasquez asked.

'One was unconscious,' Culp explained, 'but alive. The other two were conscious. They had broken limbs, I think.'

'You think?'

'He was able to stand. He said the vehicle had just winged him.'

'Could they confirm the type of vehicle?' Leroy asked.

'It was black,' Culp replied. 'From the descriptions, something like an SUV.'

Leroy looked up and down the street.

'Any sign of the vehicle?'

'No. I radioed in a BOLO, but I'm not aware of anything yet.'

'And it came in this direction? Didn't cross the line of traffic?'

'It did. It was heading west. We've taken prelim statements from the witnesses, and taken their names and addresses.'

'Really?' Leroy was impressed. 'Good work. We'll need to talk to them in more detail later.'

'I understand, Detective. I just figured while the details were fresh in their minds.'

Leroy nodded.

'I understand. These witnesses – how many, and were they on foot or driving?'

Culp checked his notes.

'There were eleven pedestrians across the street, and three driving this side. Nobody heading the opposite direction on account of the stop light on San Pedro.'

'So, fourteen witnesses in total, plus those that were taken to hospital. Which ER were they taken to, do you know?'

Johnson replied, 'The ER at California Hospital, down on South Grand.'

'Yeah, I know the place.' Leroy looked up and down

the street again, pointing as he spoke. There are cameras there, there, and there, and there. We should get a view of the incident from at least one of them.' He asked Culp, 'Did any of the witnesses get anything on their cell phones?'

'Sorry, Detective, I didn't think to ask that.'

'Don't worry. We'll pick that up when we speak to them.'

'Let's hope it doesn't go on social media before we get to see it,' Velasquez said. 'But, I'm guessing it all happened so fast, nobody would have had time to react.'

Leroy looked at her and nodded.

'Once we've viewed what's on there, we should have a handle on the vehicle, where it headed, and where it came from. We might even get a tag number.'

'Always the optimist,' Velasquez said humourlessly.

'There's always the possibility,' Leroy added, 'that the vehicle is lying crashed somewhere, if the driver was DUI – drink or drugs. Or they may have dumped it.'

'They could have gotten ill,' Johnson suggested, 'and lost control temporarily.'

'Then why didn't they stop?' Leroy asked her. 'No, there are plenty of possible explanations, but they still left the scene. It's still a hit and run.' He paused and waved as Hobson drove away, then turned to Velasquez. 'Let's make a start on the victims' possessions, and identifying them.'

'We know the man is Scott Dempsey.'

'We do. We also need to identify the second.'

'The Oaxaca lady?' Culp asked. He pronounced Oaxaca *wah-hah-ka*.

'The what?' Leroy asked.

'The Oaxaca lady,' Culp repeated. 'On her tee shirt.'

'Oaxaca is a town in Mexico,' Velasquez explained.

'I know that,' said Leroy. He paused a second, then said to Culp and Johnson, 'Thanks for all you've done, guys. We'll take it from here. Can you send us the witness statements, names and addresses?'

'You got it, Detective.'

'The Oaxaca lady,' Leroy muttered as Culp and Johnson returned to their car. 'Pamela, we need to ID her asap. At her age, she probably has family, kids. Come on, let's finish up here and head back to the station.'

Velasquez double checked the evidence bag: Scott Dempsey's wallet and cell phone, and the Oaxaca lady's pocket book and phone, while Leroy walked over to the street corner where the remaining two from the Field Investigations Unit were working.

'We're almost done here,' the lead technician said. 'We're headed back to the labs and get everything processed and uploaded.'

'We're almost through here also. When do you expect to get everything on the file?'

'By late morning tomorrow, I expect.' He must have been able to read the expression on Leroy's face, so added, 'That's the quickest I can manage.'

Leroy nodded. 'Lunchtime tomorrow is good. We have other evidence to sift through. Like identifying one of the victims.'

He left the technician to finish up and walked back to where Velasquez was waiting.

'They're getting ready to open up the street,' she said.

'Yeah, looks like we're all done here. Let's get back to the station.'

They both ducked under the tape and headed for their respective cars. As she was opening hers, Velasquez asked, 'When are we likely to see Ray?'

'Not before too long, I hope.'

'I guess it depends on how sick he is.'

Leroy was not sure how to take this, not sure exactly what she meant. He recalled he had told her Ray was sick, he implied covid; but could not be sure if she was being genuine, or if she knew what he had told her was bull, and was being sarcastic, or fishing. He decided to opt for the former.

'Yeah, I guess it does. Once we've done for the day,

I'll check in on him before I head home.'

She nodded, enigmatically.

'Did you guys get to tie everything up, by the way?' Leroy asked, attempting to change the subject.

'Pretty much. Just a couple more i's and t's to dot and cross.'

'Fine,' said Leroy. 'I'll see you back there. I want to get that lady identified as soon as we can; we know about Scott Dempsey. We're gonna have some next of kins to call on.'

## CHAPTER FIVE

LEROY AND VELASQUEZ arrived back at the station in the middle of the changeover between the day and night shifts. One of the departing detectives called out to Leroy, 'Where's Quinn? You got him working overtime again?'

'He's still out in the field,' Leroy called back, then muttering, 'Worse than a crowd of schoolkids.'

He sat down at his desk, then pushed his wheeled chair over to where Velasquez was sitting.

'First of all, we have ID'd Scott Dempsey, and gotten his address. Before we call on his next of kin, can you check to see if we have anything on him. You know, just to cover all bases. Where does he live?'

She checked.

'North Hollywood.'

'I'll go through the Jane Doe's stuff. We had cash, a TAP Card, a door key with a Mexican fob - that could figure: she looks Hispanic – but no identification.'

'She could be an illegal. That would explain the lack of identification. And the use of cash. How could she get a bank card?'

Leroy picked up the woman's phone. It was locked. He tried six stars to unlock. No luck. Then six zeroes. No luck. Then 123456. Still no luck.

'What's Spanish for password?' he asked.

Velasquez thought a second, then, '*Contraseña.*'

Leroy tried the first six letters, then the last, then the phone locked up: try *again in 15 minutes.*

'Really?' Velasquez asked.

'Worth a try.' He picked up the TAP Card. On the reverse there was a serial number. 'If I was to reach out to the MTA, do you think they could tell me who bought this card?'

'Not at this time of the day. In any case, I doubt it. You buy those at a vending machine. Put in your bank card, or your twenty bucks and get your TAP Card for a week. She's going to have used cash.'

Leroy slumped onto his own chair and sighed.

'We may have to wait till she's reported missing. I'll go talk to the Watch Commander. Let's focus on Dempsey for now.' He walked round to the Night Watch Commander's office near the station entrance. He asked to be called any time, and stressed *any* time, a missing person report came in matching the Jane Doe's description. He sent the Watch Commander the picture of the woman, then returned to Velasquez's desk. 'Anything on Dempsey?' he asked.

She leaned back in her chair.

'All I can get on him is a citation three years ago for speeding. One-fifty up the one ten freeway.'

'Jesus. What was he driving? A Maserati?'

She checked.

'An Alpine 110, it says here.'

'Then why was he walking along a street in the middle of the Fashion District?' He paused a second. 'Check if it's been ticketed in the last twenty-four hours. If he parked somewhere nearby, maybe his ticket has expired, as he obviously won't be going back to collect it.'

She checked.

'Nothing, but any validation might not have expired yet.'

'True: that might come through later, unless the car gets itself stolen.' He took a deep breath. 'It's getting late. Let's head over to Dempsey's place, and speak to the next of kin. That will get that ball rolling. Then we can call it a night; pick things up in the morning with trying to ID the Jane Doe.'

'Obviously just the two of us,' Velasquez said as she shut down her workstation.

'Excuse me?'

'I mean if Ray's isolating.'

'Right. I'll call him on my way home. Once we've been to Dempsey's place, I'll drop you back here.'

'Any chance I could take my own car?' she asked as they walked through the station to the parking lot. 'By the time we get back here, it'll be late and I have plans this evening.'

'What time are your plans?'

'Eight, eight thirty.'

'That doesn't leave us much time. Sure; take yours. I'll see you outside Dempsey's. You got the address?'


Scott Dempsey lived in an expensive looking condo on Fulcher Avenue, just off Burbank Boulevard. The journey took Leroy and Velasquez seventy-five minutes in the evening's traffic. They both took the 405 north, turning right off the freeway at the Sepulveda Basin Reserve. Velasquez parked nose to nose with Leroy's.

The building was small, only three floors, but looked exclusive, meaning expensive. At the front, either side of the path leading to the wide glass doors, was an immaculately maintained lawn.

Dempsey's condo was 2B. Leroy rang the buzzer and waited. No answer. He rang again. After a few seconds, he tried 2A. Again no answer. He rang 2C. A man's voice came out of the grill. It sounded impatient.

'Yes?'

Leroy held his badge up to the camera lens and made the introductions.

'Can we come inside and ask you a few questions?'

'What about?'

'We'll explain inside. Nothing to worry about; just routine.'

There was a click as the glass doors unlocked. Leroy and Velasquez stepped inside.

'The stairs will be quicker,' Leroy said, as he began to climb, two steps at a time. As soon as they reached the second floor, they came to door 2A, a few yards later, 2B. Leroy knocked on 2B. Nothing. He knocked again. Nothing. Leroy put his ear to the door. Nothing. At that point, door 2C opened and a man peered out. He wore a plain white tee shirt and black knee-length shorts, and was barefoot. He was short, balding, and looked around fifty. He wore glasses.

'I am 2C,' he snapped. 'You have the wrong door.'

They walked over to 2C and Leroy made the introductions again. As he let them into his apartment, he said, 'Please be quick. I'm supposed to be working.'

It was a spacious, open plan place. Adjacent to the wide window with a view of the Hollywood Hills was a large, metal and glass desk. Two yellow legal pads lay opened next to a laptop, which was also open.

'Working, sir?' Leroy asked.

'Yes,' the man replied brusquely. 'I'm a screenwriter, and I have a deadline to meet.'

'I won't keep you long. We're calling about your neighbour in 2B.'

'What of him?' As he spoke, he leaned on the glass desktop.

'How well did you know him?'

'Did? Past tense?'

'Do, I mean.'

'I see him now and again. Don't know him that well. What's this all about?'

Velasquez looked to Leroy, who nodded.

'Mr Dempsey,' she explained, 'was involved in a hit and run earlier.'

The screenwriter laughed.

'I can't say I'm surprised. I knew that would happen one day, with that fancy piece of shit he drives. Sound like a fucking airplane, too, especially at the speed he drives. So you want to know where he is?'

'Sir, you misunderstand. Scott Dempsey was the victim.'

'Fuck. Is he dead?'

'I'm afraid so.'

The man shrugged.

'Don't be afraid on my account.'

'Did he live with anyone?'

'No, but he had plenty of girlfriends.'

'Plural?' asked Velasquez.

He nodded.

'In and out, if you excuse the pun. At least three times a week.'

'Nobody regular?'

'I never saw. Just heard. This may be a fancy condo, but the walls ain't that thick.'

'No family?'

'Told you, don't know.'

'What did he do?' Velasquez asked.

He shrugged.

'No idea. Must have been a good job, to afford the rent on here.'

'You obviously do,' said Leroy.

'Not quite what it seems. I did a screenplay for Paramount a few years back. The picture did well. Still living off that.'

'What was it?' asked Velasquez.

'*The Chanting*. Heard of it? A horror pic.'

Velasquez clicked her fingers.

'You're Elliott Bronski.'

Bronski held up both palms.

'Guilty as charged.'

'What are you working on now?' She nodded over to his laptop.

'Oh, some piece of shit for Netflix. That's why I have the deadline.'

'What about the occupants of 2A?' Leroy asked. 'Would they know him?'

'2A's been empty since… since last year. The woman there OD'd.'

'And 2D?'

'You'll need to ask them.'

'Them?'

'A retired couple. Don't see much of them either. They have a place in Palm Springs. Never seem to be here.'

Leroy slowly nodded his head.

'Okay. Thanks for your time, sir. I appreciate it. We'll let you get on with your deadline. Here's my card: if anything about Mr Dempsey comes to mind, or if anybody else tries to call there, you want to give me a call?'

Bronski glanced at the card and nodded.

'Sure thing.'

Velasquez asked, 'You don't happen to have a key to Mr Dempsey's place?'

'No.'

'Would the couple in 2D?' Leroy asked.

'I doubt it.'

On the way out, Leroy said, 'I expect we, or someone from the LAPD, will be back, to effect an entry to the apartment, in the next few days.'

Bronski shrugged.

'Effect away.'

As Bronski was about to close the door, Velasquez called out, 'Good luck with the Netflix project, sir.'

Leroy and Velasquez walked back down the stairs.

Once they were outside, Leroy said, 'You'd heard of him, then?'

'Yeah, I like that kind of movie. I remembered the name. You get to talk to many people in the business?'

'The entertainment business?'

'Yeah.'

'Now and again. Some names I recognise, some I don't. I usually say I don't recognise the name, even if I do.'

'Does that piss them off?'

'Mostly. I figure they shouldn't be so narcissistic. After all, they never heard of me.'

They had reached their cars.

'See you in the morning,' she said.

'Enjoy your evening. I'm going to check in with Ray once I'm on the road. See if he's ready to come back to work, or if he's still toxic.'

'If he tested positive, he has to be off for five days.'

'Yeah. Let's hope he's not.'

They both pulled away. Velasquez followed Leroy's car down to as far as Lankershim Boulevard. Then they lost each other in the evening traffic.

## CHAPTER SIX

LEROY HEADED DIRECTLY to Quinn's house. It would not be too late when he got there; he and his wife Holly would not be in bed yet.

It was almost nine thirty when he knocked on the Quinns' door. After a few moments, Holly answered. She looked pale, although that could be explained by the absence of make-up. She was wearing a black vest, and blue jeans. Her hair was tied in a ponytail.

'Ray isn't here. If you'd called before, you'd know.'

'He's gone out?'

Holly sighed, impatiently.

'He's not living here anymore. As of six months ago. Six months, one week, two days to be exact.'

Taken aback, Leroy said, 'Shit, I had no idea.'

'But you can't be surprised, can you, Sam? You knew all along.'

Holly was referring to an incident a while back when

he came across Holly leaving a motel room with another man.

'Where is he, then?' Leroy asked.

'He's taken an apartment in Hollywood. On Schrader. You want the full address?'

'I'd better take it.'

She gave him the address. As he headed back to his car, he turned back.

'For what it's worth, Holly, I'm sorry.'

'Sure, Sam. Whatever,' she said as she closed the door.

He sat in the car for a few seconds before pulling away. He hadn't seen that coming – or had he? Looking back, there were signs. And if Ray moved out six months or so ago, that could explain a few things. Why didn't he say something?

He headed off to Hollywood, and by ten had pulled up outside a small apartment building, on Schrader and Selma Avenues, a few blocks north of Hollywood Boulevard.

Leroy found the apartment, and knocked. There was a light on, but no answer. He knocked again, this time calling out, 'Ray?'

The door eventually opened: it was Quinn, dressed as he had been earlier, looking tired and unshaven.

'Jesus, Ray. You look like shit. You want to let me in?'

Saying nothing, Quinn stepped aside, letting Leroy in.

'You spoke to Holly, then?' Quinn said as Leroy stepped inside the small apartment.

'I did.'

'You want a beer?' Quinn asked.

'Sure.'

Quinn stepped behind the kitchen counter and took two cans of Dos Equis. He pulled one open and gave Leroy the other. Leroy sat down, looking quizzically at the label on the can.

'What?' Quinn asked.

'Nothing. So, tell me about what's happened.'

'Simple. I've moved out.'

'Temporarily or permanent?'

'I think permanent. We'd not been getting along these past few months. I'm sure that motherfucker of a father of hers had been goading her on.' He paused to take a mouthful of beer. 'She used to say that I seemed married more to the LAPD than to her.'

'She'd always said that. I told you she needs to grow up, to get real. You marry a cop, that's the way it is.'

'And I think she's been seeing someone else.'

Leroy took another sip, giving himself time to think. He had never told Quinn about seeing his wife at the motel, always taking the view that it was something the two of them needed to deal with. He still had that view.

'Really? What makes you say that?' he asked, innocently.

Quinn shrugged. 'Just a vibe. No evidence. Just a feeling. Her cell would ping at odd times; she would be cagey about calls or messages; trips to the stores and coming back with nothing.'

Leroy nodded his head slowly.

'Look, Ray, I'll be honest with you. I'm really sorry you guys have split, but you need to get your shit together. Take some leave if you feel you need to, but you can't turn up for work, at a crime scene, smelling of booze like you did today, even if you aren't technically DUI. It's unprofessional for one thing; what if Perez or the captain had been there? Or what if one of the uniforms had smelt you and reported it to their supervisor? You'd better hope they didn't. Velasquez has been asking questions.'

'What did you tell her?'

'I told her you were sweating and I thought you might have a temperature. I said I told you to go home and get a covid test. But I'm not sure she's convinced; I'm sure she can smell bullshit.'

'I'll be back tomorrow.'

Leroy stood up.

'Make sure you are. Clean and sober. And negative of course, if anyone asks. Shit, Ray, why didn't you say something? This happens all the time, officers breaking up.'

'I don't know,' Quinn said, looking at the floor and shuffling his feet. He looked up at Leroy. 'Would you have?'

'Probably not,' Leroy conceded. 'You'll need to get a cab to the station in the morning.'

'I will. What happened at the scene, by the way?'

'It was a hit and run. Several injured and taken to California. Two dead at the scene. We've ID'd one of them: Velasquez and I went to his place in North Hollywood, but it looks like he was single, no family. Just a line of girlfriends. The other, a woman, we've not been able to ID yet. Velasquez thinks she might be an illegal.'

'That could explain the lack of ID. You know, not long over the border. What about a DNA check? We might have her on record.'

'That'll happen, but it takes time. In the meantime, I think we're going to have to wait until if and when she's reported missing.'

'It might be an if. Somebody might be afraid of putting themselves in the INS spotlight.'

'You got it in one. I'm leaving now. You get some sleep, then a shower and shave, then a cab to work.'

'I will.' Quinn walked Leroy to the door. 'Sam, are we okay?'

Leroy either didn't hear or chose not to answer and walked back to his car. He made a diversion to Butler and Iowa Streets, to the Station, to drop off the city car and pick up his own. The diversion probably added thirty minutes to his journey, but he wanted to go home in his own car. On this evening, especially. He noticed Quinn's own car still in the employee parking lot, and hoped not too many people saw it.

He parked at the back of his own canal-facing home just before midnight. Once indoors, he flopped onto the couch, and looked down at the file resting on the table in front of the couch. On the front of the brown manilla folder, he had written *Jordan Washington*. That was the name of a young boy who had disappeared on the way home from school a few years back. Somebody had been arrested and convicted for his murder, mainly on the strength of his guilt of some similar killings, but Jordan's body was never found. Just before he died in prison, the killer told Jasmine, the boy's mother, that he did not kill her son. At the time of the investigation, Leroy had given her his number, and said, 'Anything I can do, just call.' Years later, Jasmine took Leroy up on his offer to find out what had really happened to her son. Since then, in his spare time, Leroy had been looking at the case again, with little success. He was planning on spending an hour or two on it tonight, but it was not to be.

He was so tired. He stretched out on the couch, bunched up a cushion, and fell asleep.

He was woken by the sound of his phone ringing. Sleepily he picked the phone up from the floor. It was the station calling, the direct line for the Watch Commander. Leroy answered sleepily.

'Sam? Did I wake you up? Sorry, dumb question, but you wanted to know about any missing person report that came in matching your 20001 victim.'

Leroy was beginning to come to.

'Yeah, I just wasn't expecting it at 2:25 in the AM.'

'You did ask, buddy, but I think we've found your Jane Doe.'

## CHAPTER SEVEN

THE MISSING PERSON reported was named as Rosa Delgado. The report had come from a relative with whom she lived, in East Los Angeles. The description, physical and clothing, fitted.

Leroy arrived at the station on Butler and Iowa at seven forty-five, fifteen minutes before the day shift was due to begin. Velasquez was already at her desk. She was trawling through information on her screen. There was no sign of Quinn. She looked up as he arrived.

'Morning.'

'Hey,' Leroy replied. 'What are you checking?'

'I'm just looking through 503s in the last forty-eight hours. You know, matching the one yesterday.'

'Large and black?'

'That's what I'm homing in on. Something like an SUV.'

Leroy nodded.

'Anything yet?'

'Not around the Downtown area.'

'You want a coffee?' he asked.

'Nah, I'm good.' There was an empty mug on her desk. God knows what time she had gotten in that morning. When he returned to his desk, he said, 'I think we have our Jane Doe.'

Velasquez stopped trawling and looked up.

'We do?'

Leroy held out a sheet of paper. It was a copy of the missing persons report.

'I'd asked the night shift to let me know if there were any persons matching her description reported missing last night.'

'And there was?'

'One. A lady by the name of Rosa Delgado. She's from East LA, off Whittier Boulevard.'

'Who reported her missing?'

'A family member. Said she never came home from work last night. Not answering her cell.'

'So this relative doesn't know?'

'That's for us. That should be our first call today.'

'Fine,' she said. Looking around, she added, 'What about Ray? Is he coming in?'

Leroy checked his watch. Seven fifty-five.

'I'm expecting him.'

'He's not tested positive, then?'

'No. I spoke to him last night, and he's negative. He said he'd be in this morning. Once he's here, we'll head over to East LA.'

Velasquez continued with her trawling, and Leroy walked round to the office of his supervisor, Lieutenant Roman Perez, and updated him on the case.

Perez was working on a spreadsheet, probably containing overtime costs. He listened while Leroy was updating him, then looked up.

'Two deceaseds?'

'That's right. Four were hospitalised. Some walking

wounded. We're going to talk to them today.'

'The deceaseds, have you identified them?'

'One had ID on him. We went over to his home yesterday. A neighbour told us he was single with no dependants, but I plan to go through his apartment later.'

'You'll need someone to formally identify him. What about the other?'

'I know that. That's why I want to go through his place. Even if he does have no actual next of kin, there will be people he works with, somebody there who could identify him.'

'There must be a relative somewhere; not necessarily here. Keep me up to date, Sam,' he added, returning to his spreadsheet.

Leroy returned to his desk.

'It's eight twenty,' he said to Velasquez. 'Come on; we can't wait for Ray all morning.'

She put on her jacket and followed Leroy out of the detective suite and to the door leading to the parking lot. Just as they got outside, they saw Quinn running across the lot, from the street entrance. A cab was pulling away on Butler.

'Why a cab?' Velasquez asked Leroy.

'His own car's still here, remember?' Leroy called back, as he strode to his city ride.

Breathlessly, Quinn said, 'Sorry I'm late. The cab was late.'

'We need to get going,' Leroy said as he put on his sunglasses and slipped into the driver's seat. 'Pamela will fill you in on the way.'

Quinn began to walk around the car to get into the front passenger seat; however, Velasquez had beaten him to it, and he slipped into the back, his face like thunder.

'How are you feeling this morning?' she asked as Leroy eased into the traffic.

'I'm good, thanks,' Quinn retorted. 'You want to give me an update on the case?'

Leroy took the 10 Freeway as far as Boyle Heights,

where he merged onto the 60. A mile later he was on the exit ramp onto Whittier Boulevard, which he followed into East Los Angeles, eventually turning left onto Sadler, where Rosa Delgado's home was on the 700 block. On the way, Velasquez updated Quinn on the previous day's events, Leroy occasionally interjecting. Once she was done updating, Velasquez pulled out the Mobile Data Terminal and carried out a Social Security check on Rosa Delgado.

'What are you looking for?' Leroy asked, still looking ahead.

'Just checking Social Security records for her.'

'And?'

'Nothing. Zip. Nada.'

'So she doesn't officially exist?' Quinn asked.

'As I thought,' she said, pushing the terminal back into its slot. 'She was here illegally.'

'But she was still a victim,' Leroy said. 'Not a statistic. Not The Oaxaca Woman, as some guys are calling her.'

'The Oaxaca Woman?' Quinn asked from the back.

'She was wearing a tee shirt, which has a logo for the Oaxaca soccer club,' she explained. 'Hence the Oaxaca Woman.'

'But we have a name now,' Leroy said, ending the conversation. Now they were driving along Whittier Boulevard. Almost there.

A few minutes later, Leroy had pulled up across the road from where Rosa Delgado lived. It was a large, Spanish-style house. Leroy knocked on the door, and after a few seconds a woman opened the door. She was short - five six, Leroy guessed – in her seventies and with grey hair tied back in a bun.

'Ms Gallardo?' Leroy asked, holding out his badge. 'Isabella Gallardo? Detective Leroy, LAPD, and my colleagues Detective Quinn and Detective Velasquez.'

'You've come about Rosa?' she asked. 'Have you found her yet?'

'May we come inside?' Leroy asked quietly.

She nodded and held the door open. They waited a

second before she led them into the large kitchen.

'I'm sorry about the mess,' she muttered. 'I was just tidying.'

'Your kitchen is fine, ma'am,' said Leroy. 'You called last night about Rosa Delgado. Is she a family member?'

The woman shook her head.

'Not by blood, but we have been friends for ten years now. Just like family. Have you found her? Is that why you're here?'

'She lives here with you?'

'Yes. I moved here from Oaxaca, Mexico, seven years ago, and she and her son followed me. They both live here with me. Where is Rosa? You have found her?'

Leroy showed Isabella the photograph he had taken at the scene.

'Ma'am, is this Rosa?'

She put her hands to her mouth.

'Oh my God, yes. It's Rosa. What's happened to her?'

Leroy took the picture away.

'I'm sorry to tell you she was involved in a traffic accident yesterday. She had no identification on her; you reached out to us before we could check anything further to identify her.'

'She... she never carried ID with her. Oh my God,' she repeated, putting her hands to her mouth again. 'What about Pedro?'

'Pedro?' asked Velasquez.

'Rosa's son. He's only five years old.'

Not wanting to get frozen out, Quinn asked, 'Is he here?'

'No, no. He's at school. I shall have to go get him, tell him. Oh God, what shall I say?'

'Where is Pedro's father?' asked Velasquez. 'Does he have any siblings? Any brothers or sisters?'

Isabella shook her head.

'He's somewhere, back in Mexico, I suppose. I don't know where. He didn't come from Oaxaca. Rosa hasn't seen him in years. And no: Pedro is an only child.'

'The accident happened,' Leroy explained, 'Downtown, on the edges of the Fashion District. Would you know what Rosa was doing there?'

'She had a job there. She worked in a factory making tee shirts. She used to walk from here down to the Boulevard and catch the 66 bus there.'

Quinn said, 'So, she must have just gotten off the bus when the accident took place.'

'And was walking the last couple of blocks to where she worked,' Velasquez added.

Leroy frowned: he could see a pissing contest beginning. He turned to Isabella, but before he could say anything, she asked him, 'Where exactly did the accident take place?'

'Downtown, on Twenty-third Street, at the intersection with' - Leroy paused a second - 'San Pedro Street.'

Isabella closed her eyes and moved her index finger about as if trying to draw a map in her mind.

'Yes, that is near where she works. Oh, my God – where she worked.'

'Ma'am,' Leroy said, 'we will need somebody to come and formally identify Rosa's body. Is there somebody else we could ask?'

'No,' Isabella said, 'there is only me. I will do it.'

Leroy suggested, 'If Rosa's son is at school, are you able to come with us now? We only have a ten, fifteen, minute journey there. You could be back here long before he's due home from school.'

She agreed to go with them now. The morgue was situated at the Coroner's Office on North Mission Road, a ten minute drive from the house. One of the examiners, Leroy's old friend Russell Hobson, chatted with Leroy while Velasquez took Isabella in to make the identification. Quinn sat alone in the corridor checking his phone.

'What about the guy who came in with her?' Hobson asked.

'We know who he is,' Leroy said, 'but he seems to be

single, no family. Certainly not here, according to a neighbour. We're going to go through his stuff later to try to find somebody. No idea where he works, either.'

'Could the neighbour make the identification?'

Leroy shook his head.

'He... er, declined the invitation.'

Hobson nodded.

'By the way,' he said, 'I guess you guys haven't heard yet, but the hospital called. There's a third on its way in.'

'Oh shit, no. What's the name?'

'I don't have that here, but he was a guy in his seventies.'

'I do remember reading about an old guy on the list of injured,' Leroy said. 'So now it's three.'

'Any luck on the vehicle?'

'Nothing yet. Nothing's been reported stolen yet. I'll get one of them to check the CCTV footage, assuming there is any. Maybe we'll get lucky and get a licence plate.'

'What's up with him?' Hobson asked quietly, pointing his head in Quinn's direction.

Leroy moved closer to Hobson and muttered, 'Marital problems. But you didn't get that from me.'

Hobson straightened up and nodded.

'The vic in there: the Oaxaca woman -'

'Don't you start, Russ. Everyone's calling her that. Her name's Rosa Delgado.'

'Illegal?'

'Probably, but I don't give a shit.'

'You going to call the INS?'

'Nothing to do with me. All I'm interested in is finding out who killed her.'

'Wasn't it an accident?'

'The car didn't stop, Russ.'

'Sam, it's me you're talking to. I get you. She got kids?'

'One. A five year old called Pedro. Fucking irony that: she has a son called Pedro, and she is killed on San Pedro

Street.'

'Shit. Life really sucks sometimes.'

They ended their conversation as Velasquez appeared with Isabella, who was blowing her nose. Velasquez nodded sadly.

'Thank you for coming,' Leroy said softly. 'I know it must have been very hard for you. We'll take you back home now.'

'Thank you, Detective,' Isabella said, looking up at Leroy, 'but if you don't mind, I think I'd rather get a taxi home.'

Leroy glanced at the other two.

'I just want to be on my own for a while. Do you understand?'

Leroy nodded. 'I understand.'

'Before Pedro comes home. What will happen about Pedro? Will he be able to stay with me?'

Leroy said, 'We have to reach out to Child Support Services. They will be in touch, but as you're Pedro's nearest relative here…'

Isabella nodded. She turned to Velasquez.

'Would you mind calling a taxicab for me?'

'Surely,' Velasquez smiled and tabbed down her phone for a number. After a few minutes, they walked Isabella down to the street for her cab. Leroy gave the driver a twenty for the fare.

'Again, I'm so sorry for your loss,' Leroy said as she got into the cab. The others expressed the same sentiments, and Velasquez gave her a business card.

'This is a number for a unit who support people who have been bereaved,' she said. 'Just call that number if you need to talk to anybody.'

Isabella thanked her for the card and the taxi set off down Mission Street.

'Nice lady,' Quinn said as the cab disappeared from view.

'What about the kid?' Quinn asked.

'I'll have to do what I said,' Leroy replied, 'but it's not

a priority. He's with the best person. And,' he added, facing them both, 'our vic has a name: Rosa Delgado. Not the Oaxaca Woman. And regardless of her status, it's our job to find who did it, just as we would if it was anybody else.'

They nodded.

'And,' he added, 'we'll get there without a pissing contest. Am I clear?'

Quinn and Velasquez were both taken aback, but agreed.

'We'll head back to the station now,' Leroy said. 'Pamela, I want you to stay there and do three things. One, get a hold of that video footage. We need to see exactly what vehicle it was. If a tag's visible, we're there. Then, check through the statements of the witnesses, the ones the patrolmen got, just so that we have a full picture of what happened. And finish off looking at the stolen vehicle reports.'

'You got it, Sam,' she said.

'And Ray, once we've dropped Pamela off, we'll head over to the hospital to talk to the remaining injured – I forgot to tell you: Russ said that one of the injured had died in hospital.'

'Shit,' Quinn and Velasquez said in unison.

'Yeah, so we'll have one more next of kin to contact, one more body to ID. We'll also get into Scott Dempsey's apartment and get a handle on him. He must have family or friends or somebody who knows him.'

They were back in the car by now, all saying nothing as he drove back to the station.

## CHAPTER EIGHT

QUINN DROVE TO the hospital. On the way there, Leroy called ahead and arranged an appointment with Dr Mark Lindley, the Head of ER. Lindley said he would be available to see them, but would only have fifteen minutes or so. Leroy agreed, but interpreted the doctor's response as I don't really *want* to see the police, but conceded that it was his civic duty to do so.

On the way, Leroy wondered if Quinn would bring up yesterday's events or elaborate on his personal situation. He hoped he wouldn't; now was neither the time nor place and that was something Quinn would have to deal with himself. As Leroy had done himself, many times. Much to Leroy's relief, Quinn didn't say anything.

On arrival at the hospital, they only had to wait a few minutes for Dr Lindley. Leroy gave him an overview of why they were there, and sought his consent to speak to the remaining patients. Lindley asked if they were aware that one of the patients had died since being admitted the day before; Leroy confirmed they were. The patient who had died was Kenneth Fong, seventy-seven years of age, who had an address in Mei Ling Way, in Chinatown. Not a million miles from where they were.

To save time, Quinn spoke to two of the injured, one of whom was due to be discharged later that day, and Leroy to the third, plus to the senior nurse about Kenneth Fong. They were done within the hour, and conferred over a coffee from the Starbucks stand situated in the hospital entrance. The response from all of the interviews was that they saw very little; it was all over in a second or two. They were walking along Twenty-third Street, they heard noise: shouting, screaming, a vehicle; then they felt impact. They were the lucky ones. The nurse in charge told Leroy that Fong had both legs broken, two fractured ribs and a skull fracture, and had died of these injuries. All three of those spoken to recalled seeing Kenneth Fong and Rosa Delgado lying on the sidewalk.

'We'll go see Kenneth Fong's next of kin,' Leroy said, as he finished the last of his latte. 'His home isn't far from here. The hospital has already called the home to tell them, so we're just paying our respects and getting what information about Kenneth Fong we can. We might need to explain that we are involved as fleeing a hit and run is a felony, and we're talking manslaughter at least.'

'What about language?' Quinn asked.

'There is a wife, around the same age, apparently. She doesn't speak English, but their daughter is at the house. She does.'

It took only fifteen minutes to get to Kenneth Fong's house. The door was opened by an attractive Chinese woman, tall for an Asian, shoulder length black hair. When Leroy had introduced himself and Quinn, she gave her name as Sandra Fong, and let them inside. Her mother, a tiny, wizened, white-haired woman sat on a chair in the corner of the room, staring into space. She didn't acknowledge them.

'I'm very sorry for your loss, Ms Fong,' Leroy said to begin with.

'Thank you. The hospital told us that he had been hit by a car on Twenty-third Street. We went to see him last night, but he was unconscious. They called again to say he had died, but I'm not quite clear on exactly what happened.'

'Your father,' Leroy explained, 'and a number of other people were walking along Twenty-third when a vehicle, as yet unidentified, mounted the sidewalk and struck your father and several others.'

'A vehicle? What vehicle? Have you…?'

'As we speak, one of my colleagues is looking through the CCTV of the area to pick out the vehicle. It didn't stop, and hadn't been reported stolen.'

'So, when you view the CCTV, you can identify the vehicle? And the driver?'

'Yes, basically. The owner, not necessarily the driver, but it's a starting point. How is your mother?'

Sandra looked back at the old lady.

'She doesn't speak any English. I've told her what happened and she's kind of shut down. That's what she does; my brother was murdered a few years back, and she was like this for weeks. She'll eventually come out of it. What happens about my father's body, his personal effects? They're still at the hospital?'

'The hospital will be in touch. We won't need your father's body ourselves; all the relevant examinations have been carried out, so the hospital's free to release your father back to you.'

She nodded, glancing over to her mother.

'That's good.'

'We won't intrude any longer,' Leroy said. 'If we do need to speak with you again, we'll reach out to you; otherwise, this is my number if you need to know anything yourselves.'

'The police are involved then? It's not being treated as an accident?'

'The minute the driver left the scene it became a crime; so yes, we are involved. This card here is for a service for citizens who have been bereaved, if you need to talk to someone.'

She took the card and looked it over.

'I doubt if we will, but thank you. I appreciate the gesture.'

Leroy smiled, shook Ms Fong's hand and they left. Leroy paused on the sidewalk and looked back at the house.

'What now, Sam?' Quinn asked.

'We still know very little about the other victim, Scott Dempsey. We're going to need to gain entry to his condo and search the place. He has to have somebody who...'

His sentence tailing off, Leroy walked across the street to the Taurus.

Leroy took the 110 Freeway. They had been on the road for about thirty minutes, just passing Hollywood itself, the Capitol Records building passing on their left, when Velasquez called.

'What's up, Pamela? How's it going?'

'I've been trawling through the CCTV footage.'

'Any good? Did you get the vehicle?'

'I was able to use footage from two cameras. Two POVs. Sam, by the look of what's here, this was no accident. The vehicle - it looks like an SUV, as we suspected – was driven deliberately at those people.'

## CHAPTER NINE

LEROY LOOKED OVER at Quinn, as if to silently ask, *did you hear that?*

'Send me over the footage.'

'You got it,' Velasquez replied. 'Give me ten.'

'Once I've looked it over, I'll speak to the lieutenant as it's now a murder investigation, but as far as I'm concerned, we continue as before.'

'Should we reach out to DHS? This could be a case of domestic terrorism.'

Leroy and Quinn both looked at each other, frowning.

'Let's not get ahead of ourselves. I'll speak to Perez, and see what he reckons. What was the vehicle?'

'It was black, looks like an SUV. Something like that.'

'Send it over; we'll take a look too. We're on our way to Scott Dempsey's place; call you when we get there.'

Now they were on Lankershim, and therefore not far from Dempsey's building. By the time they had arrived, the video had arrived on Leroy's phone. Not Quinn's, so Leroy forwarded it. They both remained in the Taurus, each watching the video on their phones.

The vehicle entered the frame. According to the data stamps, it was doing fifty-three. It veered onto the sidewalk, scattering the pedestrians like bowling pins. Then it was back on the pavement, making a sharp right.

Leroy hit the pause button and tried to maximise the image.

'Look, Ray. There's no licence plate.'

'No. It's been removed.'

Leroy called Velasquez.

'Pamela, you're right; it is an SUV. Looks like a Chevy, an Explorer or a similar model. But there's no tag; not on the rear end, anyway. Can you try to get a different POV so we can see the front? I'm sure they'd have removed the front plate also, but check anyway. It made a sharp right after; that's South San Pedro Street, so have a look at the traffic cameras there. See where it was headed. Chances are you'll lose it as not every intersection's covered, but it's worth a shot.'

'And where it came from,' Quinn interjected.

'Yes,' Leroy agreed. 'Once you've exhausted possible exit routes, try the direction it came from. I know that's even more wildcard, but it might give us something.'

'That's going to take hours,' Velasquez said.

'I'm going to call Lieutenant Perez to update him,' said Leroy. 'Looking at what you sent over, the vehicle was steered onto the sidewalk, then back again. Deliberately. That means it's now a murder investigation. Murder One. Which means his precious manpower budget's going to stretch to having somebody else on the team. Which will make it easier for that kind of stuff. I'll call him now. Speak to you later.'

Leroy ended the call with Velasquez and speed dialled Lieutenant Perez. The lieutenant answered almost immediately, and listened while Leroy updated him. He said nothing until Leroy had finished.

'I appreciate you putting me up to speed on this, Sam. I'll update the captain.'

'I didn't realise he was showing an interest in this case, Lieutenant.'

Captain Robert Walker had been in post eighteen months now, and gave the phrase *handsoff* a whole new meaning.

'He would appear to be interested in this one. Sam, I'm wondering whether you need somebody else in your team.'

'Oh yes?'

'It sounds as though it might be somewhat labour intensive, all that CCTV to look through. The number of witnesses that need to be interviewed. If you can learn where the Explorer went, better still who owned it, that would help the investigation no end.'

'Lieutenant: how do you know it was an Explorer?'

There was a second or two's pause before Perez replied.

'Velasquez showed me the CCTV footage. It's not on her, Sam; I was walking past her desk, and asked how the case was going. She had no choice.'

'I see,' said Leroy. He paused a second. 'You've seen, then, that there were no licence plates.'

'I did see. That would seem to support the theory that this was deliberate. The driver knew he would be seen on CCTV.'

'One thing more, Lieutenant. Pamela asked about passing this case to DHS, in case there was a domestic terrorism angle.'

'She didn't mention that to me.'

'No. She just did to me. I think I can see where she's coming from: there'd been incidents like this in Europe, but I don't want any other agencies involved. Not at this time, anyway.'

'I agree, Sam. Let's keep that up our sleeves, but we need to make some progress soon to guarantee it's kept in the Department. I'll have a look at what resources we have available and get back to you about adding to the team.'

'I'll wait to hear. Thanks, Lieutenant.'

'Is that a serious theory?' asked Quinn. 'Terrorism?'

Leroy shook his head. 'Not as far as I'm concerned. It was just an idea Pamela came out with. Perez had spoken to her directly earlier; I just wanted to make sure he hadn't taken in some bullshit theory and the investigation gets taken over by Homeland Security or the Bureau or fuck knows who else.'

'Bullshit?' Quinn laughed.

'You know what I mean. She's almost fresh out of the Academy. Has a lot of theory, but no experience; to be able to get a feel for things; an instinct. You get what I mean?'

'I do.'

'Come on; let's look around his apartment.'

At the entrance door, Leroy rang the buzzer for 2C. He recognised the voice of Elliott Bronski.

'Yes?'

'Mr Bronski: it's Detective Leroy again. Apologies to disturb you once more, but I need you to let us in.'

'You guys want to ask me more questions?'

'No, I just need access to the building.'

'Okay.'

There was a click and Leroy and Quinn were able to get inside. On the second floor, Leroy was relieved that the door to 2C remained shut. 2B was taped off. Leroy pulled the tape away. He took out his wallet and took a ring of Allen keys.

'Strictly speaking, we should get a Department locksmith, but I don't have time for that. Just don't tell Velasquez,' he added, grinning, as he selected the right sized key and inserted it into the lock.

After a few turns, the lock clicked, and Leroy was able to turn the handle.

'Let's hope there's no alarm,' he said as he opened the door.

## CHAPTER TEN

LEROY AND QUINN stepped into Dempsey's apartment. They paused for a few seconds in the doorway, waiting and listening. Listening for the sound of an intruder alarm bleeping as it counted down to full alarm activation if the person entering had not entered a combination or a key, or a thumbprint within a specific period of time.

'No alarm,' Quinn said, as they finally moved.

'Doesn't look like it.' Leroy checked behind a couple of doors. 'If it's silent but remote, that's no problem. I can deal with a Shamu or a private security guard showing up, but I don't want the entire neighbourhood being woken up.' He closed the entrance door.

Physically, the apartment was configured in the same way as that of Elliott Bronski, only a mirror image. The furnishings were more modern, reflecting the fact that Dempsey was a younger man than his screenwriter neighbour.

'Jesus, look at that,' said Quinn looking up at the gigantic flat screen television fixed to the wall. It dominated the entire room.

Leroy whistled and stepped over to get a closer look.

'Seventy-five inches?' Quinn asked.

'At least,' Leroy said. 'I'm impressed.'

A large, plush, semi-circular sofa was positioned in front of the screen, two shades of grey, with six black cushions. Behind the sofa was a large dining table, chrome and glass. It was neatly set for six, just placemats, two place settings either side, one each end. In the centre was a candelabra with places for six candles. It was also in chrome. Leroy ran a finger between two of the place settings, leaving a trail in the dust.

There were three doors leading from the room, plain wood, painted matt black, contrasting with the light grey of the walls. One door led to the kitchen, one to the bathroom, one to the bedroom. A bookcase stood on another wall. It was modernistic in style, six shelves high, and constructed with wood, painted matt black, matching the doors.

'You can tell a lot about somebody by what's on their bookshelves,' Leroy said, looking up and down the shelves. The shelves were filled with hardbacks, matching classically bound volumes. The books comprised collections of the classics – Shakespeare, Thomas Hardy, Robert Louis Stevenson. The shelf below contained works by Steinbeck, Hemingway, and others. Leroy noticed a copy of Harper Lee's *To Kill a Mockingbird*: he had caught the Gregory Peck movie on TV the other night. He stepped back. 'It looks,' he said, 'that these are those collections you can buy online, just to fill bookshelves and impress people. Ten to one says he's never read any of them.'

'There's more here,' Quinn said. He sat on the couch and went through the collection of books resting on the coffee table, glass and chrome, a miniature version of the dining table. There were two large books on architecture, one of New York City, the other of Southern California. Next to these was a history of the Los Angeles Union Station, and under this volume was an illustrated copy of the Karma Sutra. Quinn held the volume up. 'He may not have read those books, but this looks well fingered.'

Leroy was walking over to a small desk in the corner of the room. Black wood, matching the bookcase. He looked back at Quinn. 'I'd have phrased that differently, Ray.' He sat on the black swivel chair in front of the desk. 'I'll check through here; you want to go through the bedroom? See if there's anything in there about any contacts.' He stood and went into the bathroom. 'Just as I thought,' he said, returning. 'One toothbrush. He was single, but there must be some contact info, either in there or in here.'

'What about his cell?' Quinn asked. 'He might have everything stored on there.'

'The phone was dead. The screen was badly damaged, as a result of the accident. Not that accident is the right word, now. They're trying to break into it; contact information might be retrievable, as might his call log, messages, emails.' Leroy looked around, crouching to get a view of underneath the desk. 'Is there a landline phone here?'

'There has to be a landline,' Quinn said, pointing over to the desk. 'For the internet, if for nothing else. Can't see a phone, though.'

As he leafed through the contents of the desk drawers, Leroy called out, 'He was a single man; that's obvious from the apartment. He must have a little black book somewhere. You know, a list of girlfriends. The neighbour said he had a revolving door. Unless it was totally virtual contact list. The neighbour said he wasn't a monk.'

'He wasn't a monk.' Quinn was standing in the bedroom doorway. 'Pack of condoms next to the bed. Two left. And…' He held up a set of handcuffs, bright red with three rhinestones on each cuff. 'These.'

Leroy looked at the cuffs and raised his eyebrows. 'Not standard LAPD issue. Looks like he did have company;

was it a regular relationship or did he just go in for one-night stands? No address book, or anything else like that?'

'Nothing.'

'Nothing here either. Not even memory sticks. I'm going to take this...' - as he spoke, he disconnected the disc drive - 'back with us. I'm hoping they can break into it.' He paused, the drive on his lap. 'I'm wondering if this isn't his home; rather a *pied-à-terre*.'

'You mean like a second home?'

'Kind of. You agree this place doesn't look lived in. It could be a hotel room. All nice and tidy, but there was a quarter inch of dust on that table.'

Quinn agreed. 'The wash basin in the bathroom was dry. Not been used in days.'

'There's nothing here. Let's get on the MDT in the car, see what we can find out. If we're right, a DMV check will show another address.'

'But the driver's licence showed here.'

'So it did; let's look anyway. Start with the DMV.'

Back in the car, Leroy put Scott Dempsey's drive in the trunk and got in the driver's seat. Quinn pulled the Mobile Data Terminal out from its slot and began searching. While he was doing that, Leroy checked his phone. He had had one missed call: from Stacy. There was no message; she had hung up before voicemail had kicked in. He wondered what she was calling about; after all, Lionel Lynch was now beginning a long sentence behind bars. He was about to return the call, when Quinn stopped him.

'Found him.'

Leroy put his phone away, and looked over at the screen.

'That's him, wouldn't you say?' Quinn asked.

'That's our man. What address does it give?'

Quinn read out the address, even though Leroy could see it on the screen.

'Oxnard,' Quinn said. 'That's only fifty miles away.'

'It is. Less than an hour on the 101. See if anybody else lives at that address.'

As Leroy turned onto Lankershim, Quinn checked for any other residents at Dempsey's Oxnard address.

'I'm thinking a wife and two or three kids,' Leroy said. 'You saw that place. It shouts out single man, factor in the rubbers and the cuffs, and you have somewhere he goes to get laid. His wife probably doesn't even know about the place.'

'Nobody else listed.' Quinn pushed the MDT back and sat back.

'Told you. You want to text Pamela and let her know where we're headed? We should be back at the station inside three hours.'

Leroy took Lankershim Boulevard down to the Universal City Red Line Station, then made a right on to the 101, the Hollywood Freeway, which changed its name to the Ventura Freeway as it turned west just north of Studio City. They made it to Oxnard just inside an hour.

Scott Dempsey's house was on Masthead Drive in Oxnard, an affluent-looking neighbourhood not far from the marina. The house was a large, whitewashed, colonial style building. Across the street was a group of tennis courts – as they got out of the car, they could hear the sound of a match being played – the impact of racket on ball, and the grunt which often accompanied it. They could hear the sound of children playing out back, and the splash of a swimming pool.

'I told you,' Leroy said as he rang the doorbell.

## CHAPTER ELEVEN

A MAN ANSWERED the door. In his thirties, around the same height as Leroy. Tanned, bleached blond hair.

'Can I help you?' he asked. He had a British accent.

They held up their identification and asked if they had the right house for Scott Dempsey.

'It is, but he's away at present, down in LA. Can I help?'

'And you are?' Leroy enquired.

'My name's Piers Shipley. I'm Scott's husband. You want to come in?'

Leroy was momentarily speechless, taken back by Shipley's revelation. He looked at Quinn, who appeared just as surprised. Neither made any comment as they followed him into the house, into a room at the back which doors opened onto a pool area. The pool area was deserted, but they could hear splashing and children playing from next door. Quinn looked over at his partner, giving him a *how could you be so wrong* look, but got no reaction.

Shipley turned to face them. 'So how can I help? As I said, Scott's in LA.'

'I'm sorry to have to tell you, sir, but Mr Dempsey has been killed.'

Shipley paled, took a step back. 'What? How? I don't…'

Quinn moved forward. 'Why don't you take a seat, sir? Can I get you a drink?'

Shipley sat on the edge of the couch. He waved away Quinn's offer of a drink. 'I'm okay. What happened? Where was this?'

Leroy sat on the chair opposite. Quinn pulled out a chair from under the dining table.

'It was yesterday, in LA. Downtown. Mr Dempsey was one of a number of people to be hit by a vehicle which mounted the sidewalk.'

'He was on the sidewalk? But he never walked anywhere.' Shipley paused and shook his head. 'And this was yesterday? Downtown LA?'

'You didn't know where he was?' Quinn asked.

'He's been away for a few days, through work. I wasn't sure exactly where. We've been married a few years, but it's a kind of open marriage. I do my thing and he does his. We don't normally call or message when he's away.'

'What work did he do?' asked Leroy.

Shipley sat up, paused and took a deep breath. 'He dealt with businesses. He'd raise money to buy and take over businesses which were shall we say, almost on the skids. Then make the business profitable again, and sell on.'

'Like in that George Clooney movie?' Quinn ventured. 'What was it called? *Up in the Air*?'

Neither Leroy nor Shipley had heard of the movie.

'Is that why he had the *pied-à-terre*?' Leroy asked.

'Had the what?'

'The little apartment in North Hollywood.'

'Oh, yes. It was. He used to use it if he had meetings in

the city. To avoid the drive. Sometimes the meetings went on late. Or if he wanted to entertain anybody, if you get my drift.'

Leroy's mind went back to the contents of Dempsey's bedside closet. 'And you were happy with that?'

'I told you, we had an open relationship. Very Californian, he would say.'

'And so, this latest trip to LA: he was there for a meeting?'

Shipley shrugged. 'I guess so. He'd been down there since... since Sunday, I think it was. I just assumed he was there for meetings, or just to fuck someone. Scott liked women as well, so he was spoilt for choice, you might say.'

'How much of his business dealings do you know about?'

'Not much. Very little, in fact. He never shows - showed, I guess I should say - much interest in what I did, so I didn't... you know.'

'What do you do, sir?' asked Quinn.

'I'm an actor. Now, before you say what's an actor doing living all the way up here, let me just say I'm not interested in Hollywood or movies or crap like that. I'm interested in theatre. So there's no need for me to live down there and go to casting calls every morning. I've done some work down there: a couple of plays at the Greek, one at the Hudson down on Santa Monica Boulevard. I was even going to be in a production at the Pantages – you know, the big one on Hollywood Boulevard – but that got cancelled a week before opening night. The finance fell through at the last minute, apparently. But my main source of income is a restaurant here in Oxnard. I co-own it.' He looked up at Leroy, then over at Quinn. 'I suppose you think that's a strange way for a married couple to act.'

Leroy avoided looking at Quinn. 'Not at all. It's nobody else's business but yours.'

'It started off differently: we couldn't keep our hands

off each other. We got married, and after a few years things started to change. Slowly. Don't get me wrong: when we get into the bedroom, it's still great. But the way it is now I think suits us both.'

'Where are you from, sir?' Quinn asked.

'I'm from London, England, originally. Then you probably guessed. I came out here originally for work - TV – but found the theatre. And Scott.'

Getting the conversation back on track, Leroy asked, 'So, Mr Dempsey being in LA wasn't that unusual?'

Shipley shook his head. 'No, not at all.'

Leroy asked, 'Would you know of anyone who would want to kill him?'

'To kill him?' Shipley laughed. 'No. No way. But… I thought this was a traffic accident.'

'From the street cameras, it looks deliberate. That the vehicle in question deliberately mounted the sidewalk,' said Leroy.

Quinn added, 'The other two victims are a single mother and an old man.'

Leroy said, 'Others are still in hospital. Mr Dempsey is one of three fatalities.'

Shipley leaned back and took a deep breath. 'I'm in shock about all this.'

'As far as we can figure at this time,' Leroy continued, 'there is no reason for the other two deceaseds to be a deliberate target. Hence the question about Mr Dempsey being targeted.'

Quinn added, 'The others may have been collateral damage.'

Shipley shook his head. 'Shit. I'm sorry; I don't know of anybody who would want to kill him.'

'You told us,' Leroy said, 'that he bought up companies.'

'Who would have gone bust anyway.'

'And made them profitable.'

'That's correct.'

'And that would have meant firing staff?'

'I guess so. I'd never really thought about it.'

'So maybe he could have pissed off a lot of people?'

'It's possible, I suppose.'

Leroy asked, 'Did he work out of an office? We've been through the North Hollywood place and found his laptop. Did he have an office here?'

Shipley shook his head. 'If he worked here, he'd have the laptop up there, on the table.'

'Just the laptop?' Quinn asked.

'That's right. He backed everything up on the Cloud.'

'What was his trading name?'

'It was *Scott Dempsey & Associates*.'

'And associates? So he wasn't working alone?'

'No, no. It was just Scott. He used the Associates tag to give himself some credibility; to give the impression he was more than a one-man band.'

'Okay,' said Leroy. 'We have his laptop. Do you know the password, or do you know where he would have recorded it?'

Shipley shook his head. 'Now you're asking. Wait a minute: he did tell me once. He was away somewhere, and left the laptop here. he called me to look up something on a spreadsheet.'

'And he told you the password?' Leroy asked.

'Yes, but I can't...' Shipley clicked his fingers. 'I remember, it was something to do with Satan.'

Leroy and Quinn looked at each other.

'I've got it,' Shipley said. 'It was *Satanspants69*. All one word. Uppercase S, lower case the rest. Unless Scott changed it afterwards.'

'I've got that,' said Leroy. 'Thanks for your time, Mr Shipley. And I'm sorry for your loss. The LA Coroner's Department will be in touch with you about Mr Dempsey's remains and about identification of the body.'

Shipley nodded and stood up. 'No problem. Is this where you guys give me the number of a bereavement counselling service? I've seen that on TV, but there's no need.'

Leroy nodded. 'I'll just give you my card, then. If you have any questions, or if anything comes to mind, just give me a call. And likewise if we need any more information or have any more questions, we'll reach out to you. By the way, what type of car did Mr Dempsey drive?'

'It's an Opel Speedster. Tan coloured.'

'Do you know the tag number?'

'Yes, it's…' Shipley thought for a second before giving them the number. Then Leroy and Quinn said their goodbyes as Shipley showed them to the door. The children next door were still playing in the pool, splashing and shouting.

'Let's get back,' Leroy said, briskly leading Quinn back to the car. As he drove off Leroy was about to remark to Quinn that Dempsey and Shipley had a strange marriage, but thought better of it.

## CHAPTER TWELVE

BACK AT THE station, Leroy headed for Velasquez's desk, while Quinn picked up two cups of coffee.

'How's it going, Pamela?' he asked.

She was hunched over her workstation. Upon Leroy's arrival, she leaned back in her chair and pinched the bridge of her nose. She was clearly tired.

'You're going to tell me no luck, aren't you?' Leroy said.

She pushed her chair back a few inches and folded her arms. 'The problem is, there aren't cameras at every intersection, and Downtown…'

'Has one hell of a lot of intersections.'

'That's the problem,' she conceded. 'I managed to get three, four blocks, that's all. I did a scan of the surrounding area – you know, directions it could have gone, but zip. The same for the direction it might have come from.'

Quinn arrived with coffee. Passing Leroy his, he asked, 'What about the licence plate?'

She shook her head. 'The image isn't distinct enough. I've tried enhancing, zooming in, but the angle isn't right in any locations. I can see they're California plates, but that's about it.'

'Can you get anything on the plates?' asked Leroy. 'If you can't get the number in its entirety, then two or three digits would be something. We could reach out to DMV, maybe get an extrapolation. We know the type of vehicle.' He turned to Quinn. 'You want to give Pamela a hand with that while I update Perez?'

'Sure thing.' Quinn sat at his own desk and booted up his PC.

'Go through the images: if we're lucky, there was at least one stop sign.'

'There wasn't,' Velasquez said.

'No? Shit. What are the chances Downtown? Well, every time you get a good image, freeze, and zoom in. The more digits we get, the easier it'll be to work with DMV. Depending on the angles, if we get really lucky, we may get the whole plate.'

Leroy left his partners working on the CCTV, and wandered down the corridor to the office of Lieutenant Perez. The door was ajar, and Leroy could hear the lieutenant was on the phone. Leroy knocked and put his head around the door. Still talking, Perez waved for Leroy to go in and sit down. After a few seconds, he ended the call and looked up at Leroy.

'Sam, just the person,' he said, almost breezily. 'How's it going?'

Leroy knew he meant how was the case going, not a general question about his well-being. He updated the lieutenant on the situation so far. As Leroy spoke, Perez sat quietly, nodding at various points. When Leroy was done, he spoke.

'Any more thoughts on the terrorism angle? Domestic, I mean.'

'Briefly. Pamela raised it as a possibility. But personally, I don't buy it. Nobody has claimed any responsibility for it, and they would have done by now if it was a terrorist act. Domestic or otherwise.'

'But it was clearly deliberate? A nut job?'

'That's certainly a more likely explanation. But if it was, then why just that location? Why not do it again on the next block? And the next?'

'So what's your theory then?'

Leroy scratched the back of his head. 'My gut feeling, and that's all it is at this time, is that it was deliberate, premeditated, and that the driver was in all probability aiming for somebody on that sidewalk.'

'So it's now a homicide investigation?'

'Definitely, without a doubt. We're approaching on two levels. One: to ID the owner and hopefully the driver of the vehicle. We know what the vehicle was - that's the easy part – but we need the licence plate number. None of the CCTV footage shows the plate in its entirety, so I've got the others scanning what we can, getting a digit or so here, another digit there, to get a full number. Or get as much as we can and reach out to DMV with what we have.'

'If it's on CCTV while it's at a red then you stand a better chance.'

'We don't have any stop signs, no reds. What are the chances of that? The problem is, not every intersection has stop lights. But we're expanding the radius of the search: if we lose it at one place, we might pick it up at another. Pamela's doing the same, but in reverse, trying to track where it came from.'

'Any success?'

'Not yet, but the more views we get of the vehicle, the better the odds. The rear plate had been removed; we may get lucky with the front.'

'Stolen?'

'No vehicle of that description has been reported stolen. Not in the Greater Los Angeles area, in the last five days.'

'But you'll need to keep checking that. If the vehicle was stolen, the owner might not be aware yet. It could have been taken from the garage at LAX and the owner's in Paris or Tokyo or somewhere.'

'We're on that.'

'You said you were approaching this from two angles. What was the other?'

'The other angle is starting with the victims. So far we have three dead and two still in hospital.'

'Three dead? I thought there were only two.'

'We had word earlier that a third had died. So from the fatality point of view we have...' Leroy used his fingers to count off the victims. 'In no particular order, we have a white middle aged guy who specialised in buying up companies who were near Chapter 11, making them profitable - which mean firing most of the employees – and selling the company on.'

'Scott Dempsey?'

Leroy paused and stared at Perez for a second before continuing. 'Correct. Number two was a single mother from Mexico, who was on her way to her badly paid job in the Fashion District.'

'Er – what's her residential status?'

'I have no idea, and I don't care.'

'Do you plan to reach out to the INS?'

'I have no intention of reaching out to the INS,' Leroy replied, vehemence in his voice.

'Okay, okay. That works for me. The third?'

Leroy waited a few seconds, before saying, 'The third was an elderly Asian who died in hospital from his injuries.'

'And the other two? The walking wounded?'

'Hardly walking wounded, Lieutenant. They're still at the hospital. One is a twenty something woman - Caucasian - also headed for work, and the other a 7/11 cashier – a man in his sixties – who was headed home from work.'

Perez nodded, closing his eyes. Leroy knew that this meant he was assimilating the information. 'So you're saying Scott Dempsey was the likely victim?'

'No, I'm not saying that at all. They are all victims, aren't they? I'm saying Scott Dempsey is where we're starting. We have his work laptop and password.'

'Where did you get his password?'

'Ray and I have just got back from Oxnard, where we spoke to Dempsey's husband.'

'His husband? But didn't his neighbour say he had women in his apartment?'

'Apparently Scott Dempsey was something of a swinger. Like a pendulum, it appears. We found, er - accessories in his apartment.'

Perez frowned. 'So if he has a husband up there and women down here, do you think there's a motive in there somewhere?'

'I'm not thinking anything at the moment. We're not going to head down a blind alley. There's no reason to think the husband is a person of interest at this time. We have Dempsey's password, so we can access his laptop. I'm hoping we can learn about his business dealings, and they might give a lead into any likely persons of interest.'

Perez nodded. 'Okay, that all sounds logical. Anything else you want to tell me?'

Leroy frowned. 'About what?'

'There's a rumour going around that Ray's split up from his wife. Also that you guys had an argument at the scene. Is that correct?'

'Jesus Christ, those guys out there are worse than…' Leroy paused. 'Yes, that's true, to a point. I wouldn't say split; more a temporary separation. Apparently they've been having difficulties for a while, like everybody does. I'm sure it'll resolve itself. And as for an argument at the scene – that's fucking bullshit. I don't know where that came from, but I didn't think he was focussed enough. I sent him home to get his shit together. He has days and days of personal time owing. I told him to use some of that. Pamela and I are able to handle things.'

'He's in today: how is he?'

'He's dealing with it. Is there anything else, Lieutenant?' Leroy stood up to leave.

'One more thing. You have an appointment five fifteen with the Chief.'

'What? With the actual Chief?'

'The actual Chief.'

'Snell?'

'That's the man.'

'What about?'

'He wants an update on this case.'

'What the hell for? He's never...'

'I know, I know, I know. He seems to be showing an interest in this case. I've already had two calls from his office about how you were getting on. Maybe he wants to hear it from the horse's mouth, as it were.'

'That's just swell,' Leroy muttered as he left the lieutenant's office.

## CHAPTER THIRTEEN

CHIEF OF POLICE Robert Snell worked out of an office on the third floor of the LAPD Headquarters at 100 West 1$^{st}$ Street, a block away from City Hall, and situated between Main and Spring Streets.

For Leroy, the timing couldn't have been worse, in terms of the investigation – he wanted him, Quinn, and Velasquez to get started on the two avenues of enquiry – and in terms of the hour. The appointment was five fifteen – right in the middle of rush hour. At this time of day, the journey would take at least an hour, so that meant he was wasting two hours behind the wheel when he could be looking for a killer. And why the hell did Snell want a personal, face to face update on the investigation?

After a seventy minute drive along Santa Monica and Beverley Boulevards, fortunately not encountering too many red lights, Leroy eased the Taurus into a space in the underground parking garage at Headquarters at five minutes after five. He had just made it.

Previously, after leaving Perez's office, he returned to his desk and updated Quinn and Velasquez on where he was headed. He told them to split the camera footage between them and to view as many images of the SUV as they could to get the licence plate number. When they had a number, and hopefully a name, then they were to call him. At least he would have a result to give to the Chief.

He had heard nothing as he neared the end of his journey, so as he made the right onto Normandie, he called Quinn.

'What have you got so far, Ray?' he asked. 'I'll be seeing the Chief in thirty minutes.'

'We're starting to build up pieces of the plate,' Quinn replied. 'It begins with a 9, then OY, we think.'

'Can't be an O,' said Leroy. Only the second alpha character can be an O. or a Q, or an I. It must be a C. Or a G. Anything else?

'View from other angles: last three numbers are a 1; then either an 8 or a 3. That goes for both second and third numbers.'

'So could be 33, 88, 38, or 83.'

'You got it. But we still have some way to go.'

'Well, keep at it till around six, unless you get the whole tag earlier. If you're doing this for too long, you'll be in danger of missing something. Pamela must be punch drunk by now.'

'I think she is.'

'Give it another half hour, then go home and get some rest, both of you. We'll not be able to reach out to DMV until the morning in any case.'

'But if we get the whole number, Sam…'

'I know, but it'll keep till the morning when we're all fresh.'

'You got it. What are you going to do?'

'I'm due to see Snell five fifteen to bring him up to speed on the case. Then I guess I'll call it a day myself and go home. The traffic's shit, so I guess I'll get back late.'

'You'll tell us tomorrow what he said?'

'I will. I can't imagine what he will say. I'm hoping he's not going to try and steer the investigation in a particular way. Look, Ray; I'm here now. You and Pamela keep searching until five thirty, then I'll see you both at the station in the morning.'

'Sure. I'll text you if we get a full result.'

'That would be good. Try and make it around five twenty. That will make us all look good.'


The appointment was at five fifteen and it was now five twenty-two. Leroy had been sitting outside Chief Snell's office since five ten.

'He shouldn't be much longer,' Snell's red-headed secretary tried to reassure him. Leroy smiled weakly. As he sat there, his mind wandered over to a scene in the first Dirty Harry movie where Callahan has a meeting with the mayor. When the mayor, played by John Vernon, asks what Harry has been doing, Harry replies that he had been sitting in the outer office for the last forty minutes waiting on him. Leroy thought about saying that, but thought better of it.

Eventually, the door opened, and two uniformed officers – grey-haired, so probably senior – walked out. A third uniformed officer followed a few seconds later. Leroy recognised him as Chief of Police Robert Snell. Leroy had known Snell for a few years, although their paths had not really crossed until his promotion to AC. Prior to that, he was the Director, Office of Special Operations, where he and Leroy had very little contact.

Leroy stood and nodded at the two departing officers. One nodded a brief acknowledgement to him, to which Leroy reciprocated; the other just walked past. Leroy turned to Snell.

'Detective Leroy?' Snell asked.

'Chief,' Leroy replied, shaking Snell's hand.

'Thank you for coming. This way.'

Resisting the temptation to ask if he had a choice, Leroy merely replied, 'No problem, Chief,' as he followed Snell into his office.

This was the first time Leroy had been in this room, which seemed ten times the size of Lieutenant Perez's office. The walls were painted light green, contrasting with the light oak colours of the woodwork and furniture. A door led from the room directly behind Snell's desk, which Leroy assumed was to the Chief's private bathroom. Dotted around the room, two on three of the walls, were black and white prints of the city from what Leroy guessed were the forties and fifties, maybe sixties, long before the massive level of construction that had gone on Downtown over the last couple of decades or so. Behind the Chief hung two framed commendations; Leroy did not bother to read the detail. Two photograph stands were on his desk: one of a woman, and the other of two children. So Snell had a family after all.

Snell was tall, easily over six foot, sturdily built, and with a full head of silver hair. He had a deep tan, which looked recent. On the previous occasions Leroy and Snell had met, the Chief was wearing a suit and tie; today he was in uniform: black pants, shirt and tie, contrasting with his silver hair. Leroy wondered if the uniform was for his benefit, as if to make some impression on him. If it was, it had failed. Leroy also noticed the shape of Snell's stomach underneath his shirt, and speculated that if the Chief was conscious of the beginnings of a paunch, wearing black would hide this, in the same way that weight-conscious women sometimes dressed in black in the perception that black made them look slimmer. As Snell sat down behind his large desk, Leroy came to the conclusion that he was being fanciful, and that this was just the beginnings of middle age spread; quite normal. Snell made a couple of strokes on his keyboard, then looked up at Leroy. Leroy stood in front of the desk.

'Take a seat, Detective,' said Snell. 'You're leading the

Dempsey investigation?'

Leroy was momentarily taken aback at hearing the investigation referred to in this way, but soon recovered his composure. 'Yes, Chief.' he replied as he sat. 'The murders of Scott Dempsey, Rosa Delgado, and Kenneth Fong, plus the attempted murder of two others, still in hospital.'

'Of course, yes. Tell me what progress you've made.'

Leroy took a deep breath and repeated what he had told Perez an hour or so ago. 'We're approaching the investigation from two angles. One being the vehicle involved.'

'What type of vehicle?'

'A black SUV.'

'Licence plate?'

Leroy sighed audibly and continued. 'A black SUV. We have CCTV footage of the incident and it seems clear that it was deliberately driven onto the sidewalk. Therefore, it's a murder and attempted murder investigation.

'So far, none of the CCTV images have given us a full view of the front licence plate - the rear had been taken off - so my team are viewing what we have, from different angles, to build a full picture. In the event that we can't get a full picture, we already know three or four digits, we can reach out to DMV in the morning to extrapolate and get the owner's details.'

'Stolen?'

'That's a possibility, even a probability, but there are no reports of black SUVs being stolen in the last seven days. Of course, it could be that the owner doesn't know it's been stolen; it could have been taken from a parking garage, at LAX, for example.'

'But once you have the owner...'

'Yes, once we have the owner, things will move much faster.'

'An arrest?'

'Assuming the owner was driving; yes, an arrest.'

'You said you have two approaches.'

'Yes. We're looking at the victims, with a view to establishing a motive.'

'Scott Dempsey had something to do with rescuing bankrupt companies, is that right?'

'Kind of, Chief. He'd buy up failing companies, make them profitable, then sell them on.'

'I see.'

'One aspect we'll be looking at is that, by making them profitable; well, that's going to mean downsizing the workforce, firing people, so there might be a motive there. There's also the question of where he got the finance to buy the companies in the first place, and if and when he paid it back when the concerns were sold off. We went to visit his husband up in Oxnard earlier; now we have his laptop and password, we can check out his business dealings.'

'Any partners? *Scott Dempsey and Associates*, wasn't it?'

'Business? No, according to his husband, he worked on his own. He used the *Associates* tag to add some credibility, to disguise the fact that he was a one-man show.'

Snell nodded. 'I see. Anything else?'

'Well, one possible aspect. According to the husband, he used to sleep around. They lived up in Oxnard, but he had a condo in North Hollywood. The husband said Dempsey used to use the place to meet women. He liked to swing,' he added, noticing a look of discomfort on Snell's face. 'We found a set of handcuffs in his bedroom there, so that's another possible line of enquiry.'

'How many of you are working on the case?'

'Myself, Detective Quinn and Detective Velasquez.'

'I'll speak to Captain Walker and ask him to arrange for you to have more in your team. That should move things on nicely; get a result quicker. But I'd like to be kept up to speed on this one. Thanks for coming in. Anything else you need?'

Leroy paused a second.

'Two things, sir. I've only told you about one of the victims. There were two other deaths.'

'Yes, I know about them. The mother and the elderly Asian.' Snell paused a second. 'And I expect you to give equal consideration to them. There's no reason to give Scott Dempsey priority over the other two. A senior and a woman whose residential status is questionable are still victims.'

'They were never otherwise, Chief. The other question is: why the interest? At your level of seniority, sir?'

Snell cleared his throat. 'There's concern over at City Hall at safety on the city's streets. Tent City seems to be expanding and that has brought an increase in levels of crime. For an incident like this, for a killing on the streets in broad daylight in Downtown; well, let's say the Department – and you, Detective Leroy – are under the microscope. Am I clear?'

'Three killings, sir; maybe more to come. And yes, you are crystal clear.'

'I appreciate you coming in, Detective,' said Snell, standing up and walking over to the door. 'Remember to keep me up to date, and if there's anything else you need, please reach out.'

'I appreciate the additional team members, sir,' said Leroy as he followed Snell to the door.

'If there's anything else,' said Snell as Leroy stepped into the outer office.

After saying goodbye, Leroy headed straight down to the parking garage. He sat silently in the car before starting the engine. What the hell was that all about? He had the feeling he was being shaken down, that he was being manipulated.

He sat for a few moment more, then decided it was time to go home.

He started the engine and slowly took the Taurus out of the garage and up the ramp onto the street, still with a feeling of unease.

## CHAPTER FOURTEEN

LEROY DID NOT go straight home.

He decided to call Stacy Chen. He had taken a rain check when they were about to go for lunch the other day, so maybe as he was Downtown today, he could collect on that.

'Sam,' she said, picking up after two rings. 'How you doing?'

'I'm Downtown. I've just finished a meeting at 100 West 1st. Are you busy?'

'You mean can you collect on that rain check?'

'Yeah, kind of,' Leroy laughed.

'Are you hungry?' she asked. 'I'm craving some Mexican food.'

'That sounds good to me. Where did you have in mind?'

'I'm thinking *La Tostaderia*, in the market. Where are you parked?'

'I'm in the parking garage here at HQ, but I'll drive round and park at the market. See you in thirty?'

'You got it. It's going to be busy there. Meet you at the foot of Angels?'

'See you soon.'

In the rush hour traffic it took Leroy ten minutes to move his car from the garage at Police HQ to the Grand Central Market parking on Hill Street. He parked on the second floor and walked down the steps to Hill Street, where he saw Stacy waiting by one of the orange columns at the base of Angels Flight. She was wearing a grey jacket and light blue skirt, and was carrying a thin black leather case.

'Hey,' she smiled as he approached. 'Hungry?'

'Always.'

They crossed Hill Street and walked into the market. She led him to the *La Tostaderia* stand. The smell of cooking as they passed through the market was enticing: Leroy was slightly hungry so far; now he was ravenous.

They reached the stand, waited in line for a few minutes, then ordered. Once they had their food, they sat at a metal table away from the aisle. She ordered Octopus Tacos, which comprised charred octopus, yuzu sauce, ginger aioli, daikon, cucumber and bean sprouts; Leroy chose fish ceviche tostada: chilled white fish, tomato, cucumber, red onion, avocado, cilantro, all with freshly squeezed lime juice. Both had a cold beer. Stacy insisted on paying.

'Thank you,' Leroy said, taking a bite. 'Bon Appetit.'

'You don't mind this kind of food?' she asked.

'I practically live on street food.'

'You probably told me already, but are you single?' she asked, casually.

'Yes, I'm afraid so,' he replied, noticing the casual way she asked. He could tell fishing when he saw it.

'So, street food and microwave dinners all the time?'

Leroy nodded and waited until he had finished his mouthful. 'Pretty much, yes. You?'

'I'm single, also, but I try to cook at least three nights a week. But I have regular hours. Long hours, and I need to work some evenings. But I generally know in advance.'

'That makes it easier. What are you working on at the moment?' As he spoke he noticed two uniformed officers walk past the stand. There was no recognition on either part.

'It's a complex case. Money laundering and trafficking. Third day in.'

'Trafficking? Over the border?'

'Where else? They seemed like two separate investigations, but after a while, it became clear they were connected.'

'What's the LA connection?'

'The arrests were made here. Do you know a Detective Castillo? In Major Crime Division?'

'Can't say I have. Is he dealing?'

'*She* is.'

'Sorry. She. But wouldn't the Feds be dealing?'

'They are, but... and this is where it gets complex. Castillo was involved with the money laundering investigation to begin with, then it escalated.'

'Okay, I get it.'

'And, by the way: Lionel Lynch is appealing.'

'You have to be joking. Appealing what? The conviction or the sentence?'

'The conviction. Can you believe it?'

'On what grounds?'

'That he didn't do it.'

'So more work for you?'

'A heap more. Just when I have a new case on. I hope it gets thrown out at first base. I don't want to get taken off this one, just to work on that scumbag's appeal.' She used a napkin to wipe the corner of her mouth. 'How was your day?'

'That crime scene I got called away to the other day,' Leroy said. 'That one.' He related to her what had happened so far on the case.

She nodded. 'So if I read you right, once you've ID'd the vehicle, and the driver, it's pretty slam-dunk, yes?'

'In theory, it is. But it all seems too easy.'

Stacy laughed. 'I wish.'

'What I mean is: yes, once we have the vehicle, we can identify the owner - not the driver – but it's certainly a massive step forward.'

'You mean it could have been stolen?'

'It could have, yes. There are no reports in the last couple weeks of a black SUV being stolen, but as my partner pointed out, the owner could have parked at LAX while he went on vacation for three weeks, and know nothing about it.

'Also, you have to be blind not to see the dozens of traffic cameras around. Surely, you'd consider the possibility - probability, if not guarantee – that one of those cameras is going to pick you up.'

She took another bite of taco. Some food dropped onto her paper plate. 'I see what you mean.'

'That's why I'm a tad uneasy about it being so straightforward. Another thing about the investigation is – and this is why I'm over here – is that I was summoned, I mean invited, to update the Chief about the case.'

'That isn't usual, I assume.'

'No way. I kind of asked, but he gave me some crap about the mayor being concerned about street crime, but I knew it was bullshit. And he knew I knew it was bullshit, I could tell. So far, we have three fatalities: a guy named Scott Dempsey, who was a corporate downsizer.'

'One of those guys who basically fires everybody until a company makes a profit?'

'That's it. The other two were Rosa Delgado, a single mother, and Kenneth Fong, a seventy-seven-year-old Asian. Two others are still in hospital. But he kept referring to it as the Dempsey case. Even after I pointed out that Dempsey wasn't the only victim, he kept talking about him.'

'Maybe he was telling you the truth. Maybe he is under

pressure from City Hall.'

Leroy pulled a face. 'Nah. I could tell. It was bullshit. He was only interested in Dempsey. If it was about street crime, then what about the other victims? They were just as much his statistics as Dempsey.'

'And you're sure it was deliberate?'

'Pretty definite from the CCTV.'

'So it's homicide?'

'It is.'

'So what about motive?'

'Can't figure one out yet. Delgado and Fong, and the injured in the hospital – they all seem quite innocuous, unless there'd anything we don't know. The nature of what Dempsey did for a living might have pissed somebody off.'

'Enough to kill him?'

'Possibly. We're going to look into his business tomorrow. We might get a break there.'

'Unless you get the vehicle first.'

'Unless we get the vehicle first.' He pushed his empty plate to one side. 'Look, thanks for the food, but I'd better get off. Early start in the morning.'

'Same here,' she said as she gathered up her case. 'Plus I have some things to go through tonight. I won't be in bed before twelve.'

Taking her last sentence at face value, Leroy said, 'You must let me return the favour. Soon.'

'I will,' she said as they made their way through the thinning crowds to Hill Street.

'Where are you parked?' he asked.

'I'm in the office lot. Only a couple blocks away.'

Leroy nodded. 'Thanks again. Speak soon.'

Stacy began to walk past the market and towards 1st Street while Leroy crossed over Hill Street to the parking garage. He was soon out of the garage and heading home. An unexpected meal date: he was planning on stopping off at the In-n-Out on Sunset in Hollywood. He wondered what was the healthier: a Double Double with fries or a fish taco.

## CHAPTER FIFTEEN

Leroy was almost home when Quinn called.

'Sam, where are you?'

'I'm almost home. What's up?'

'We've found the vehicle.'

'You guys still at the station?'

'Yeah, we're just clearing up.'

'So who's the owner and where?'

'That's the thing, Sam. It's a Ford Territory; black, as we know. It's part of a fleet of hire cars.'

'Shit. No, it shouldn't make any difference. Where's the company based?'

'LAX. SoCal Hire Services.'

'Good work, both of you. I'll try and get a warrant arranged for the morning. I'll see you both at the station usual time, then we'll head down to the airport. Is Pamela still there also?'

'She is; about to go home.'

'Tell her well done.'

Leroy heard Quinn's muffled voice say, 'Sam says well done.' Then, 'She said, "You're welcome."'

'Cool. See you guys tomorrow.'

After parking behind his Venice house, Leroy sat in the darkened car, thinking. So the car in question was not privately owned; the killer had hired it. In theory, it would be a simple matter of seeing who had hired the vehicle. Leroy's only concern was, that whoever hired the Ford Territory had now left the country, in all probability without returning it. The timing sucked, as they had no choice but to wait till morning.

Once home, he put in a call to Judge Valeria Santos. She tended to be Leroy's go-to judge if he needed a warrant. He had testified many times in her courtroom, and she was normally amenable if he needed a warrant out of hours. He kept a warrant template on his laptop, and Judge Santos said that if he brought it to her house between seven and seven thirty the next morning, she would check it over, and, if happy with it, sign it. Leroy thanked the judge and said he would see her in the morning. She lived in Beverly Hills – a detour for him, but a journey he would be prepared to make as it was preferable to going to the courthouse later in the day. It just meant a very early start next morning.


He wanted to get down to LAX as soon as practicable. The judge had said between seven and seven thirty. He completed the warrant template and printed it the night before, and set off from home just before six, before sunrise. The traffic was more or less as he had anticipated, but was able to pull up outside the judge's Beverly Hills house ten minutes before seven. As a courtesy, he waited in his car until seven o'clock precisely.

Judge Santos lived in a house which was modest by some of the neighbouring standards. Off Wilshire

Boulevard, it was set back from the street by a nicely manicured lawn either side of a narrow path leading to wide black double doors. He could hear a chime from inside as he pressed the bell.

Momentarily, the door was opened by a tall, thin woman wearing a black dress and white lacey apron.

'The judge is expecting me,' Leroy said. 'Detective Leroy.'

'Yes, come this way, please,' the maid said, her voice almost a whisper and with a trace of an accent. She led Leroy to the rear of the house and the kitchen where Judge Santos was sitting at a breakfast bar with a cup of coffee and a copy of the LA Times. She looked up as he entered the kitchen.

'Good morning, Judge. I appreciate you seeing me this early.'

'It could have been earlier.'

'Excuse me?'

'Was that your car parked outside the last ten minutes?' she asked, a trace of a grin on her face.

'Um, yes. I left at six to avoid the traffic. I didn't want to intrude. You said seven.'

'It wouldn't have been an intrusion,' she said as she put down the newspaper. 'You have the warrant?'

'I do.' He pulled it from his pocket, opened it, and passed it over. She took it and adjusted her glasses.

'You want a cup of coffee while I read this? she asked as she began reading the warrant.

'I'm good, thanks, Judge.'

She took about ten minutes to read the warrant. Leroy noticed that she actually read it twice: through the first time, then two sips of coffee, then a second. The second time, she said, 'Yes, I read about this. Awful. And this is the vehicle in question?'

'We believe so, Your Honour, yes.'

She signed the warrant and passed it back. 'Here you are. Good luck with your investigation.'

'Thank you, Judge. I appreciate your time. Have a good

day.'

As Leroy turned to leave, the maid appeared - he had no idea where she had been while he was with the judge - and escorted him to the door.

Warrant in hand, Leroy walked briskly down to his car, and joined the rush hour traffic back to the station.

He arrived in the parking lot the same time as Quinn, who waited for him as he parked so they could walk in together. Velasquez had already arrived and was chatting with a uniformed officer, holding a paper cup of coffee. She followed Leroy and Quinn to their desks.

'What's the plan today, boss?' she asked.

Leroy unlocked a desk drawer and took out Scott Dempsey's laptop. 'We have this,' he said, opening it, 'and we have his password. Or what his husband says is the password. If it isn't, we may need to reach out to him again. Hopefully, he'll have details of his business dealings on there; maybe there are some names there, names of somebody with a grudge. Somebody Dempsey pissed off in a big way. In the meantime, we should get the details of whoever hired the SUV.'

'Sam? You got a second?' It was Lieutenant Perez calling from the end of the corridor.

Leroy waved an acknowledgement at the lieutenant, and turned to Velasquez. 'You want to make a start on the laptop now, just to make sure the password works.' With a grin, he jotted the password down and passed the paper to Velasquez.

She looked at it, and did a double take. 'Nice password,' she said. 'Tasteful.' She started to boot up the laptop while Quinn did the same with his desk PC.

'It looks like Perez wants me,' Leroy said. 'We'll head on out when I'm done with him.'

Leroy walked down to Perez's office; as he approached, he heard Velasquez call out, 'We're in!' He tapped on the lieutenant's door, which was slightly open. Perez was on the phone, but motioned for Leroy to enter.

Perez ended his call and asked Leroy, 'How did you get

on with the Chief last night?'

Leroy took a couple of steps into the office, but remained standing. 'I updated him on the investigation, and our progress so far. I took him through how we were approaching it: the driver of the vehicle on one hand, anybody who might have held a grudge against Dempsey on the other. He's the most likely motive for a homicide, although not the only victim.' He paused a second. 'I had to remind him about that.'

Perez put one elbow on the desk and rubbed his temple. Leroy was sure he heard a faint groan. 'I'm sure he's aware of that, Sam. How were things left?'

'He said he wanted to be kept in the loop, to be updated. Personally.'

'He wants *you* to call him?'

Leroy shrugged. 'He just said updated personally.'

'He would have meant he wanted to be told about progress directly, which I admit is unusual for him. Look – do me a favour, will you? I don't want to be wrong-footed by him or his office a second time: when he called yesterday, I didn't know what the hell stage you guys were at. So keep *me* up to date every step of the way, and I'll feed things back to him.'

'That works for me, Lieutenant. There is one more thing he said. He said he'd arrange for a bigger team. As well as Quinn and Velasquez. He said he would speak with the captain about that.'

'What was his rationale for that?'

'To speed things up. Said there was a lot of pressure from the mayor's office.'

'What do you think? Do you need anybody else?'

'It wouldn't hurt, I guess. I've no problem supervising three or four detectives.'

'I'll talk to the captain then. I might try to pre-empt things. There is the cost to consider, though.'

Leroy grinned. 'You have a good day, Roman.' He turned to leave, but Perez called him back.

'There's just one more thing, Sam.'

'Yes?'

'Close the door, will you?' Leroy did so, and took a step forward. Perez asked, 'You are keeping Velasquez as part of the team aren't you? I know you and Quinn have been partners for a time, but she won't learn much if she's just sitting at a desk while you and he are swanning around out there.'

'That's bullshit. Has this come from her? Has she said something to you?'

'No, no. Nothing like that. I've just noticed her at her desk on the computer, doing her own thing. On her own. You need to make her part of the team.'

'I will. I do, I mean. I'm just curious as to where this came from.'

'I told you, it doesn't come from anywhere. I just noticed her there, that's all.'

'Well, she *is* being included, but I'll bear what you said in mind.'

''That's all I ask. Thanks, Sam.'

Leroy walked back to their desks. He was slightly annoyed. Velasquez was sitting in front of Dempsey's open laptop, Quinn sitting close behind. They were having a conversation about something on the screen.

'Found anything?' Leroy asked.

Velasquez and Quinn both looked up. 'All we've seen so far,' she explained, 'is a list of companies. Each has a separate folder. This one we're looking at right now, has accounts for the last five years, a copy of a few annual reports, and a list of personnel.'

'I've had an idea,' Leroy said. 'Pamela, you've spent the last few days looking at a screen. Before your eyesight finally calls it a day, let Ray look at that this morning. You can come with me down to LAX, to the car rental company.'

'SoCal Rentals?' she said.

'That's them.'

'Sure thing, boss,' she said, pushing her chair back and standing up.

'You okay with that, Ray?' he asked.

Quinn changed chairs. 'You got it,' he said. Leroy could not help but notice the expression on Quinn's face.

## CHAPTER SIXTEEN

THEY WITHDREW A city car and, Leroy driving, eased into the late rush-hour traffic. Leroy headed for the 405 and took the freeway as far as the Pepperdine University at Westchester, then Sepulveda down to the airport.

'Why can't we just get details of the rental over the phone?' Velasquez asked on the way there.

'I want to cover all bases. I want to look at all the records they have. Places like this don't always give out clients' personal details – it depends on their company policy – without a warrant, so I'm just trying to pre-empt that.'

'We have a warrant?'

'Yup. I have a judge; I call her my go-to judge. I reached out to her on the way home last night and arranged to call into her house on the way to work this morning to pick it up. It's much quicker than going through the usual channels and waiting hours at the courthouse. So if we get any *I want to see a warrant* crap, we already have that covered.'

She nodded. 'Smart.'

'It's the sort of thing you figure out over time. There's always different ways of doing things. Always keeping within the law and Department policies, but different. You just figure out what's best for you. Mainly with experience. There's also the likelihood that we'll need to impound the vehicle.'

'For forensic tests?'

'Yup.'

'But surely it'll be cleaned and valeted by now?'

'I'm sure it will be; I'm expecting it to be. But it's very hard to be one hundred percent clean. Anyway, we'll need the warrant to get the car. Nearly there: LAX two miles.'

SoCal Rentals was based on the first floor of parking garage P7, across from Terminals 7 and 8. Leroy parked in one of the empty spaces and walked in to the office structure. There was one clerk behind the counter. He was finishing a transaction with a lady customer.

'Here you are, ma'am,' he smiled, handing her a set of keys. 'Bay one. Have a nice day.' As soon as she turned to leave, his face switched to look at Leroy and Velasquez. 'Good morning, sir and ma'am. Welcome to SoCal Rentals. How can I help you this morning?'

The smile faded when Leroy showed his badge and introduced himself and Velasquez. 'I'm interested,' Leroy said, 'in this vehicle. Who had hired it, and where it is, to begin with.' He passed a business card with the licence plate number written on it.

The clerk swallowed. 'I'll need to speak to with my supervisor first.'

Leroy shook his head. He passed over the warrant. 'No, you won't. Speak to your supervisor later, by all means, but if you don't give me the information I need *now*, you'll be speaking to this judge first.'

The clerk swallowed again, and was beginning to sweat. 'Okey dokey,' he said, trying to disguise his signs of panic. He typed in the tag number and waited for his screen to populate. He began to read from the screen. 'Ford Territory one point five litre. Gasoline. Automatic transmission. Front wheel drive. Black.'

'Who hired it last?' Leroy asked impatiently.

'The last hire, sir,' the clerk read, 'was seventeen days ago. Returned nine days ago, to a -' He stopped as Leroy swung the screen round to look at it himself. Leroy showed Velasquez the screen. Leroy double-checked the licence plate number – everything matched.

'I need to see the vehicle,' Leroy said. 'Is it out there?'

'No,' the clerk replied. 'The vehicles out there are only the ones awaiting collection. The remainder of our fleet are stored on a secure lot the other side of the airport.'

'Somebody is there with the fleet?'

'24/7.'

'Okay. We'll head on out there. Where the other side of the airport?'

'It's on the perimeter. Off Northside Parkway. There's no company signage, just the lot behind security fencing.'

Leroy nodded at Velasquez to confirm what they had been told, then turned back to the clerk. 'Thanks for your help. We'll be in touch if we need any more information from you.'

On leaving, Leroy made a quick check on the vehicles parked in the vicinity to double check that the Territory was not there; once satisfied, they exited the parking garage and headed out of the airport. Leroy made for Lincoln Boulevard, soon taking the exit for Northside Parkway. As soon as they had left Lincoln, they could see a medium sized lot containing thirty to forty assorted vehicles.

'That must be the place,' said Leroy as he indicated and made a right into the compound. A red and white striped bar hung over the entrance, with an intercom. Leroy leaned nearer, and called out, 'Police.'

Momentarily, the bar lifted, and as Leroy drove the twenty yards to park, a man came out of the prefabricated office building. He walked over to the car. 'The office told me you were coming over,' he said as Leroy and Velasquez got out of the car.

They showed him their badges and Leroy said, 'This is the vehicle we're interested in. Black Ford Territory. This is the licence plate number.'

'I'll just check where it's parked,' the clerk said. 'Save time.'

Leroy nodded. 'We'll wait here.'

A minute later, he returned holding a set of keys. 'Third row, in the centre.'

They followed him along the third row and stopped in the middle, where the car was parked. The make and the model matched, to their records, and to the images on the CCTV. The licence plate matched.

Leroy held his hand out for the keys. 'I'll bring them back in when we're done. Thanks.'

The clerk reluctantly handed Leroy the keys and walked back to the office. Leroy waited till he had gone, then clicked the open button on the key fob.

'It's been cleaned,' said Velasquez, running her hand over the shiny black hood.

'And valeted,' said Leroy, looking inside.

Velasquez looked inside too. 'It smells brand new. So we're screwed, then?'

'Not necessarily,' Leroy said quietly, looking over the interior. 'As I said, it's very difficult to be a hundred percent clean. Even with a fancy valet cleaning.' He walked to the front of the car and crouched. Ran his fingers over the bumper. Looking up at Velasquez, he said, 'Slight dents here. Feel.'

She did so, and nodded. 'I can feel.'

He stood up. 'I'll reach out to SID, and get them to come and collect it. Then they can check every square inch. Every square millimetre.' As they walked back to the office, he called the Scientific Investigation Division and requested a pick up. 'It will be around ninety minutes,' he told Velasquez after he hung up.

Back in the office, he asked the clerk, 'Have you any records here of when the vehicle was last hired? Or do you use the same database as the airport office?'

'The same,' came the reply.

'The vehicle has been cleaned and valeted,' Velasquez said. 'When and where is that done?'

'Once a vehicle is returned, it's checked over at the airport office. Then it's taken to be serviced, gassed up and cleaned. That's all done at a garage off Sepulveda.'

'So it's fully cleaned and prepped when it gets back here?'

'Under the hood and interior, yes. It's taken through the car wash before it's driven over to the airport for a pick up.'

'At the Sepulveda garage?'

The clerk nodded.

'I'll need details of this garage.'

'Surely.' The clerk gave them the name and address.

'We're going to need to impound the vehicle. I have a warrant here.' He showed the warrant to the clerk, who said, 'I'll need to talk to my supervisor.'

'That's your prerogative, but a pick-up will be here in ninety minutes. We'll give you a receipt for it.'

Leroy and Velasquez wandered back outside into the sun. Leroy pointed as he spoke. 'There are cameras there, either side of the gate, here, at the office; there at each corner of the lot. So good coverage.'

'What kind of time frame are we looking for?'

'I think start now. Then work backwards, keep going until you see something. Pick the POV showing the vehicle.' He paused. 'And that will change, depending on how many times it was moved.'

'So that means more CCTV trawling then?'

Leroy looked at her and winced. 'Yeah, I'm sorry.'

'I guess there are boring parts to any job.'

'Believe me, seventy-five percent of this job is boring. At least these days, you can view everything in the comfort of the station.'

'As opposed to?'

'Back in the day, you would have had to have stayed here, sitting through dozens of VHS tapes. Go back as far as the last known hire.'

She nodded. 'Sure thing, boss. I'll go get the footage emailed over to me.'

'I'm going to check out the lot.' While Velasquez went back inside, Leroy wandered around the car pound. Coverage here was good, he felt. Two cameras by the gates, one on the office building, and one on each corner.

The clerk came outside. Leroy turned and said, 'The place seems to be well covered.'

'Yes, security is good here.'

'I hope so. We believe the vehicle was used in a homicide two days ago.'

'But,' the clerk said, 'it's been here all the time.'

'Not according to CCTV of the incident.'

'How long will you have it for?'

'I'm not sure. It might be needed as evidence. But we'll let you know. Once we can release it, we'll return it.'

The clerk nodded and went back inside, crossing with Velasquez.

'All done, boss,' she said. 'It's waiting for me back at the station.'

Leroy nodded. 'Good. The pick up's going to be an hour plus. You take the car back; I'll get a ride with the pick up.'

'You're going to stay here?'

'I will. I want to make sure the car's secure until we take it, and to get an idea of what happens when you drive off.'

'You think he'll tamper with the vehicle?'

'I've no idea, but I don't want to leave it unattended. I don't want it touched, even by you and me. Make a start on the CCTV when you get back. I won't be too far behind; then I can see how you and Ray have gotten on.'

## CHAPTER SEVENTEEN

LEROY WATCHED AS Velasquez drove out of the car pound and back to the station. He would wait for the SID pick-up truck and get a ride back with them. As she got out of view the guy behind the desk in the office came out, half walking, half running.

'Anything else I can do for you?' he asked. He seemed stressed that Leroy was still there.

'No, I'm just waiting here for the pick-up.' The guy half nodded, turned, and went back inside.

On the perimeter of the lot, just inside the chain-link fencing, was a small knoll, covered in patches of grass, half green, half brown. Leroy sat on the knoll as he waited. One reason he had sent Velasquez ahead, was that he wanted to make sure there was no tampering with the Territory, and to gauge the general activity here.

He had been there five minutes when two men appeared from the rear of the building. Dressed in blue overalls, they ignored Leroy, and walked over to a red Nissan Sentra. The Sentra was gleaming in the morning sun, but both men took chamois leather cloths from their overall pockets, and began buffing the vehicle, chatting loudly as they worked. It sounded as if they were speaking in Spanish. Clearly the Sentra was being prepared for a rental.

His phone pinged. He reached down and took it out of his belt pouch. It was from Stacy. She enjoyed the meal the night before. It was no big deal if he already had plans for Friday evening, but if he was free, was he interested in seeing a stand-up comic, of whom Leroy had probably never heard, at the Laugh Factory on Sunset. He messaged back that he appreciated her invitation, that he was interested, and in fact would look forward to it.

He noticed he had two voicemails. One was from Quinn, the one he had heard already, and hadn't deleted it; the other was from Jasmine Washington. Reluctantly, he put the phone to his ear to listen to the message.

Every so often, Jasmine would call Leroy and ask if he had any news for her. Each time he would say not at this time, but he was still working on it. She need not worry; he would not forget.

This time was no different, but as he slipped his phone back into its pouch, he tried to remember when he had last looked at the file. Over a week at least: he promised himself he would resume tonight. Maybe after being away for a few days, he would be able to see something he had missed before.

As he waited on the knoll, he looked up at an airplane which was coming in to land. The noise of the planes was constant, loud, but after a while, you got used to it, talking louder over the sound of the jet engines. Leroy watched as the aircraft crossed the sky, getting lower and lower. The tail-fin was red, and he tried to figure out which airline it belonged to, and where it had come from, but by now, it was too far in the distance for him to make out any logo.

The arrival of the pick-up truck brought Leroy out of

his reverie. He stood up as the barrier rose, and directed the driver over to where the Territory was parked. He still had the keys.

Leroy watched as the Ford was loaded onto the truck, gave the office clerk a receipt, and jumped aboard with the two drivers.

The truck took the 405 Freeway, and Leroy got the driver to drop him at the bottom of the off ramp at Cotner Avenue. He would then get back onto the freeway across the street. It was a twenty minute walk from there to the station at Butler and Iowa Avenues. He considered looking for a cab, or getting Quinn or Velasquez to come get him, but the walk would save him some gym time this week. He saw a black and white on the corner of Cotner and Olympic, but decided not to get them to drop him off. He had been told several times by the Watch Commander that, 'My patrol cars are not for you detectives to use as goddamned taxicabs.'

Once back at the station, he considered giving Perez an update, but decided to wait as at the moment there was not much to update him on. Velasquez and Quinn were both at their desks, Velasquez at the large PC screen and Quinn on Scott Dempsey's laptop. They both looked up as he arrived.

Velasquez spoke first. 'I've started on the POV from the camera on the office structure. You get a good view of the Ford from there.'

'And it's not moved?'

'Negative. I'm viewing at sixteen times the normal speed, keeping focussed on the vehicle. But, no movement yet.'

Leroy nodded. 'What about you, Ray? Any luck?'

## CHAPTER EIGHTEEN

QUINN PUSHED HIS chair back and looked up at Leroy.

'So far, I've been able to identify two companies Dempsey had had dealings with in the past three months. The most recent was a printing company based in Boyle Heights. He bought it out in February this year. Sold it in August.'

'At a huge profit, of course,' said Leroy.

Quinn referred back to the laptop. 'Seven point eight million.'

Leroy whistled.

Velasquez asked, 'February to August. Six months. So what happened in those six months? He fire all the staff?'

'Pretty much. He did make other economies: smaller premises, for example. Put up prices, also. But when he bought the company, there were nine workers. When he sold it, there were four.'

'Personnel costs being the highest of any concern,'

Leroy said. 'Do we have details of the five who were fired?'

'We do. Names and addresses.'

'Where does he get the cash from to buy the company?' Velasquez asked.

'Bank loans.'

'I'm guessing,' Leroy said, 'that he had a track record in turning companies around, so he was able to get the money from his bank. They knew they weren't throwing money away on some shit concern; they knew they were going to get their dough back.' He paused, taking a mouthful of coffee. 'So we have names and addresses of five people who would have reason to be pissed at Dempsey?'

'We do,' Quinn confirmed.

'So that printing company was sold off at a seven point eight million profit in August. What was he working on when he died?'

'Yeah,' Quinn said, turning back to the screen. 'That seems to be a larger, er, project. He bought it out June thirtieth. Paid fifteen million for it.'

'Jeez,' breathed Velasquez. 'Same source?'

'The same. *Tool World*. A small chain of hardware stores. Has stores Downtown - Sixth Street – and in South Pasadena, Florence, and Anaheim.'

'So he bought them out end of June, while he was still downsizing the printer's,' Leroy said. 'Busy guy. But didn't Shipley say he worked on his own?'

'He did,' Quinn nodded.

'As you say,' Velasquez said. 'Busy guy.'

'How far had he gotten on the hardware chain?' Leroy asked.

'Difficult to tell,' Quinn said. 'All I can find on here, inside the *Tool World* folder, are financial statements for the last five years, profiles of regular business customers as opposed to walk-ins.'

'I thought they were stores?' Velasquez asked.

'They are, but they seem to have been building up an

online side to the business.'

'That would have been forced on them by the pandemic,' Leroy said. 'But there was no reason to discontinue it. It's still business. What about employees? Anything about laying people off?'

'Nothing I've found so far. There is a sub-folder with a list of employees, but no hit list.'

'Looks like he got interrupted,' Leroy said.

'Yeah,' Velasquez added. 'By a black Ford.'

Leroy nodded. 'All five thousand pounds of it.' He finished his coffee and tossed the paper cup away. 'Good work, guys. Keep at it; I'll go update Perez.'

He walked down the corridor to the lieutenant's office, his phone pinged. He paused and checked it. It was a text from Stacy about tomorrow night. She had the tickets for tomorrow night. The performance started at eight thirty, and where and when did he want to meet up? He replied that eight thirty tomorrow night was good for him, and he would love to pick her up, but did not know where she lived. He finished the message with a wink emoji. Grinning, he put his phone back into its pouch, and tapped on the lieutenant's door.

Perez motioned for Leroy to enter, and sat listening attentively as Leroy gave him a progress update.

'So you're saying,' he asked, once Leroy had finished, 'that the SUV was stolen from the lot to kill Dempsey?'

'It depends on your definition of stolen. According to the rental company's records, it was not hired out during that period. Which means it was stored on that lot. But we know it was Downtown at least part of that time. So that means it was removed, used, and replaced. It had to have been: if somebody saw it stored there, and said, "Look, there's a car I can use as a murder weapon. I'm going to steal it," they're going to just dump it. They're not going to take it back, are they?'

'So why was it returned? And are you sure you have the right vehicle?'

'Why was it returned? I have no idea at this time. And,

yes: we are sure. The licence plate matches, the make and model match. And I found a dent on the front bumper which I think is consistent with impact with a human body.'

Perez nodded. 'Where is the vehicle now?'

'Forensic have it. I've asked them to go over it with fine toothed comb. It's been cleaned and valeted, of course.'

'But that would be standard practice with a car rental company.'

'I know, but even that would be comparatively superficial. I'm hoping they find something that could lead us to a driver.'

'Okay,' the lieutenant nodded. 'Ray says he's going through Scott Dempsey's business folders. Is there anything there which could link him to a potential killer? The Chief -'

Perez was interrupted by Velasquez, who burst into his office.

'Sorry, Lieutenant, but... boss, we have a face.'

Quickly, Leroy gave Perez some context. 'Pamela's been viewing the CCTV for the car rental pound, where the Ford has been stored. Excuse me, will you?'

Leroy hurriedly followed Velasquez back to the desk. He noticed that Perez was following. They gathered around Velasquez's desk while she replayed the footage for them.

It began with the Territory being driven along the row of parked vehicles. It was night, and the brake lights went on as it stopped. Then the reverse lights as it turned in a quarter circle to park, the brake lights going on and off. Then the running lights as the engine went off. After a moment, under the light from the pound floodlights, they could make out two figures exiting the vehicle.

The camera the footage of which they were viewing was the one attached to the office building, so the two men who were walking towards the camera were clearly heading to the office. As they got nearer, Leroy said,

'Freeze it there.' Velasquez hit the pause button.

Even allowing for the fact that it was dark, and the floodlights were in the background, there was a reasonably clear image of the two men. One was tall, youngish. He bizarrely wore sunglasses, was clean shaven, and wore a dark leather jacket. The other was shorter, and stockier. He had a dark beard, and was wearing a dark coat and beanie.

'Well?' Leroy asked, talking to himself as much as the others. 'Anybody know these guys?'

## CHAPTER NINETEEN

VELASQUEZ ENLARGED THE frozen image so that the two faces filled the screen. Leroy, Quinn and Perez looked at the screen. Quinn and Perez shook their heads.

'The one with the beard is strangely familiar,' Leroy said eventually. 'But I can't put a name to it. The other one – no idea.' He looked over at two other detectives, Swann and Quinto, who were at their workstations. 'You guys recognise these jokers?'

Swann and Quinto rose and walked over to Velasquez's screen. Both leaned over to look at the images. Quinto shook his head. 'What do you think, partner?' he asked Swann, who stood up and shook her head.

'Never seen either of them. Sorry, Sam. Lieutenant.'

They wandered back to their desks as Leroy looked over at Perez. 'Would you authorise us to use LACRIS here?'

Leroy was referring to facial recognition. The LAPD

does not have a platform of its own, but has access to the Los Angeles County Sheriff's Department database, known as the Los Angeles County Regional Identification System, or LACRIS. Use of the system is heavily regulated and governed by state law, following concerns raised about privacy and civil liberties. Facial recognition is not considered the same as identification; a criminal investigative search is the only form of facial recognition allowed on LACRIS. There can be no connectivity to a surveillance system, including body cameras, or to the DMV, or social media, or other open source platform. Users have to be properly trained, and its use by the LAPD has to be authorised by a Supervisor, which meant that, as Leroy was running the investigation, its use would have to be authorised by Leroy's Supervisor, namely Lieutenant Perez.

'Yeah,' Perez nodded. 'I'll authorise it. Let's set it up on your desk.'

Leroy sat at his own workstation and logged into the system. He pushed his chair back to enable Perez to type in his own identification and password. Then Leroy uploaded the facial images from the CCTV. It was now a matter of waiting, as LACRIS compared these images to the DMS, or Digital Mugshot System. Any match would not be able to be used in evidence, but merely assist Leroy's team in identifying the person.

'How long is this likely to take?' Velasquez asked, as the program began running.

'I'm hoping not too long,' Leroy replied, checking the time. 'But don't expect too much. It might not even come up with anything. While we're waiting, do you want to print off a hard copy and we can get it shown to the others in the station?'

'I don't need to get it printed,' she said, pressing some keys on her phone. 'Here: it's on my cell.' She held her phone up, so Leroy could see the two men's faces on her screen.

'Shit, that's impressive. Can you send that over to Ray

and me?'

'No problem, boss.' Momentarily, both Leroy's and Quinn's phones pinged.

'That's great,' Leroy said, looking at the images which had just come through. He nodded over to his workstation screen, where LACRIS was still running. 'Keep an eye on that. I'm going to have a word with Double-R.'

Double-R was the Watch Commander Ronny Rosenberg. He and Leroy had had a good working relationship for years, which always came in useful if it was a matter of liaison between the detectives and the uniformed division.

Leroy picked up a coffee and Snickers bar on his way to the Watch Commander office, and laid them in front of Rosenberg, who was currently on the phone. Rosenberg quietly acknowledged the offering, but retained a puzzled look on his face. Once he ended the call, he looked up at Leroy.

'Much appreciated as always, Sam; but what's the occasion?'

'No occasion, Ronny. Just a friendly gesture. Plus I need a favour.'

Rosenberg laughed. 'So there is always a price to pay.'

Leroy held out phone. 'These guys here: we're trying to identify. Could you send the images out, so your guys can say if they know them?'

Rosenberg put on his glasses and checked Leroy's phone. 'I don't need to. I can tell you who the bearded one is. Not the other, though.'

'You being serious? Who is he?'

'Let me just verify.' Rosenberg turned to his keyboard and typed some search parameters. 'There,' he said, swivelling his screen to Leroy could see.

Leroy read the name on the screen. 'William Mitchell.' The picture on the mugshot was almost identical to that on the CCTV image.

'Yeah,' Rosenberg said. 'I recall him now. Our paths have crossed once or twice before. Mean SOB, as I remember. Has done a stretch for robbery, three years; then four and half for assault. Is he in the picture for that four eighty?' Four eighty is the call code for a hit and run.

'It's a one eight seven now. The CCTV showed the vehicle was driven deliberately onto the sidewalk. Three fatalities so far, two still in hospital.'

'That would be his MO. Like I told you, Sam, I don't know who the other guy is, but I can get his picture out, if you want.'

'It's okay, Ronny. Mitchell's details should be enough. Is there an address?'

'There is.' Rosenberg copied the address and passed the note over to Leroy. 'Good luck, Sam. Go get that scumbag off the streets. You want backup?'

'That might be an idea. Thanks.' Leroy looked at the address. 'Fountain and Mariposa. Could a car meet us there in an hour?'

'You got it. No problem.'

'Thanks, Ronny. I appreciate that. Keep the Snickers.'

'I will.' With a grin, Rosenberg opened a desk drawer and theatrically brushed the candy bar into the drawer.

Leroy returned to the desk. Velasquez spun round.

'It's still checking.'

'Tell it not to bother. I have a name and address.'

'How did you get that?'

'Ronny Rosenberg, the Watch Commander. He's dealt with our guy before. His name's William Mitchell, lives on Fountain and Mariposa.'

'And the other?'

Leroy shook his head. 'No, just Mitchell. But I would guess once we have Mitchell, that will lead us to the other. Ronny is arranging a back-up Shamu to meet us there around twelve thirty.'

'We'll need that?'

'Double-R believes so. Best to be prepared. Ray: keep on with Dempsey's business files. You might want to reach out to Financial Crimes. They might be able to identify any criminality going on, that might have been a motive. Ronny's given me a name and address for the guy in the beard and beanie. I'm taking Pamela over to bring him in.'

'Sure thing, Sam. What about the LACRIS search? You want me to stop it?'

'No, let it run. Sure, we know who William Mitchell is, but we also need to identify the other one. The one who wears shades at night. Jeez.'

The most direct route from the station to Mitchell's house would be to take Santa Monica Boulevard; however, at this time of day a less direct route would be quicker. Leroy took the 405 north to Sherman Oaks, then the 101 to Hollywood, then Franklin Avenue into Little Armenia, where Mitchell lived. He took Mariposa Avenue down to the intersection with Sunset Boulevard. Across Sunset, he saw a black and white parked outside a school. He pulled up in front of the patrol car. As he parked, two uniformed officers got out. They introduced themselves as Officers Silva and Clarke. Silva was the senior.

'Lieutenant Rosenberg told us to meet you here, Detective,' Silva said.

'The address is 1360,' Leroy said. 'Over there we have 1310, so we're talking five buildings away.'

'A lot of residences in this street are gated,' said Clarke. 'Would that complicate things?'

Leroy sighed and looked up and down the street. 'It might. We could lose the element of surprise. Anybody know the name of the next cross street?'

'Alexandria,' volunteered Officer Clarke.

'Alexandria,' Leroy repeated. He turned to Velasquez. 'Can you and Officer Clarke here, go round to the back of the premises, just in case he tries to run? Silva and I will go to the front of the house. Let me know when you're in position.'

'Sure thing.' Velasquez led Clarke along the alley which ran by the side of the building numbered 1330. It ran through to Alexandria Avenue, then they were able to cut through to the rear of 1360 Mariposa. Velasquez called

Leroy to confirm they were in position.

'Okay,' Leroy directed. 'Let's go.' He and Silva checked their service weapons and walked down to number 1360. It was the first of a number of actual houses, as opposed to apartment buildings. Set back slightly from the street, it had no gate or fence. The screened front door was situated on a small raised wooden porch. You could tell the house had once been painted a shade of terracotta, which probably looked smart when fresh; now it was grimy and faded. The front windows were also screened: on one of the panes the screen was torn, and you could see that the glass had not seen water or soap for a long time. In fact, the whole house had the air of neglect about it.

Leroy put his ear to the screen on the door. He could not hear anything. He glanced over at Silva and shook his head.

Then he waited a couple of seconds before knocking on the door.

## CHAPTER TWENTY

THERE WAS NO answer.

Leroy knocked again.

Again, no response. He and Silva listened for any sounds from inside the house, or round the back. If Mitchell had tried to flee from the back of the house, they would have heard Velasquez and Clarke raise the alarm. Silva tried to peer through the gap in the window screen but the interior was in darkness.

Leroy considered whether to effect a forced entry, but was interrupted by a voice.

'Are you looking for William?'

Leroy and Silva turned in the direction of the voice. An elderly man had just come out of the house next door, accompanied by a German Shepherd.

'Yes, we are,' Leroy said, 'but it looks like he's not in.'

'He'll be at work,' the man said, restraining his dog, which was keen to begin its walk.

Leroy stepped over to the chain link fence. 'Do you know where he works?'

'As far as I know,' the neighbour said, 'he's working at that gas station Downtown.'

'Which gas station would that be?'

'The one on Alameda. You must know where I mean; it's a block away from the train depot.'

'I know the one,' Silva said.

Leroy looked at her and nodded. 'Yeah.' He turned back to the neighbour. 'Thank you for your help, sir. Appreciated.'

'You're welcome,' the neighbour said. He stepped off his porch and paused. He nodded to Silva, who was wearing uniform. 'He's not in any trouble, is he?'

'No, no, nothing like that,' Leroy lied. 'Just routine. Thanks again. You have a good day, sir.'

Leroy watched the neighbour and his dog get to the sidewalk, and get out of view. He took out his phone and called Velasquez. 'Pamela, he's not here. A neighbour told us he works at the gas station on Alameda and Cesar Chavez. Meet us back at the cars and we'll head up there.'

It took Velasquez and Clarke five minutes to make their way back to where they had parked. 'When we get to the gas station,' Leroy said, 'we'll be okay to park on the forecourt, but you guys will need to park out of sight. I'm sure he's not expecting a visit; I don't want him to get spooked by a black and white and run.'

They headed Downtown. The gas station in question was situated a block up from Union Station. Where North Main and North Alameda Streets cross, there is a small island, and the gas station is located there. On arrival, Leroy pulled up on the forecourt, next to the air pressure hoses. Silva and Clarke parked their patrol car out of sight behind the hotel across North Main Street. Once everybody was in place, Leroy and Velasquez went inside the gas station.

Leroy immediately recognised William Mitchell behind the counter. He was taking a cash payment from the driver of one of the vehicles at the pumps. He glanced up for a second as Leroy and Velasquez entered the premises, then returned to his transaction. Leroy and Velasquez stood in line behind a woman. Once he had served her, Mitchell asked them, 'Which pump?'

Leroy held out his badge. 'No pump. William Mitchell?'

Before Leroy could say anything else, Mitchell moved. Adjacent to the counter was a door leading to a back office area, locked with a press-button keypad. The counter had two till positions, one of which was closed, with Mitchell manning the other. Only a few years ago, Leroy could have leapt over the counter to give chase; however, now, since the pandemic, thick clear plastic prevented that.

Two other drivers had joined the line: Silva called, 'LAPD!' as she and Leroy ran past them and out onto the forecourt. Now with weapons drawn, they ran around the side of the building, to North Main Street. Velasquez and Silva, also with weapons drawn, were calling out to Mitchell, who had by now exited the gas station building, and had made his way across the busy street. Mitchell was ignoring them, and continued running in the direction of East Cesar Estrada Chavez Avenue.

Fortunately, the traffic here was one-way, heading north, which made it easier for Velasquez and Clarke to cross in pursuit. Silva following, Leroy ran down the sidewalk, across the street from Mitchell, hoping to head him off.

They were near the intersection when a bus passed by, slowing down slightly owing to the weight of traffic. Once it had moved on, Mitchell was nowhere to be seen.

'Fuck!' Leroy called out. 'Where is he?' He spun round on the corner, feverishly trying to see where Mitchell had gone.

On the corner of Main and Chavez is the Maple Immigration and Income tax Services, on the second floor above a closed and shuttered market. A curved staircase led up to the offices. Leroy gestured to Velasquez and

Clarke to check up there. There was nowhere else for him to have gone. While they climbed the steps, Leroy did two three sixties.

'How the fuck could we have lost him?' he called out to Silva, who was two feet away.

Silva looked around too; then, 'Detective, there he is!'

Somehow Mitchell had made it across the street and was disappearing into Olvera Street.

Olvera Street is known as 'the birthplace of Los Angeles', and is the oldest street in the city. It is a Mexican marketplace, recreating a romantic and historic 'Old LA' with a narrow, tree-lined block-long street filled with stalls, gift shops, and restaurants. Leroy and Silva crossed over and followed Mitchell through the *pueblo.*

He was running in a straight line, running very fast. Leroy was not sure if he and Silva could keep up with him. He was slightly faster than Silva, but could feel himself getting out of breath. For a middle aged man, Mitchell was surprisingly fit.

'Out of the way! LAPD!' he would cry periodically, and the people in the streets browsing at the items on the various Mexican stalls, or perusing the menus outside the eating places, moved aside. Both he and Silva were brandishing their weapons, but there was very little reaction at this from the people they passed. Maybe they were running too fast for the weapons to be noticed.

At the very end of the street, on the right, is a Mexican restaurant *La Luz Del Dia*, literally Daylight. Outside the brick adobe is a covered patio, where around a dozen people were brunching. Mitchell made a sharp left, and ran along the patio, pushing one of the servers out of the way, causing a tray filled with drinks and two plates of *huevos rancheros* to scatter onto the ground. Some of the diners screamed, but Mitchell carried on through the patio, leaping over the low fence at the end. Leroy and Silva continued along the street itself, having to fight their way through a crowd of tourists being led by a guide.

At the end of the street is a large and ornate wooden

cross, standing on four circular steps. It is a common tourist photograph location: Leroy had himself been asked, when off duty, if he would mind taking a photograph of a family, or a group of tourists. Before selfies took over.

This time, though, there were no tourists on the monument, although a couple of dozen onlookers were gathered in a wide semicircle.

The patrol car was parked on Los Angeles Street, and Velasquez and Clarke were standing, feet apart, at four and eight o'clock, pointing their weapons at William Mitchell, who was on his knees, his hands on his head.

## CHAPTER TWENTY-ONE

WILLIAM MITCHELL WAS now sitting in Interview Room 2. Within thirty minutes of making his phone call, his lawyer, a forty-something who wore his hair and clothes like it was the nineteen eighties, arrived at the station. The lawyer's name was Rogers ('with an s') McQueen. Leroy was sitting across the table from Mitchell and McQueen; Quinn and Velasquez were watching the CCTV screen outside. Leroy was ten minutes into the interrogation when Lieutenant Perez wandered over and began watching.

Leroy opened his laptop and began to play the video from the car pound.

'You were seen here, on CCTV, parking a black Ford Territory, here in an automobile pound on the outskirts of LAX.'

Mitchell looked across to his attorney. 'No comment.'

Leroy pressed the Play key, and they watched the video. He paused it when Mitchell and the other men appeared. 'Is this you?'

Mitchell looked across to his attorney. 'No comment.'

Leroy asked, 'Where were you between eight and nine AM two days ago?

Mitchell looked across to his attorney. 'No comment.'

Leroy said, 'Can't you answer a question without looking at him?'

Mitchell looked across to his attorney. 'No comment,' he said, then sniggered. McQueen kept a straight face.

Leroy leaned forward, his elbow resting on the table. He spoke softly, looking at both Mitchell and McQueen. 'Look, let's stop jerking around here. We both' – he looked at McQueen – '*all* know -'

McQueen cut in. 'Detective, I'm here purely to advise my client. I do not *know*, anything.'

'Sure,' Leroy said. 'As you say.' He turned to Mitchell. 'As we both *know*, it was you there, on the CCTV, parking and getting out of that vehicle. That's obvious, even though it was dark. And we all know, from other CCTV footage, that the vehicle in question was used in a hit and run between eight and nine AM two days ago. A hit and run in which three people died, and several are still hospitalised.'

'Is there a question in there, Detective?' asked McQueen.

Leroy said nothing, just stared at Mitchell and McQueen.

Outside, Lieutenant Perez chuckled. Quinn looked over to him. 'What's funny, Lieutenant?'

'Sam's interrogation technique. To just sit there and say nothing, waiting for the silence to get uncomfortable so somebody can't help speaking. It's normally the lawyers.'

Inside the interview room, it took thirty seconds for the silence to get uncomfortable. McQueen asked, When was that taken?'

Leroy pointed to the date and time stamp on the screen.

'And when was the alleged hit and run supposed to

have taken place?' McQueen asked.

'When this vehicle allegedly hit a sidewalk full of people, allegedly killing three of them, and allegedly injuring even more? It was then and then.' Leroy jabbed the screen with his finger as he spoke.

McQueen looked over at his client, then leaned back in his chair, tapping his pen on his yellow legal pad. 'So, let me get this right. Two days elapsed between this alleged hit and run and when my client was seen leaving the vehicle. Quite a time gap, wouldn't you say, Detective? More than enough time for somebody else to do whatever they did with the vehicle, return the car, and for my client to make use of it.'

With a straight face, Leroy said, 'So it *is* your client on here?' He touched the laptop screen with his index finger.

Outside, Lieutenant Perez chuckled again. 'Just remind Sam to keep me up to speed on this,' he said, returning to his office.

'Will do, Lieutenant,' said Quinn, just as his cell phone rang.

Back in the room, Leroy asked Mitchell, 'So why were you parking the car then? As your attorney has conceded that this is you here.'

McQueen looked up from his legal pad, his face reddening slightly, then shrugged as Mitchell looked over at him.

Mitchell said, 'I work for the place.'

'As well as the gas station?'

'There's no crime in having two jobs, is it? Fucking cost of living.'

'So, we've established that this is you here. Not your long lost identical twin.'

Mitchell looked across to his attorney. 'No comment.'

Leroy looked up at the camera in the room in frustration. 'Jesus Christ, you've just admitted you work there.' He paused and took a deep breath. 'Be right back.' He got up and exited the room, and walked back to his desk, where Velasquez was watching the screen.

'You want me to listen to what they are saying?'

'Not much point. We can't use it. Any progress on the other guy?'

She shook her head. 'Nothing. LACRIS is finished running. No match on the other guy. But it identified Mitchell.'

'As we did ourselves earlier. So much for technology. His partner obviously doesn't have a record. Look, can you get onto the car rental company? Verify that Mitchell does work there. Text me if they can't verify.'

Leroy returned to the room.

'We're verifying,' he said, 'that you do actually work for the car hire company. What do you do there?'

'I drive the cars to and from the terminal. Before and after the hire.'

'And who is that with you?'

Mitchell looked over at his attorney, who clearly had no advice.

'It's a simple enough question. You admit you work there, and that this is you on the screen. So who is the other guy?'

Mitchell hesitated for a second, then said, 'His name is Sergei Zhurov.'

'Sounds Russian.'

Mitchell shrugged. 'Guess so.'

'He works there too? What does he do?'

'Same as me.'

'Where does he live?'

'Don't know.'

Leroy stood up. 'Be right back again.'

Outside, he asked Velasquez, 'What did the rental company say?'

'They confirmed he works for them. Part time. Moves cars around, mainly between the pound and the airport, and to and from the gas station to wash and fuel up. You said to text you only if he didn't work there.'

'I know, I know, but I need you to call them back. Mitchell has named the other guy as Sergei Zhurov.'

'Russian?'

'Sounds like it. Call them back, confirm Zhurov does work for them as well, and get his address. Tell them we're not concerned with Zhurov's immigration status, which we're not. Remind them they've seen the warrant if you have to, and tell them not to reach out to him. If they do, they could be charged with obstruction.'

'Could they?'

Leroy shrugged. 'Where's Ray?'

'He had a call from Financial Crimes. He's taken Dempsey's laptop to West First, so they can go through the accounts with him. He said he'll be back later.'

'Okay. Progress, I hope. I guess it's too soon to expect anything from Forensics about the car.' Leroy returned to the interview room, calling over his shoulder, 'Text if you get anything about Sergei Zhurov.'

As Leroy entered the interview room, McQueen asked, 'Are we nearly done, Detective? My client -'

'Almost,' said Leroy as he sat down. 'For now. We're verifying what you said about Sergei Zhurov, and getting his address. So, are you going to tell me where you were that morning, or are we going around in circles again?'

Mitchell's eyes met his attorney's; then he replied, 'I was at home.'

'Not at work, or going to work?'

'I start at the gas station at noon, and if I'm working at the pound, that's usually after eight at night.'

'Can anybody corroborate that?'

'I live alone.'

'I see.' Leroy paused. 'That's all for now. Thank you for your cooperation so far.'

Mitchell looked at his attorney.

McQueen asked, 'So Mr Mitchell is free to go?'

'I didn't say that. He arrived here 12:25PM, three and a half hours ago. That means I can hold him for another forty-four and a half hours.'

McQueen spluttered, 'I prot -'

'You know the law, Mr McQueen. He'll be in a holding

cell. This is a murder investigation.'

## CHAPTER TWENTY-TWO

THEY HAD SERGEI Zhurov's address. Baldwin Street, Lincoln Heights. As before, with William Mitchell, Leroy had arranged for a patrol car to meet them at the location.

'We'll wait here,' Leroy said. 'They'd better not be too long.'

They remained parked across the street, three buildings down from Zhurov's.

The address in question was a small apartment building; Zhurov lived on the third, the top, floor. On the wide driveway at the front a man was servicing a motorcycle. The bike was propped up, and he was crouching by the side of the machine, using a spanner to tighten something.

'Do you think that's him, Sam?' Velasquez asked.

Leroy looked over. 'Could be.'

'Does he look Russian, do you think?' she asked.

Leroy looked at her. 'What does a Russian look like?

He's not wearing a Cossack hat, black boots, and drinking vodka. And I can't hear *Lara's Theme* playing.'

'*Lara's Theme*?'

'*Dr Zhivago*. The movie. It doesn't matter. He is wearing a leather jacket, though.' Leroy checked the time. 'Where the fuck is that back-up? We'll give them five more minutes, then I'll call Double R again.'

Leroy waited three more minutes before running out of patience. 'We're going to lose the moment if we don't act now,' he said as he climbed out of the car.

Velasquez followed. 'What about back-up?'

Leroy looked over his shoulder. 'I have you.'

They paused to let a car pass, then crossed over. The man working on the motorcycle looked up as they approached.

'Can I help you?' he asked, standing up. He had an accent, which Leroy took as Russian.

Leroy held out his badge. 'Are you Sergei Zhurov?'

'I am. What's this all about?'

'We need you to come to the station with us. We have some questions to ask you, concerning your employment with SoCal Rentals.'

'Am I under arrest?'

'Not at this time, but we would appreciate your cooperation.'

'Which police station are we going to?'

'West Los Angeles, sir,' Leroy replied politely.

'Can I put my bike away first?' Zhurov asked, pointing over to an open garage door.

Leroy nodded. 'Surely.'

Zhurov kicked away the support pedal. He made to reach for the handle bars, but moved his body slightly to the right.

'Gun!' Velasquez called out, drawing her weapon. Leroy instinctively took a step back and drew his. Both covered Zhurov.

'Stand perfectly still. Hands on your head,' Leroy ordered. Zhurov complied. 'Cover me,' he said to

Velasquez, as he stepped behind Zhurov, and lifted up his leather coat. Inside, tucked into Zhurov's jeans, was a gun. Leroy pulled it out by the barrel and passed it to Velasquez. He then pulled out a set of handcuffs from his own pocket and cuffed Zhurov's hands behind his back.

'About time,' said Velasquez as a patrol car pulled up outside. Two uniformed officers got out.

'Where the hell have you been?' Leroy called out.

'Sorry we're late, Detective,' the lead officer said. 'We got delayed by an eleven sixty-five.'

'By a -?' Leroy shook his head in exasperation. 'Now you're here, put him in your back seat. We're taking him to West LA.'

'Anything we can do for you here?' the officer asked.

'I don't think so.' Leroy turned to Velasquez. 'Once he's booked in, I'll reach out to Judge Santos for a warrant to search here and Mitchell's house.' Turning back to the officer, 'Could you guys wheel the bike into that garage, then seal it up with tape? We'll be back later.'

The officers led the handcuffed Zhurov to the patrol car and locked him in the back seat. Velasquez had put the gun into a clear evidence bag. She held it up. 'What do you think?'

'It looks like a Ruger,' Leroy said. 'Lightweight?'

She held it in the palm of her hand. 'Yup.'

Once the property was secured, they took Zhurov to the station. He was booked in, and Leroy and Velasquez returned to their desks.

Leroy took a deep breath. 'It's four PM now. It's been a long day. You get off home now, if you like. I'm heading Downtown to get the warrants. You want to meet here at seven in the morning? Then we three can head over to Mitchell's place, as he was here first, then back to Zhurov. We have at least another thirty-six hours before we have to release them. That should give us enough time.'

'What about the extra personnel the Lieutenant said he was going to give us?'

'He's gone quiet on that. I'm going to update him on

the way out, so I'll follow that up. I suspect he's concerned about the cost, so he's trying to kick the can down the street. I'll ask, anyway.'

'I don't need telling twice. I'll clear up here and go.'

'If Ray checks in, tell him the same. See you back here... seven in the AM?'

Before setting off, Leroy checked in with Lieutenant Perez. He updated the lieutenant, who had the attitude of *I'm really too busy to hear this, but I have to because I need to update the Chief later.* Leroy broached the subject of the extra manpower, only to be told that Perez was working on it. Leroy grinned as he left the office: just as he suspected, Perez was delaying the extra officers as he was worried about the cost of the investigation. But at this time, Leroy was not sure that extra detectives were needed. They had the two drivers in custody; surely it was only a matter of time?

At the Downtown courthouse on West Temple Street, there were no delays in Judge Santos issuing the warrants. With the documents in his inside pockets, Leroy walked to the exit, where he ran into Stacy Chen.

'Still okay for tomorrow evening?' she asked.

'Absolutely,' he said. 'I'll need to know where to pick you up.'

The address was in Hollywood, a street off Franklin Avenue. Not a street Leroy knew, but he would find it. They agreed seven o'clock the next evening.

On the way home, he called Quinn. He had almost finished at Financial Crimes, and was about to leave himself.

Leroy updated him. 'I've told Pamela to get off home; you do the same, but we need to meet at the station seven in the morning so we have an early start on searching their homes. We can keep them for forty-eight hours. They're both being represented by the same lawyer, surprise, surprise. A seedy little shit by the name of Rogers McQueen. He's played up about them being held overnight, but there's nothing he can do. How have you got on?'

'The guy at Financial Crimes has been going through what was on the laptop, but said to leave them everything so they can analyse the accounts.'

'Shit, you didn't leave the laptop there?'

'No, they downloaded everything. Said they have specialised software for this type of thing.'

'Fine. Let them get on with it. I'm really more interested in the names of anybody who he might have pissed off.

'So, tomorrow, we'll meet at the station at seven. We three will go first to William Mitchell's place, as his forty-eight hours expire first, then up to Lincoln Heights for Zhurov. Our next steps may well depend on what we find there. I'll also reach out to Forensic, see what they've found on the Ford.'

'So I'll just head off home now?'

'Yup, see you seven in the morning.'

'You off home too?'

'On my way now.'

'You feel like getting a drink?'

'I would do, but I've some more things I need to get done before I'm done for the day.'

There was a pause.

'The Washington kid?'

Leroy sighed. 'Yeah. I've let it drop for a while, but she still calls me every so often.'

'Why don't you just say you've taken it as far as you can? You wouldn't be lying to her.'

'Wouldn't I? Have I? Taken it as far as I can, I mean? It may well come to that, but I want to be able to look her in the eye and say I've given it my best shot.'

'So that's your homework tonight?'

'It sure is. You get off home now, Ray. See you seven in the morning.'

'Yup. You take care, Sam.'

'I will. You too, brother.'

Leroy headed west on the I-10. After a few miles, he

noticed the signs for La Brea Avenue. To exit the freeway there would mean only a slight diversion into Hollywood. He considered heading up to Franklin Avenue to check out where Stacy lived. Just in preparation for Friday night; so he knew where to go. Then he remembered he was no longer seventeen years old, and carried on along the freeway.

## CHAPTER TWENTY-THREE

LEROY STOPPED FOR food on the way home. Street food.

He pulled up alongside *La Isla Bonita*, a Mexican cuisine truck in Venice, on Rose and Third.

The smell of the taco, its beef and onions, its refried beans, its *salsa roja*, filled his car, making him even hungrier. He was tempted to pull over and consume the taco there and then, but as he was so close to home, he would do the civilised thing and eat at home.

He was soon indoors. There was no need to even nuke the taco in the microwave to heat it up again, it was still hot. He took a bottle of beer from the fridge, unwrapped the food, and sat down at his table.

In the middle of the table lay a manilla folder. The folder contained thirty-five sheets of paper. Thirty-five xerox copies. The entire murder book for Jordan Washington.

Leroy had borrowed the file from the records

depository some time back. He was aware that as part of due diligence checks, files were reviewed every year or two. He did not want to draw attention to the fact that he had possession of the file, so he returned it after three weeks, having copied the entire book.

He slid the folder over, cursing as a ball of *salsa roja* dropped out of his taco and on to the table, missing the folder by a quarter of an inch. He wiped up the salsa and began to leaf through the xeroxes.

After ten minutes, he placed the papers back onto the table. There was nothing new here. He leaned back in his chair and took a long mouthful of beer. Other times when he had reached a dead end, he would drive over to Jordan's school, walk around the neighbourhood. Sometimes doing this would give him an idea.

He rubbed his eyes; doing that would not help tonight. Maybe he had come to a dead end.

Then he had an idea.


Quinn arrived home. Or to the place he had been renting. He still didn't consider it as home. He was halfway through the lease, and had no idea what he would do when the lease expired. He got indoors, threw his keys onto the kitchen counter, and flopped onto the couch. He sat in the dark.

This was what it was like, coming home to an empty house.

Just like Sam.

He wasn't sure about Pamela.

Before he moved out, he could guarantee an argument about something within thirty minutes of getting home. Something or nothing. And he didn't have to cook.

The flip side to all this was that he no longer had to listen to Holly going on about how wonderful her father, whom she worked for, was. Holly was the archetypal daddy's girl.

He had stopped off at Albertsons on Crenshaw the previous night to stock up on microwavable meals for one, so had a well-stocked freezer. Tonight was chili con carne.

As the microwave heated up the food, he opened the fridge for a beer. 'Shit,' he muttered, seeing he was out of beer. He looked around for some wine, but there was none – wine was Holly's tipple anyway – but eventually found an almost empty bottle of Jim Beam. There was around two inches left at the bottom of the bottle, so he poured that into a glass, and added the same amount of tap water.

After eating, he picked up his phone, and trawled through various apps, checked messages and emails. Nothing of any more there. No missed calls.

He was secretly hoping for a call from Holly asking him to come home, but tonight, he was hoping in vain. Maybe he should go and see her. It had been three weeks since any contact. Not tonight, though: he was too tired and too full of Jim Beam. He would leave it until the weekend, then he would have to decide whether to call her first or just show up.

'Fuck,' he whispered, looking up at the ceiling. How could such a basic decision be so complicated?


Velasquez had just arrived home to the smell of cooking. Home for her as a second floor condo in West Hollywood, off Crescent Heights Boulevard. She dropped her bag on the floor and headed for the kitchen, where the smell was coming from. Her partner, Gabriela Diaz, was busy over a stove.

'Hey,' Gabriela said, smiling and looking up.

'Hey back,' Velasquez said, embracing Gabriela. 'That smells good.'

'Me or the pasta?'

Velasquez laughed. 'Both.' She poured herself a large glass of Merlot and perched on one of the kitchen stools.

'How was your day?' Gabriella asked, straining the

pasta.

'Long. Long and tiring. And we have an early start tomorrow.'

Gabriela looked over. 'How early?' she asked.

'I have to be at the station by seven.'

'Girl, that is early. Look, this will be another half hour. Why don't you take a bath or something? Chill for a while.'

'I think I will.' Velasquez picked up her Merlot. 'How was your day?'

'Same old, same old.' Gabriela was the manager of one of the offices in a film and TV studio on North Cahuenga. The office closed promptly at five, and so Gabriela was always home first. 'They're preparing one of the stages for a new TV show.'

'Not a cop show, I hope?' Velasquez hated cop shows, always saying they were so unrealistic. Her main gripe at the moment was shows set in LA where the characters would say, 'see you in thirty minutes' before setting off. In Los Angeles, you can't get anywhere in thirty minutes.

'No, it's a teen comedy.'

'Anybody famous in it?'

'You heard of Victoria Read?'

'Never heard of her.'

'Nobody famous then.'

Velasquez picked up her wine and left for the bathroom.

'See you in thirty,' Gabriela called out.

'You got it, honey,' Velasquez replied from the hall.

## CHAPTER TWENTY-FOUR

LEROY, QUINN, AND Velasquez were all in by seven the next morning.

Velasquez arrived at six forty-six, expecting to be the first to arrive. She hurried round to their desks to get into place before Leroy arrived, almost skidding to a halt when she saw Quinn sitting at his desk, leafing through paperwork.

He looked up.

'Hey. Morning.'

'Morning,' she replied awkwardly. 'Couldn't you sleep?'

Laughing slightly, Quinn said, 'Something like that.'

'Is Sam in yet?'

'He's around somewhere. He said he's been in since just after six.'

She looked around the empty office, looking for Sam. 'I'll get coffee. You want some?'

'I'm good, thanks.' As if to evidence that, he moved his cup around the desk.

She left her bag on her desk and set off to get coffee. As she was about to leave the room, she bumped into Leroy who was coming back.

'Hey,' he said, breezily. 'You ready to head out?'

'Sure. I'm just getting coffee.'

'Bring it with. We're all ready to rock and roll. I've just been checking on our guests.'

'How are they?'

'Well, I'm expecting to get several phone calls from their lawyer today.'

'McQueen?'

'That's the one. Quoting Miranda at me, but he knows as well as we do how long we can keep a suspect for. I'm just hoping we find something today.'

'I'll be two minutes.'

'See you in the lot. I've drawn a city car.'

Velasquez got her coffee. When she returned to their desks Leroy was nowhere to be seen and Quinn was shutting down his PC.

'Where's he gone?' she asked.

'Out in the parking lot.'

'Man,' she said as they walked out, 'what's he on?'

'Haven't you noticed yet?' Quinn grinned. 'Sam's a morning person.'

'And you're not?'

Quinn shook his head. 'You?'

'I thought I was, but not like him.'

When they got outside, they saw a maroon Chevrolet Impala idling in the parking lot. Leroy was in the driver's seat.

'Jump in, you guys,' he said. 'We have rush hour traffic to beat.' Quinn and Velasquez had barely fastened their seat belts before, with a squeal of tyres, the Impala headed for the Butler Avenue exit.

'I'm expecting some heat today,' he said, as they got onto Santa Monica Boulevard, 'from McQueen.'

'We have until tomorrow morning, don't we?' Quinn said.

'Oh, yes; and he knows that, but he'll try and bullshit us. I'll just remind him of that and tell him to fuck off.'

'What about the lieutenant?' Velasquez asked.

'About updating him, you mean? He hadn't gotten in yet, or answered his cell. I just left him a voice message. He's more interested in keeping the Chief happy, so I can't see him getting twitchy about how long they're being held for.'

'What about the extra manpower?' she asked.

'That seems to have gone cold. Perez is obsessed with budgets and the cost of everything, so I'm guessing he's just kind of kicking that can down the street for as long as he can. I'm cool with that, anyway. I think it was just the Chief saying that to make a point.'

'Why is the Chief so interested in this case?' Quinn asked.

'Over and above every other homicide on our books? I have no idea; neither has Perez. He kept referring to it as the Dempsey case, so you can see where his interest lies.'

They took Santa Monica Boulevard inland and into Little Armenia. There was no need for any discretion today, so he parked directly outside Mitchell's house. Faced with the court order, Mitchell had no choice but to give Leroy permission to take his door keys.

As they stood on the porch, before inserting the key in the lock, Leroy paused and looked around.

'What is it, Sam?' Quinn asked.

'That neighbour we saw last time: I was just checking he wasn't around.' Leroy shrugged, unlocked the door, and they stepped inside.

It was as Leroy had remembered it from his first visit. The blinds were down and the screens were dirty, so with bright beams of sunlight coming in through the gaps, the room had an air of neglect and decay.

The room smelt dirty. Velasquez sniffed. 'Nice.'

Quinn looked around the room and agreed.

'We'll split up,' Leroy said. 'I'll go through here and the bathroom; Ray, you take the bedroom or bedrooms - there might be two – and Pamela, you take the kitchen. You all got your gloves?'

'The kitchen?' Velasquez asked indignantly. 'Why me in the kitchen?'

Leroy paused a second; then, 'For fuck's sake, it's only a room. I'll check the kitchen when we get to Zhurov's. Are we good?'

Velasquez said nothing as she went into the kitchen. Quinn did not know whether to grin or just not react; he chose the latter. 'I think there's just one bedroom; I'll go check in there.'

'Not that anybody has a bug up their ass,' Leroy muttered, then called out, 'Take lots of pictures.'

He looked around the room, trying to figure out where to start. Centre was a three-seated sofa, with wide arms. It appeared cream, but in the light it was difficult to tell whether it was actually cream, or a dirty white. A flat screen television set stood on a small three-drawer table. A pair of boots and a pair of sneakers had been thrown in the corner of the room.

He went to the three drawers first. In the bottom drawer were half a dozen magazines, several months old. They were a mixture of *Hustler*, *Barely Legal*, and *Classic American*. The final title related to classic cars. Back in the old days, Leroy might have flicked through the porn; now he just looked at the cover and put the publications back in the drawer. Maybe Mitchell was old-school; Leroy assumed most people got their porn online these days.

The next drawer up contained some pens and pencils and a packet of tissues. Leroy wondered if the tissues related to the contents of the bottom drawer. Nothing of any interest there: he opened the top drawer. This contained three more recent copies of *Barely Legal* and a *TV Guide*. Leroy took pictures of everywhere he looked.

Sighing, he closed the drawer, and stepped over to the couch. He knelt and felt under each cushion. Nothing.

Then he looked under the sofa. Apart from several months' worth of dirt, fluff, and debris, he was able to pull out another magazine. That month's issue of *Classic American*. This time he did leaf through the magazine, before tossing it onto the couch.

He wandered into the hallway and found the bathroom.

The toilet bowl had not been cleaned in months. Fighting the urge to gag, Leroy put the seat lid down and checked inside the cistern. He looked around the room. The bathtub itself had a distinct tidemark all around, just below the top. He pulled the shower curtain to one side: On a plastic shelf fixed to the wall were containers, one of shower gel, one of shampoo. There were black mould stains in the top corner.

Above the equally tidemarked washbasin was a wall-mounted cupboard. Leroy opened the mirrored door. There was not much in the cupboard. Two shelves containing a still wrapped toothbrush and unused toothpaste. Two boxes of Tylenol. He stood in the doorway. He took one more picture, then called out, 'Anything, you guys?'

Velasquez appeared. 'Nothing. Zip. The kitchen's clean.' She paused. 'Well, kind of,' she added, pulling a face.

'I know what you mean,' replied Leroy, nodding his head to the bathroom.

They wandered into the bedroom.

'Anything?' he asked Quinn.

Quinn put his hands on his hips. 'Anything?' He showed them what he had found.

In the top drawer of the bedside cabinet was a small clear plastic bag containing a white powder.

'More importantly,' said Quinn, 'is what's in here.' He opened the other drawer. It contained a survival knife, six inches long, serrated on one edge.

'Looks like an Apache,' Leroy murmured.

The drawer also contained a handgun.

'A Ruger,' Velasquez said. 'Just like Zhurov's.'

'SR1911,' Leroy added. 'Cartridges?'

'Box in the drawer. Half empty.'

'Shit,' said Leroy. 'Anything else?'

'No, everything else – the drawers over there, the closet – is clean.'

'Okay. Let's bag everything up, and head over to the other place. You guys take plenty of pictures?'

Quinn and Velasquez nodded their conformation.

'Cocaine?' Quinn said, as he bagged up the bag of powder.

'I'd guess so. That quantity looks like for his own personal use, but we'll take it, anyway. It might lead to something else.' He paused and looked around. 'Any laptop, iPad or anything?'

Quinn and Velasquez shook their heads. 'Maybe he just used his cell phone?' she suggested.

Leroy nodded. 'Could be. Right, let's get over to Lincoln Heights.'

They locked the evidence in the trunk. Before pulling away, Leroy said, 'So we have a hunting knife, and a gun. Why would he need a hunting knife in LA? And the gun. We need to check if it's stolen, and if he has a permit. There was no garage, so we've covered everything.'

'I checked the yard out back,' Velasquez said, 'but that was clean. Not even a shed.'

'We did find stuff,' Leroy said, 'but not as much as I hoped for. Nothing linking him to the hit and run.'

'We have him on the CCTV,' Velasquez said.

'Yeah, but parking the vehicle a day or so later. Just circumstantial. The DA's office won't run with that, but he does have questions to answer about the knife and gun.'

Leroy fired up the ignition and drove off.

## CHAPTER TWENTY-FIVE

THE CONTRAST BETWEEN William Mitchell's house and Sergei Zhurov's apartment could not have been more marked. Whereas Mitchell's place was untidy, grim, grimy, and just plain smelly, Zhurov's was more modern, clean, tidy, and inviting. Not dissimilar to Dempsey's.

You could be forgiven for thinking nobody lived there.

It was like one of those homes furniture and decorating companies use to publicise their goods in catalogues.

Only Leroy and his team knew that Zhurov lived there.

'This is a man's home,' Velasquez said, gazing around the place.

'I'm glad I didn't say that,' Quinn remarked.

Leroy looked over at her. 'What makes you say that, Pamela?'

'There aren't any feminine touches. Look at the pictures on the wall: they're functional, like you see in hotel rooms. No flowers, nothing feminine. Check the bathroom.'

'Maybe it's a place he used when he's in LA,' Quinn suggested. 'Like Dempsey.'

'Yeah,' she said. 'But he had his bike here. He was servicing it outside. His stuff was in the garage.'

'I'm inclined to agree with Pamela,' said Leroy. 'This is his home. The home of a single man.' After a pause, he said, 'Let's make a start. Once we've done here, we can get something to eat. Ray: you check the bedroom again. Pamela, you search in here, and that looks like an office out there I'll check the kitchen and bathroom.'

'Sure thing, boss,' said Velasquez, clearly pleased at not being sent into the kitchen.

Quinn began to search the bedroom. The drawers contained nothing but clothes; by either side of the bed were two collapsible tables, each with a small lamp. The only other pieces of furniture were an empty wicker laundry basket, a chair, and a large closet. The closet contained half a dozen jackets, many more shirts and pants, all neatly folded or hung. Six pairs of shoes rested at the foot of the closet.

In the kitchen, Leroy was almost envious of the size of the room, and how neat it was. Zhurov seemed to have every type of kitchen gadget known to mankind. The cupboards were full of non-perishable foodstuffs, cartons, tins. In one drawer was at least fifty little containers of spices, curry, Cajun, buffalo, onion powder, cayenne, paprika. Leroy had no idea there were that many types of spices. Another drawer contained five bottles of vodka, one of which was open. The fridge was fully stocked too: milk, eggs, cheeses, and four bottles of white wine.

Nothing Leroy was hoping to find.

Next, he checked the bathroom. As he expected, it was spotless. Leroy could well have been in the Mondrian. The walk-in shower contained three glass shelves of assorted gels and shampoos; likewise the shelves in front of the wash basin was filled with varying aftershaves and colognes.

Again, nothing Leroy was hoping to find.

In the living room, Velasquez found nothing of any consequence. She searched everywhere; the sixty-five inch TV was mounted to the wall, and she even checked the gap between the set and the wall.

Leroy joined Velasquez in Zhurov's office, a small room off the main living room. There was just enough room for a desk and chair. The desk was more a table, glass and chrome. A personal computer rested on the table, the disc drive on the floor underneath.

'No drawers,' she said. 'Where does he store everything?'

'Maybe he keeps everything on that,' said Leroy nodding to the screen. He looked around the office. There was a calendar, not in English. There were no notes or reminders scribbled onto the dates. 'Spotless, so tidy,' he muttered. 'And yet...' His voice trailed off.

'And yet what?'

'Something here's not right. But I can't...' He clicked his fingers and pointed to the opposite wall, where there was an air conditioning vent. He walked over to the vent. 'Look,' he said.

'The AC?'

'Yes, but the vent is crooked. It's not fitted on straight. Is that consistent with the rest of the place? And here.' He ran his fingers over one of the screwheads. 'The paint here's been scratched off. Ray?'

Quinn appeared. 'Yo?'

'Do me a favour, will you? Go back to the car and bring up the screwdriver kit.'

'Sure thing, Sam.'

'Do you see what I mean?' he asked Velasquez. 'Everything in this place is so tidy, so in order, so in place; but that's not.'

She nodded. 'Now you've brought it to my attention, it stands out a mile.'

Quinn returned with the screwdrivers. Leroy picked out one, and took the first screw out. Then the next three. Then he was able to lift the vent off the wall, exposing the bare metal duct. He switched on the flashlight on his phone, put his head into the duct and looked left and right.

Quinn and Velasquez looked at each other as he pulled out a laptop bag, which he put on the desk and unzipped.

'Jeez,' he said, as he lifted out a large bundle of stacked dollar bills. Then another. They were fifty and hundred bills, neatly stacked and banded. Velasquez began to sort through the bundles.

'Each bundle of fifties contains a thousand bucks,' she said.

'And the hundreds?' Quinn asked.

Leroy answered. 'Two five.'

'That makes a total of thirty-five thousand,' Velasquez said.

'Pictures,' Leroy said, as he went back to the duct. 'I'll see if there's more.' He reached further into the duct. The others looked up from the cash when they heard a muffled 'Fuck me.' Leroy stepped back from the vent hole. Velasquez gasped when she saw he was holding an assault rifle. He laid it down on the desk next to the money. 'I think it's an M16,' he said.

'Why has he got -' Quinn began to say, only to be silenced by Leroy's raised index finger as he went back into the duct.

Gradually, he brought out another rifle. Then another. Then another. Then two more.

Eventually, all ten assault rifles were laid on the desk, next to the bag of thirty-five thousand dollars.

Leroy looked at Quinn, then Velasquez, then back at the pile of ten M16s.

'Jesus Christ,' he breathed. 'What the fuck have we stumbled on?'

## CHAPTER TWENTY-SIX

LEROY LEANED INTO the duct again. Using one of the M16s as a hook, he pulled out a light blue holdall. He put the bag on the desk and unzipped it.

'I wondered where we'd find this,' he said, as he fished out box after box of cartridges.

Quinn picked up one of the boxes. 'M193s.'

'Yeah,' Leroy said. 'The normal ammo for the M16, as I recall.'

'The boxes look intact,' Velasquez observed.

'Just waiting to be used,' Quinn added, grimly.

'Twenty cartridges in each box,' Velasquez said. 'How many boxes, Sam?'

Leroy counted the last few boxes out loud. 'Fifty-seven, fifty-eight, fifty-nine, sixty. That's it: sixty. Sixty boxes in all.'

Quinn said, 'Sixty boxes of twenty cartridges...'

'Twelve hundred rounds,' Leroy said, his gaze fixed on

the pile of boxes. 'One of you take a look in the duct, just to make sure there's nothing left.'

Velasquez switched on the flashlight on her phone and leaned into the duct, looked both ways. 'All clear here.'

'What now, then, Sam?' Quinn asked.

Leroy said nothing, his gazed fixed on the boxes of cartridges.

'Sam?' Quinn repeated.

Leroy snapped out of his reverie. 'Let's get this stuff locked and secured in the trunk. I think we're done here. No, wait: there was a garage, wasn't there? Where he stored his bike.'

'You expecting more in there, then?' Quinn asked.

'Not expecting much. The garage was in an open space, can't be seen from here. And if he's using the AC to store stuff, I can't see him using a less secure garage. But we have to look, anyway. But before we do: there must be vents like that one in the other rooms. We need to check behind those, also.'

They spent the next thirty minutes unscrewing and removing the vents in all of the other rooms. All were on the wall, except for the kitchen and bathroom, which were on the ceiling. Quinn stood on a chair and checked those. All were empty.

'So it's just this stash here,' Leroy said. 'As if all this wasn't enough.'

Leroy and Quinn each cradled five rifles and carried them down to the car. Velasquez put the blue holdall containing the cartridges and a black holdall containing the cash over her shoulders and accompanied them, her own weapon at the ready. She took the car keys from Leroy and reversed up the driveway to stop six feet from the garage, allowing the trunk to be loaded discretely and not in full view of the street. It also partially obscured the garage while they were searching it.

Leroy unlocked the garage and pushed open the metal door. He and Quinn went inside while Velasquez stood in the entrance, her hand resting on her Beretta 92. Quinn wheeled the bike out of the way. He leaned it against the wall and took a step back. 'Not bad,' he said, nodding. 'I could get at least six for something like this.' Quinn considered himself something of an expert on motorcycles, and had developed a side-line in trading them on eBay, much to Leroy's amusement.

'Six what?'

'Six grand, of course. It's a Honda CB650R. I reckon about nine thousand new, but second-hand, I've sold similar for around six.'

'You can make Zhurov an offer when he begins his sentence, but let's focus on in here. I'll be happier when those M16s are secured properly.'

The contents of the garage comprised a couple of cans of oil and a metal box of tools. Two chairs, one of which had two legs broken, stood in the corner, one on top of the other. There was an old table standing up against the wall, with remnants of various paint spillages. On one of the rusty metal shelves next to the table were three half gallon paint cans. Leroy took them off the shelf and rummaged for a screwdriver. He found a large bladed one and prised the lids off the paint cans. Each can still contained paint, between one third and two thirds, red, white, and blue. The blue was mid-way between light and dark. A skin had formed on the surface of each paint.

'Not been used for a while,' Leroy muttered. He looked over his shoulder to check on Velasquez, then added, 'I don't recall any of the rooms being this colour.'

'They weren't. So why would he be keeping cans of red, white, and blue paint?'

'Same colours as the American flag,' Velasquez said from outside.

Leroy rubbed his chin. A thought flashed through his mind about whether to shave before his evening with Stacy later. 'Yeah, I had that feeling as well.'

Quinn dug through the drawer where Leroy found the screwdriver. 'There's just crap in here.'

'He kept anything of importance in the apartment. Or in

the AC.' Leroy rubbed his hands down his clothes. 'Come on; let's close up here, and get that shit stored in a secure place.'

Quinn took one more look at the Honda, then wheeled it back into place. Leroy closed and locked the garage door, put up a length of police tape, and joined the other two in the Impala. He made a left once on the street, and headed back to the station.

That day, Sergeant Willy Keith was on duty accepting and registering evidence brought in for storage.

He looked open mouthed as Leroy and Quinn laid ten M16 assault rifles on the desk, followed by the light blue holdall containing twelve hundred cartridges, followed by a black holdall containing the cash.

'Everything okay, Willy?' Leroy asked breezily. 'You want to get these checked in? You'll need to cross reference them with the Ruger we brought in yesterday.'

Keith swallowed and checked the items, logged in and recorded them, then locked them in the wire cage at the rear of the room, and printed out Leroy a receipt and inventory.

'Anything else, Sam?' he asked.

'Just these.' Leroy passed over the evidence bag containing the handgun and knife from Mitchell's house.

'A separate listing?' Keith asked.

Leroy nodded. 'Affirmative. Different suspect.'

Keith's supervisor, a grizzled veteran Sergeant Al McMurray walked past with a clipboard. He looked over at what Leroy had brought in. 'Busy morning, Sam?'

'Busy morning. You wait till this afternoon.'

McMurray grinned and sat at his desk to answer his phone. Leroy took the inventory for Mitchell's item and he and the others walked round to their desks.

'You guys want to make a start on what we brought in?' Leroy asked. 'Check out the guns first; are they registered with those jokers in there, were they reported stolen, do they have permits, the usual stuff. I'm going to update Perez, give him the opportunity to kiss the Chief's ass.'

'What about the knife?' Velasquez asked.

'It seemed to be clean, but we can still get it up to Forensic later, in case there is any trace on it. But the guns will give us a quicker result, and might enable us to hold them for more than forty-eight hours. I'll need to speak with Perez about the M16s.'

Perez waved Leroy into his office, and Leroy began to update the lieutenant. Perez was keying data onto a spreadsheet, half listening as Leroy brought him up to date. Until Leroy mentioned the ten M16s.

'What?' he said, looking up at Leroy. 'Run that past me again. Ten…?'

'Ten M16s.'

'Loaded?'

'No, but with twelve hundred rounds, and thirty-five thousand.'

'Thirty-five thousand dollars?'

Leroy nodded. 'All in fifties and hundreds. Velasquez has backache now.'

'This is more than a hit and run, Sam.'

'Obviously. The evidence we have at this time for Mitchell and Zhurov for the hit and run is only circumstantial. We were still working on that when we came across all of this. I had no idea a search of their homes would bring this up.'

'Do you think they're related? The weaponry and the hit and run, I mean.'

'At the moment, I have an open mind on that. I was planning on treating it as another line of investigation.'

Perez sat back in his chair. 'You still got that FBI contact?'

'Callaway? I have, but I was going to say this looks more like a Homeland Security case.'

Perez nodded. 'You could be right. I'll give the Chief a

call, run it by him. He'll be wanting an update, anyway. Have you questioned the suspects about this?'

'Not yet. We can hold them both until tomorrow. There was small amount of cocaine - I think it was cocaine – at Mitchell's place, but only enough for his personal use. Ray and Pamela are checking out the two guns, ownership, use, and like that.'

'Does the Russian know you found his M16s?'

'He's Latvian, or so he said on the way here. He and Mitchell will know about the handguns and the knife. They were in plain sight on Mitchell's place, and Zhurov was carrying when we arrested him. That's why he was arrested. I'm sure they'll be discussing that with their lawyer.'

'Lawyer? Singular?'

'They have the same one. Coincidence? But the cash, the M16s and M193s were hidden, so he won't be expecting us to have found them.'

'When are you planning on bringing those into the interrogation?'

'I think I want to wait for a response, some guidance, from DHS. We can hold Zhurov for another twenty-four hours.'

'Good idea,' said Perez. 'You get on, and I'll put a call into the Chief.'

'What about the captain?' Leroy asked on his way out.

'I've been keeping him in the loop but the Chief wanted to be appraised personally, which is what I'm doing. Walker seemed just as bemused as I was about the Chief's interest in the case.'

'So you'll let me know about DHS?' asked Leroy as he left the office.

'I will. Good work, Sam.'

Leroy left Perez and walked back to his desk. He was met halfway by an excited Velasquez.

'Sam – you need to see this.'

## CHAPTER TWENTY-SEVEN

'LOOK AT THIS here,' she said, pointing to the screen on Quinn's desk. Quinn eased his chair back to give room, and Leroy bent slightly to read what was causing so much excitement. The handgun they found in Mitchell's house had been reported stolen early the previous year, from a hotel room in Las Vegas.

Leroy straightened up and folded his arms with an air of satisfaction.

'Good,' he said. 'That means we have something we can charge him with. Something concrete. We'll need to establish his story as to how he came about the gun. I'll take book he'll refuse to talk to us without his lawyer being present. I'll get that set up. While I'm on that: Ray, can you go back the last six months for any murders or stabbings in LA County where the weapon wasn't recovered, but the wounds match the dimensions of his survival knife. Pamela, can you do the same for Zhurov's handgun; I think we'll need to deal with the M16s separately. I'll try talk to our guest.'


It took just over an hour to set up Mitchell's interrogation. As Leroy had expected, Mitchell exercised his constitutional right to have his lawyer present. By the time McQueen could be reached, and made it over, sixty-five minutes had elapsed. Once Mitchell and McQueen were in place, Leroy gave a weary sigh and flopped into the chair across the table. He had been told on a training course many years ago, that if the interviewer appeared tired, subconsciously the suspect would be more cooperative in order to speed up the process. Leroy did it when he remembered, but was never sure if it ever worked, or was just an urban legend.

He opened up the laptop he had brought in with him.

'During the search of your home, we found a small quantity of cocaine.'

'That's just for me,' Mitchell said. 'Only for me to use when I can't sleep.'

Rogers McQueen looked up from his legal pad. 'Detective Leroy, you cannot be serious. Are you telling me you have summoned me over here just to talk about a tiny quantity for cocaine, which cannot be anything than for my client's personal use?'

'No,' said Leroy, as he swung the laptop round. 'But we also found this.' He showed them an image of the knife, and then tabbed to a picture of the gun. 'And this.' He looked up at Mitchell. 'Do you recognise them?'

Mitchell looked at the photographs, then back to McQueen, who gave no reaction. 'Yeah. They're mine. I keep them next to my bed. For safety.'

'For safety?'

'Absolutely. LA's a dangerous place.'

'Let's start with the knife.' Leroy flicked the image back onto the laptop screen. 'Why do you keep a knife like that? And why is it next to your bed?'

'I told you: LA's a dangerous place.'

'Really?' said Leroy, sarcastically.

'Okay. I use it for when I go hunting.'

'For when you go hunting. And where do you go hunting? And what do you hunt?'

'Up in the hills. In the canyons. I might find some game. A deer or something.'

'So you'd use that knife to kill a deer? And how would you catch the deer first?'

Mitchell shrugged. 'Also to protect myself from cougars while I'm out hunting.'

'Protect yourself from cougars,' Leroy repeated, then looked Mitchell in the eye. 'The knife looks clean – on the surface. But it's going to forensic to check it *is* clean. That there's no dried blood, tiny particles of blood left on it, on these teeth here. And if there are any traces of blood - human, not deer or cougar – then well…'

Leroy's and Mitchell's eyes locked. Leroy said nothing; waiting for Mitchell to react. He did not.

'Let's park the knife for now,' Leroy said as he swiped the photographs. 'The gun. The Ruger. Is this yours?'

'Yeah, it's mine.'

'According to police records, the gun was stolen from a room in the Nobu Hotel in Vegas last year.'

'I don't know anything about that.'

'How did you come by the gun?'

'I bought it from a guy in a bar.'

'A bar. Which bar?'

'Here in LA. I forget which one.'

'So what was the name of the guy in the bar? Obviously not a licenced, registered firearms dealer.'

'I don't remember his name. A white guy.'

'When was it last used?'

'Don't recall. A long time ago.'

'Where?'

'Hunting, probably.'

'You mean to shoot the deer before you slit its throat

with your survival knife?'

Mitchell said nothing.

Leroy asked, 'You have the paperwork for the weapon?'

'What paperwork?'

'What paperwork? A bill of sale, your Firearm Safety Certificate, your Safe Handling Demonstration.'

Mitchell said nothing.

Leroy asked, 'Are you the legal owner of the weapon?'

Mitchell's eyes darted over to McQueen, who gave a small nod.

'I told you, I bought it from this guy.'

'So are you saying you are the legal owner?'

McQueen interrupted. 'Detective, my client has already answered that question.'

'I'm just trying to get a straight answer to the question. Is it yes or no? Are you the owner?'

McQueen gave a discrete nod to Mitchell who looked over at him before responding.

'Yes,' Mitchell replied.

'So you have all that paperwork?'

'It's around somewhere.'

'Sure it is.'

McQueen looked up at Leroy. 'Detective, are you prepared to charge my client? He has been detained here since yesterday morning without any charges.'

'There will be charges,' Leroy replied. 'We have until tomorrow morning to prepare them. So far, we're talking about illegal possession of a firearm. That's before a forensic examination of the survival knife your client keeps by his bedside. Plus, your client says he bought the gun in a bar here in Los Angeles. The gun was reported stolen in Vegas. That means a stolen weapon crossed the state border. That means it's a federal case, and I'm sure the FBI will have some questions to ask your client.' He shut the laptop and stood up. 'We're done here for now.'

*****

After Leroy had left the interview room, he arranged for Mitchell to be taken back to the holding cell. He reiterated to the supervising officer that Mitchell and Zhurov had to be kept separately and could not be allowed to communicate, regardless of how full the cells were. He also arranged for Rogers McQueen to be escorted out of the building. Then he returned to Quinn and Velasquez.

'We have at least two charges.'

'Possession?' Quinn asked.

'Yes, unless he can find the magic paperwork, which he won't. And he bought the weapon illegally. And it's a stolen firearm, which was taken over the state line.'

'So that means we'll have to hand over the investigation?'

'I don't know yet. I'll need to speak with Perez again before -'

'Sam,' Velasquez interrupted. She was on the landline and had one hand over the mouthpiece. 'I have Brent Powers, Department of National Security, asking for you.'

## CHAPTER TWENTY-EIGHT

'DETECTIVE LEROY? BRENT Powers, Department of Homeland Security, Los Angeles Office here.'

'This is Detective Leroy. Thanks for coming back to me so promptly.'

'No problem. I guess then that you knew your department had reached out to us. Sometimes a supervisor will call us for advice or assistance, and not tell their subordinates, and the call comes as a surprise. Not always a welcome one, I might add.'

'No, I requested that my lieutenant call you guys.'

'Now we got that out of the way, I'm concerned at what your guy told my supervisor. Ten assault weapons, and one hell of a lot of ammunition.'

'Yeah,' Leroy confirmed. 'Ten M16s, and twelve hundred rounds.'

'I'm calling out of our LA office; we're on East Olympic. I'll drive over to you, take a look at what you have. Then we can talk about next steps. I'll see you within the hour.'

Quinn and Velasquez looked up at Leroy.

'He's coming over,' Leroy said. 'Wants to see the M16s. In the meantime: Ray, can you chase Financial Crimes. See if they have gotten anywhere with Dempsey's accounts. If that's the wrong avenue to take, let's close it today. Pamela: keep on at that car pound CCTV. Just make sure there was no other activity with the vehicle. I'll check out the handgun Zhurov had tucked into his pants. If that's illegal as well, then we can charge them both. Just because Mitchell and Zhurov are doing God knows what with illegal weaponry still doesn't put them in that vehicle at the time of the hit and run.'

It took Leroy twenty minutes to ascertain that this Ruger had also been reported stolen, this time four months earlier from an address in Los Feliz. As Leroy sat organising the various folders in the murder book, Watch Commander Ronny Rosenberg appeared at his side.

'Sam? He's out front, asking for you.' Rosenberg handed him a business card. BRENT POWERS DEPARTMENT OF HOMELAND SECURITY.

'Thanks. I'll go get him.' Leroy got up and followed Rosenberg to the front desk. At the desk, Leroy recognised Powers immediately. He was at least six six tall, almost half that wide, and his blond hair sported a military style buzz cut. He turned to Leroy. 'Detective Leroy,' he asked, holding out a hand.

'I'm Leroy. Sam.'

They shook hands, and Leroy led him to the murder room. 'Come this way, Agent Powers.'

'Let's skip all that bullshit,' Powers replied, following Leroy along the corridor. 'I'm Brent. You're Sam, right?'

'That works for me,' said Leroy. 'Here's the rest of the team: Ray Quinn, Pamela Velasquez.'

They all shook hands. Even Velasquez was impressed by Powers; his hand must have been twice the size of hers.

Powers turned to Leroy. 'First, I need to see the M16s.'

'They're downstairs, in the secure storage area. This way.'

As Leroy led him down the stairs, Powers said, 'Too bad it's a Friday afternoon. I was looking forward to a weekend off.'

'I'll bear that in mind for next time,' Leroy quipped as they arrived.

'Jesus H,' said Powers, as he saw the haul for the first time. He reached out for them, then stopped. 'They been checked for prints?'

Leroy nodded. 'Yup. It's okay to handle them. They were all clean, by the way; no prints whatsoever.'

'Hmm,' Powers muttered as studied one of the rifles. 'I'm wondering if they've ever been fired. Recently, I mean.'

'They all looked clean. No smell of GSR.'

Powers studied three others. 'These are pristine. Virgins. Where's the ammo?'

'Here.' Leroy slid the boxes of cartridges along the counter top.

Powers checked the sealed boxes and whistled. 'Twelve hundred rounds.'

'That's what we figured. What do you think?'

'I'm not sure yet. Tell me about the guy who had them. Where were they hidden?'

'In an AC duct. Very well hidden. We only found them by chance. There was something else; I don't know if this means anything. The guy had a garage, containing three cans of paint, quart size. Red, white, blue. All around half full.'

'Red, white, blue?'

'Yes, Pamela said the colours of the flag.'

'Would you say the guy fits the profile of a white supremacist?'

'He's white. Thirty three. He's not American, though. Latvian.'

'Latvian? I'm not aware of any intelligence about guys from there. How much longer can you hold him for?'

'We brought them both in yesterday.'

'Both? I thought…?'

'Our primary investigation is for a hit and run.' Leroy gave Powers a run-down on the investigation so far.

'So finding these,' Powers asked, 'was just a coincidence?'

'Surely. We don't know, as yet, if the other guy, Mitchell, has anything to do with these. But both of the suspects were found to be in possession of stolen handguns: this guy, the Latvian, was carrying; the other had it next to his bed. With a survival knife.'

'So you can charge them?'

'Yes, I can. We've only just established that this guy's weapon is stolen. My plan is to wait a little longer today, before they're charged. Then there's no time to get them into court before Monday. I don't want some judge freeing them on bail for the weekend.'

Powers grinned. 'Covering all bases?'

'Something like that.'

'Where will they go for the weekend?'

'The Men's Central Jail on Bauchet.'

'Is that the place Downtown?'

'That's the one,' Leroy nodded.

'We'll pick this up in the morning,' said Powers. 'Oh, shoot: it's Saturday. Are you guys okay to come in?

'I am. I was planning on coming in anyway; I have the suspects to deal with. I can't speak for Ray and Pamela though; they weren't due to. I'll speak with them.

Powers dismissed this. 'If they can't, they can't. Nine tomorrow?'

'That works for me. One question.'

'Shoot, Sam.'

'The other guy, Mitchell – his weapon was reported in Vegas, so it's travelled over the state line. What about -'

Powers held out a hand. 'I'll stop you there. I know what you're going to say. DHS gets first dibs on this. If it turns out the handguns aren't relevant to our investigation, then they can have it.'

Leroy nodded. 'Works for me,' he said again.

## CHAPTER TWENTY-NINE

Leroy had arranged to pick up Stacy at seven that evening.

She lived in a small house on Grace Avenue, five hundred yards up the hill from Franklin. It was of an unusual design, part of the second floor jutting out over the freshly blacktopped driveway. Relatively modern, certainly newer than the neighbouring properties. Leroy speculated that the land on which Stacy's house stood once belonged to one of the houses next door, the owner selling off this valuable real estate. He wondered if she owned the house, or was renting, maybe from her neighbour.

He parked on the drive, in front of her silver SUV, and walked to the door. There was no bell, so he knocked loudly on the brown oak door. After a few seconds, the door opened.

'Hold on, Sam,' a voice called out as Leroy caught a glimpse of Stacy disappearing into a side room. Or rather, he caught a glimpse of a black minidress disappearing into a side room.

'No hurry,' he called back. 'We've plenty of time.'

Momentarily she reappeared. Wearing that black minidress, her dark hair worn down to her shoulders – a contrast as he had only ever seen her with it worn up. She wore black shoes and a matching clutch bag. She smelled good. Leroy approved.

He was wearing a white polo shirt under a dark blue jacket and grey pants. His hair was so short there was very little he could do with it, but he had bothered to shave. Stacy liked the smell of his aftershave. She approved.

Leroy had booked them a table at Musso and Frank's Grill, on Hollywood Boulevard. Not a place he frequented often, but as Stacy was providing the tickets for later, he thought it would be the place to go. Not far from Stacy's house either, and soon he was pulling into the parking lot off North Cherokee.

The restaurant, at 6667 Hollywood Boulevard, opened in 1919 and was named after its original owners Joseph Musso and Frank Toulet. It is the oldest restaurant in Hollywood and has been called 'the genesis of Hollywood'. Since those days, the restaurant has retained its original character, which includes high ceilings, dark wood panelling, and red booths. The bartenders and waiters dress in the same red jackets that they have worn for decades. Some have worked there for forty years and more.

When the restaurant opened, the financial and political centres of Los Angeles were based Downtown, not an easy journey at that time. This made it possible for the restaurant to attract the intellectual and bohemian clientele who were beginning to spend time in Hollywood.

By the thirties, the restaurant was firmly established as the centre of Hollywood's cultural life. The Screen Writers Guild was across the street, and Stanley Rose's bookstore was next door. Many of the writers of the hard-boiled fiction which Rose preferred, such as Raymond Chandler and Dashiell Hammett, spent endless hours in the bar of Musso and Frank. By the forties, the restaurant was so firmly identified with the Los Angeles literary scene, that aspiring writers would also drink there, as a way of emulating their role models.

Then there was the film industry. Musso and Frank has always been part of the movie world social life, keeping a separate back room for its studio clientele; not just screenwriters, but actors, directors, and producers. Tom Mix, Jack Warner, Humphrey Bogart, Mary Pickford, and Orson Welles are just a few, and this association continues to this day.

Musso and Frank has also found its way into popular culture, featuring in feature films and television series, *Ed Wood*, *Ocean's Eleven*, *Once Upon a Time In Hollywood,* to name a few.

All this was not lost on Leroy, as he would have researched the place before booking a table. No point taking Stacy somewhere if she would not be impressed. His normal go-to eating place in this part of town was the eponymous *Off Vine*, less than a mile away, across Sunset Boulevard, but he was banking on Stacy being drawn into the Old Hollywood-style glamour and atmosphere of the place.

'At the risk of using a cliché,' Stacy said as Leroy handed over his car keys to the valet, 'but do you come here often?'

'All the time,' he replied as they walked inside. 'Once a week at least.'

'Really?'

'No,' he laughed. 'This is my second in ten years. What about you? This is almost your local restaurant.'

She looked around the room. 'I don't think so. I think I would've remembered.'

After an appropriate delay, one of the red-coated waiters brought two menus. Stacy ordered an appetizer of Meatballs and Polento, followed by Turkey A La King; Leroy chose an Avocado Cocktail, followed by Spaghetti and Meatballs. All accompanied by a bottle of Inception, a 2018 vintage from Santa Barbara. While they were waiting, Leroy took a beer, and Stacy a cocktail: City Lights, comprising Bulleit Bourbon, Green Chartreuse, Aperol, and fresh lime juice.

Conversation during the meal revolved mainly around their jobs: the cases Stacy was working on. Leroy noticed she was careful not to give him too much detail, just enough for him to get the flavour.

'You've heard all about me and my job,' she said, as they ordered dessert. 'Now tell me about yours. Tell me about the case you're working on.'

She already knew something about what he was working on as he had told her the other day at the market. He leaned forward and updated her, including the two arrests, what they had found, and the involvement of DHS. Both told their stories quietly and discretely.

She pulled a face at the mention of the rifles. 'Man,' she said, sipping her wine, 'what would someone be doing with ten M16s? That's worrying.'

'That's an understatement. I'm meeting with the guy from Homeland Security in the morning.'

'Is that the only case you're working on? As if that wasn't enough. Don't you guys have primary and secondary investigations, like that?'

'That's all I and my team have at this time.' He paused. 'But I kind of have a secondary of my own.' He then proceeded to tell her about Jordan Washington.

'You mean you've been working on that on your own, in your own time? In the evenings?'

'Pretty much, yeah.'

'Have you come up with anything?'

'Nothing. But I've decided to try a new approach.'

'What's that? Tell her the case was closed for a reason? Sorry; that sounded callous. It must be so awful for his mother.'

'Don't worry. That's what Ray says. I just want to try one more thing.'

'And what's that?'

'Well, so far I've really been going over what the original investigators did; you know, validating the statements they took; I've spoken to more of the folks who live across the street from the school. Not really a new approach.'

The waiter brought over their desserts: New York Cheesecake and Key Lime Pie. They decided to split each dish fifty-fifty. Leroy ordered two coffees.

'You were telling me about your new approach,' she said, taking a spoonful of pie.

'I'm going to look at Trejo himself. His story, his past, his background. See if I can come up with the truth from that angle.'

Stacy nodded thoughtfully.

'If that comes up with nothing, then I guess I'll have to tell her I've come to a dead end. Either the trail's gone cold, or Trejo was messing with her when he retracted his confession. Not that he actually confessed.'

'Doesn't the LAPD have teams who look at cold cases? I mean, isn't this a cold case?'

'The Department does, and this is; but it's always a question of priorities. The resources, the cost. You know the story, I'm sure.'

She nodded. 'It always comes down to money. Always has. Always will.'

Leroy nodded.

'Anyway, Sam,' she added, 'at least you can say you did what you could do. You went the extra mile for her. Not many cops would do that.'

'That's also what Ray says.'

'Then maybe he's right.'

Leroy finished his coffee and beckoned the waiter for the check.

## CHAPTER THIRTY

LEROY HAD NO idea that Ray Quinn was less than three miles away. Twenty blocks to the east along Hollywood Boulevard, on the corner of Rodney Drive, is a discrete, red-bricked building, housing *Cheetahs*, a basement dancing club.

Ray Quinn sat alone at a tiny circular table, nursing his second bourbon and ice of the night. That old saying was right: two is too many and three isn't enough. The waitress shimmied past, carrying empty glasses on a little circular tray. She was wearing little more than a bikini top, with a white lacy apron over a microskirt, and lacy back stockings. He asked her for another.

'Sure thing, honey. Be right back.'

While he waited, Quinn downed the very last drop of the bourbon, took in the remaining ice cube, and sucked that, trying to get any remnants of the whiskey.

After a few minutes, the waitress returned with her

little silver tray.

'Here you go, honey,' she said, placing the glass on a cheap little mat on the table. She had two other drinks on the tray, and turned to deliver those.

'Thanks,' Quinn mumbled. He put a folded twenty on her tray. 'Don't go far.' He realised she had noticed his wedding ring, and awkwardly put his right hand over his fingers.

'Don't worry, honey,' she said. 'This place is full of guys whose wives don't understand them.'

Quinn looked up at her. 'My wife does more than not understand me. She's not with me anymore. I had to move out.' He took a shot of bourbon. 'She's probably fucking some other guy right now.'

She already had a hand on his shoulder; now she moved it up his neck and ruffled the back of his hair. 'And you need some company.'

He looked up at her. 'Wouldn't say no.'

She touched his hair one more time and left to deliver the other drinks. She returned a few moments later, and began to wipe the table with a cloth. 'You need to go to the men's room,' she said quietly.

'What?'

'There's a machine on the wall sells Trojans. I have stuff to do behind that curtain. Bring a fifty.'

Surprised, Quinn finished the whiskey and went to the restroom as he had been instructed. He peed, then bought a pack of three condoms from the dispenser. Back out in the bar, he saw the waitress go behind the black velvet curtain.


Not too far away, in her apartment in West Hollywood, Pamela Velasquez was lying on her couch. She was resting her head on the lap of her partner Gabriela. They had eaten, and were on the couch, watching *Stranger Things*. Each had a glass of Merlot, Velasquez holding hers upright on her stomach.

She looked up at Gabriela. 'I'm fighting to stay awake.'

Gabriela ran her fingers through Pamela's hair and stroked her forehead. 'You've had a long week.'

'Yes.' She was aware she had not given Sam a definitive answer as to whether she would be in the office the next morning. The career officer in her told her she should; but the partner of gorgeous Gabriela told her she should stay home. 'A long week.'

She had the feeling, though, that her fatigue was more to do with the Merlot than with the LAPD.


When the red-coated waiter brought the bill, Stacy tried to agree a fifty-fifty split, but Leroy refused.

'No way,' he said. 'This is on me.'

'But Sam,' she protested.

'No arguments. You're providing the tickets for later.'

She sheepishly looked down at her napkin. 'I'll come quietly. They were complimentary.'

Leroy laughed. 'At least you're honest. It's still on me, though. Next time is on you.'

'Okay,' she said as they got up and walked out to the parking lot. Leroy was optimistic that there would be a next time.

The second part of their evening was at The Laugh Factory, a stand-up comedy spot on West Sunset. The performance was due to start at nine thirty, so after a leisurely drive along Hollywood Boulevard, down Highland Avenue, and along Sunset, and a not-so leisurely attempt at finding a parking space they arrived at the venue with ten minutes to spare.

'That's one of the perks of the job, then?' Stacy asked as they crossed the street. The venue was on the corner of Sunset and Laurel Canyon Boulevards: the other side of Laurel Canyon was a Chevron gas station. Leroy knew the manager of the station, who agreed that he could leave his car on the far end of the forecourt.

'It helps sometimes.'


Back at *Cheetahs*, all the unspent passions, frustrations, and stresses of the last few months were reaching their release. Standing with her back against the wall, the waitress had wrapped one arm around Quinn's neck, the other pushing up against a shelving rack for support. With every one of his thrusts she let out a cry, as did he. He was breathing heavily, grunting with every movement.

They stood immobile once he had finished, both needing the pause to get their breath back. Then Quinn took a step back from her, fixed his clothing, and wordlessly and hurriedly left her behind the curtain. He slowed his pace once he was back in the bar, and, as casually as he could muster, left.

Outside, he ran the first twenty yards up Rodney Avenue to where he had parked. Breathlessly, he leaned against one of the small yucca trees planted on the edge of the sidewalk. He bent down, putting his hands on his knees as he panted. Then leaned back on the tree, and rubbed his hands over his face. He looked back down at the bar, then turned to walk the last few yards back to his car.

He unlocked his car, but before getting in, leaned on the side and looked down the street one more time. Hollywood Boulevard was at the end of the street, the cars and vans and buses still making their way along, even at this hour.

Friday night in Hollywood.


The stand-up comedians were not the best or the funniest Leroy had seen, but he was enjoying himself. It was probably more the company he was keeping than the quality of the routines. He tried and failed to memorise some of the gags so he could repeat them next week.

It wound up just after eleven. As the applause died down, Stacy looked over at him and said, 'It's been a long week. Would you be able to take me home?'

'Absolutely,' he said, pulling her chair out for her.

It took a while to get back to Stacy's street, as the roads were very busy, as Leroy expected. Even taking the deserted cross streets back did not really save any time. Eventually he pulled up on her driveway.

'Thanks for the show,' he said. 'I really enjoyed it.'

'Thanks for the meal. I really enjoyed that.' With her hand on the door handle, Stacy asked, 'Did you want to come in for a while?'

Leroy had to be honest. 'I'd love to, I really would. But I have an early start tomorrow. I need to be at the station by eight.'

'You work too hard, Detective,' she said, and leaned over. She brushed his lips with hers, gently, softly. Leroy responded, aching to feel inside her mouth, but that would not be the thing to do tonight. After a few seconds she withdrew.

'I'll call you?' he part said, part asked.

She nodded. 'Call me.'

From inside the car, Leroy waited until she was safely indoors, then reversed onto the street to begin the not so short journey home.

## CHAPTER THIRTY-ONE

HE HAD WOKEN early. Earlier than he had planned.

Sam Leroy rubbed his eyes and sat up in bed.

It was not dark, yet not fully light; otherwise the rays of the early morning sun would be flooding through the window into his bedroom.

He checked the time, and groaned. There was no way he was going to get back to sleep now. It was not as if he had gotten to sleep early. It was almost midnight when he got back the night before. On the drive home, he kept thinking about his evening with Stacy, and whether he did the right thing in declining her offer to come in. He was being honest with her when he said he had an early start Saturday morning, but would he have done the same thing years ago?

Unlikely.

He knew exactly what would have happened had he gone inside, and he would have been frantically driving home in the even earlier hours of the morning to shower and change before work. He used to keep a change of clothes in his locker for occasions such as those, but had had so little need for that in the past few years that he never replaced it last time he used it.

Still, he had a feeling she wanted him as much as he wanted her, and a little bit of denial might make her want him even more.

As well as thoughts about Stacy, the two investigations he was working on were on Leroy's mind. The first was the Jordan Washington case, which would not go away. Not go away because Leroy would not let it. He made himself a cup of hot tea and sat on his back porch, and thought through his next steps. As he had probably decided already, he would look more at Robert Trejo: his background, his history, his record, everything he could. That had to be something for the weekend. Then there was his actual case. Still, the evidence they had for Mitchell and Zhurov was very weak and circumstantial, for the hit and run at least, although it looked like the Zhurov angle was morphing into something else, something more. Ironically, Leroy was not that interested in the ten M16s and twelve hundred rounds they had found at Zhurov's place: he knew other agencies would deal with that. His main concern was who was driving when Rosa Delgado, Scott Dempsey, and Kenneth Fong were mown down. In a sense, he perversely hoped that Zhurov was not involved in the hit and run: the last thing he wanted or needed was a pissing contest with Homeland Security. He had been through this with the Bureau on more than one occasion, and it was never helpful. He understood that from their point of view ten assault weapons and possibly more was higher on the priority list than three people being run over, but the hit and run was his case, and he was determined to get the person or persons responsible, and have them face justice.

It was these late night ruminations which led to him being awake till gone one, and so it was a tired Leroy who eventually dragged himself out of bed and into the shower. Before showering, he stumbled into his kitchen to make himself a cup of very strong coffee. From his kitchen, he could just about make out one of the canals which give Venice its name, and just got a glimpse of two men in small boats rowing, calling out to each other. Too noisy for this early in the morning, he thought.

After showering, dressing and a second mug of coffee, he decided to head to the station. He was going in primarily to liaise, as Brent Powers put it, with DHS. Leroy was not sure exactly what that meant; certainly he had every intention of his team being equal partners with Powers and his team.

The place was deserted when he arrived, the streets almost empty as he drove in. He pulled in at a McDonalds drive-thru on the way to pick up breakfast. There had been a rain shower in the night, and the streets were still wet. A third cup of coffee later, and he was sitting at his desk, finishing off his egg and sausage McMuffin, with biscuits in place of a bun.

His plan was to cover what Pamela had done, just to satisfy himself that no stone was left unturned. He had seen other investigations where things had gone in the wrong direction because what was obvious was deemed to be the solution, rather than looking as thoroughly as they could. Jordan Washington was a case in point.

He retrieved the video from the car pound. Started at the moment when Mitchell and Zhurov parked the Ford, and walked towards the camera. Then he put his index finger on the search backwards key, drained his coffee cup, and watched, his finger remaining on the key.

As the recording reversed, at 16 times normal speed, Leroy watched the cars come and go, people come and go.

He sat up. A black Ford Territory was being driven away, out of the pound. He stopped the recording, went back (or forward) a few seconds, and watched again. This had to be the same vehicle: when they checked the pound the other day they saw no other. Leroy tried to make out who was driving, but the windows were tinted, and the camera faced the passenger side. The driver must have approached the Ford concealed by the vehicles parked behind.

Leroy checked the time and date stamp. This was day one, five hours after the hit and run. He would need to check a camera with a different point of view to confirm that was the vehicle in question, as well as checking activity up to and past (or before) the time of the incident. He reflected that they might have saved time by first looking at footage from the cameras pointing at the entrance, but it was too late now. He made a note of the time the Ford left, then continued monitoring the parked vehicles.

He was soon aware of somebody standing behind him. He turned to see Brent Powers.

'Morning, Sam.'

'Hey, Brent,' replied Leroy. 'I didn't expect to see you this early.'

Powers looked at his watch, a gold Rolex. He was wearing white sneakers, blue sweatpants, and white tee shirt, with a DHS logo on the left breast. A contrast with the light grey suit, white shirt, and dark blue tie he was wearing yesterday. Perhaps the sweatpants were his Saturday smart casual. 'I'm an early riser. The other guys are out in the parking lot. You want to meet them?'

'Why not?' Leroy logged off and followed Powers outside. In the parking lot was an SUV. Shiny black, tinted windows, not too dissimilar to the Ford Territory. The nearside door was slid open; four figures were sitting inside.

Powers and Leroy leaned inside and Powers introduced his colleagues, three men and one woman. All were dressed in varying versions of Saturday smart casual, except for one of the men, who was wearing a light blue suit, white shirt, and light blue tie. Two of the men and the woman wore sunglasses, even thought they were sitting inside a car with tinted windows.

'Hi, guys.' Leroy straightened up and looked at Powers. 'So, what's the plan?'

'We're headed out to the Latvian's house. Then we're going to tear it apart.'

'Excuse me?'

'Tear it apart. Search every square inch. I'm working on the basis that if you guys can find ten M16s and a shitload of ammo, then who knows what else the bastard has hidden. No offence, by the way.'

'None taken. You have a warrant for all this?'

'We do. Signed by a federal judge last night. You coming with us? If you do, it can only be an observer; DHS-LAPD liaison, that kind of thing.'

'Yes, I'll come with you.'

'Great. And he's in the jailhouse?'

'Both he and William Mitchell are Downtown, waiting on their court appearance Monday.'

'And William Mitchell is…?'

'He's the other guy we arrested in connection with the hit and run. He was carrying a piece as well.'

'What's his connection with the Latvian?'

Leroy explained about the car pound and about seeing Mitchell and Zhurov get out of the Ford.

Powers chewed on the end of his sunglasses. 'It's a bit… tenuous, don't you think?'

Leroy was getting irritated by this man. 'That's as far as we've got at this time.'

Powers said, 'Our interest is just in Zhurov. Nothing you've told me gives me reason to change that.' He paused a second. 'You want to ride with us? Room for one more.'

'I'm good. I'll meet you there.'

'As you wish,' said Powers, sliding the door shut. 'See you there.'

Powers climbed into the driver seat and drove off. Leroy turned and hurried inside. He made a note of where he had reached on the time stamp, and went back out to his car.

By the time he arrived at Zhurov's place, the SUV was

parked on the drive, one agent sitting guard inside. Leroy leaned in.

'Hi again. The others inside?'

The agent nodded.

Leroy nodded back and went inside. He met Powers in the doorway. It was like the place was being ransacked, which of course it was. Drawers and cabinets had been pulled out; the air conditioning vents had been taken down, leaving the bare vents exposed. Powers was holding what looked like a child's games handset.

'We use robots,' Powers explained. 'To save one of my guys having to do a Bruce Willis and crawl through the ducts, which in most places isn't physically possible, we send this little guy, and he relays what he sees to this screen here. Infrared of course, as it's dark inside one of those mothers.'

Leroy nodded, pretending to look impressed. 'I'll wait outside,' he said. 'There's not much to observe here.'

'As you wish. Let me tell you something: if we find anything that's of no interest to us, but may be to you, we'll give you the nod.'

'I'd be obliged,' said Leroy. 'As long as your warrant covers it.'

'It will.' With that, Powers turned back to the search. Leroy left and went back outside. He hoped they'd find something, the mess they would be leaving.

## CHAPTER THIRTY-TWO

As Leroy made his way outside, Quinn called.

'Sam, where are you? I'm at the station.'

'I'm at Zhurov's place, with Powers and his Homeland Security team. They're tearing the place apart.'

'His team? I thought just he was coming back today.'

'Him and four others. They're all dressed in their Saturday best smart casual. They look like the fucking Book of Mormon.'

'Looking for more M16s?'

'Kind of, I guess. Or anything else.'

'Do you think they know something, and aren't telling?'

'I've no idea. He got four other people ready quickly. He's not giving much away.'

'They might find something for us. You know, not a Homeland Security matter, but evidence for us.'

'That's what he said. He told me they have a warrant,

but didn't show it to me. So I'm not sure about that aspect of their search.'

'Surely that's not our problem?'

'It could be if they do find anything for us, and decide to share it. Without a properly executed warrant, it's inadmissible.'

'Sure. Why are you there?'

'He invited me along, as an observer only, he stressed. As a kind of DHS-LAPD liaison. Let's hope that works both ways. But at the moment, I'm not involved in what they're doing inside. I'm just out here by the car.'

'Have they searched the garage yet?'

'It doesn't look like it, yet. He knows about the paint. He says the colours might be significant. Started talking about white supremacists.'

'In LA?'

'Not the most obvious place, I agree.'

'Do you need me to come over?'

'There's no point. No need for both of us to waste our Saturday morning.'

'As I'm here, what do you want me to do? I have all day.'

'Before I left for here, I began to look at more of the CCTV from the car pound.' He updated Quinn on what he had seen. 'Can you pick up where I left off, and go further back. You'll also need to check the footage from the POV of the camera pointing at the gates. Good chance of getting the licence plate that way.'

'Okay,' said Quinn. 'I'll get on to it. Is Pamela coming in?'

'I've no idea. I've not been in touch with her. I left it up to you guys as to whether you came in. It's overtime.'

'There's no sign of her. Maybe she has a life.'

Leroy was unsure whether that was bait intended for him to take, but he ignored it. 'I'll be back once we're done here. I guess their next steps will depend on what if anything they find here.'

'At least we have Zhurov charged with something.'

'We do. And Mitchell. Fingers crossed the judge doesn't free them on bail Monday morning. Powers left one of his pals out here, guarding their SUV. I'll see if I can get anything out of him. Let me know, Ray, if you come up with anything on that CCTV.'

They ended the call, and Leroy sauntered up to the black SUV. The passenger door was slid open, and he could see one of the agents sitting by the opposite window. Blue sweatpants, grey tee. He was wearing sunglasses, even though the windows were tinted and he was reading something on his phone.

Leroy rested his hand on the roof and leaned in. 'Hey.'

The agent looked up, grunted something unintelligible, and returned to his phone.

Leroy then asked, 'You guys at DHS being kept busy?'

The agent looked up. 'There's normally something going on,' he said, before returning to his phone. From the very brief glance Leroy managed, it appeared the agent was playing a game on the phone.

Leroy nodded, and returned to his own vehicle. No point even attempting a conversation with this guy. He leaned on the side of his car, pushed his shades up to the top of his forehead, and pulled out his phone. He checked his messages. He was looking for one from Stacy. All morning he had been wondering if and when he would hear from her. Nothing so far. Was it too early in the morning? Maybe she liked to sleep in on a weekend: he was hoping he'd find out eventually. Or was he expected to make the first move?'

He sent a message. Was she okay? He enjoyed last night, and hoped she did too. He stared at his phone screen, just in case a reply came though immediately. It didn't. Then he noticed she was last online six twelve the previous evening. That was before he picked her up. He would just have to be patient and wait.

He then trawled though other messages and emails, of which there was nothing of any consequence, apart from one from his nephew Dean. His sister still lived in New

York with her husband and two children, as did his widowed mother. He would occasionally get messages from Dean, maybe with a joke, maybe with a picture of something he had made or drawn. Today it was a picture of a Lego Millennium Falcon. Leroy replied that it was very impressive and hoped to see it himself real soon. He had recently considered a trip back to New York to see his family: maybe over Thanksgiving weekend; that wouldn't be too long. Maybe taking Stacy with him; or was that being too premature and fanciful? In any case, he was not going anywhere until this investigation had been closed.

At least there were no messages or calls from Jasmine Washington. So far.

He put his phone away and stretched. He was still tired. He was uncertain how long he would be here; he had no intention of wasting a Saturday just waiting on those guys in there. He still had no idea what Powers really meant by liaison, and Dilbert inside the SUV certainly wasn't giving anything away.

He decided to give it another thirty minutes; then either go inside and see what was happening - they hadn't even touched the garage yet – or just head back to the station.

At that point, Powers appeared in the doorway, and walked over to Leroy.

## CHAPTER THIRTY-THREE

CASUALLY, LEROY PUT his phone back into its pouch and looked up at Powers as the agent approached.

'Still here?' Powers asked, grinning.

'Still here. Still liaising. Have you found anything? More weapons, more ammo?'

Powers shook his head. Folding his arms, he leaned on Leroy's car. 'No. And I think we've covered every square inch in there. We're going to take his laptop. I'm surprised you guys didn't take it already.'

Irritated, Leroy asked, 'Laptop? We didn't find any laptop.'

Smugly, Powers nodded. 'Yeah, a laptop. You said something yesterday about cans of paint.'

Leroy inclined his head over to the garage. 'Yeah, red and white and blue. Half used. In that garage.'

Powers walked over to the garage, and pulled down the police tape. 'Jerry!' he called out, to which the guy sitting in the SUV jumped out. Powers held out the key fob and locked their vehicle.

Leroy slowly followed them to the garage. By now they had opened the door and were inside. Powers was checking the cans of paint.

'All half empty,' he said to Jerry. 'Or half full, depending.'

'Red, white, blue,' added Jerry. 'What do you think?'

Powers shrugged. 'I reckon we're almost done in there,' he said, scratching his head. He pointed to the rest of the junk stored in the garage. 'Let's go through this shit first.'

'I'll leave you guys to it,' Leroy said. 'I'll go liaise somewhere else.'

'Are you headed back to your office?'

'I am. I still have a murder investigation. A triple murder.'

Powers said, 'We're going to need to speak with your Latvian buddy.'

'He's still at the Central Men's Jail.'

'You told me already. How long will he be there?'

'He's due in court Monday eleven AM. So I suggest you go see him asap, in case the judge frees him on bail.'

'We'll head over this afternoon.'

'You seem to be planning on charging him with something; after all, you found – sorry, we found – ten M16s.'

'That's a certainty,' Powers confirmed. 'You're obviously intending on charges yourselves. The fact that we've taken him into custody doesn't stop you doing what you need to do.'

'And if we need to talk to him some more?'

'He won't have disappeared into a black hole. All you guys need to do is reach out to us if you have to talk to him again, or charge him.'

Leroy could feel his phone vibrating. Two vibrations. A message. Maybe Ray had found something. He nodded. 'So you found nothing of any use to you guys?'

At that moment, Jerry called out. 'Nothing here.'

Powers turned to the garage. 'You want to just load the cans of paint into the back? Make sure the lids are on securely. Also, check for any brushes that have traces of red, white, or blue paint in the bristles.'

Jerry waved his acknowledgement. Powers clicked the fob to unlock the SUV, then turned back to Leroy.

'That answers your question, Sam, doesn't it? No; no, we didn't.'

'Those M16s were well hidden.'

'If there'd been anything else,' Powers replied, 'we'd have found it. You guys got yourselves a lucky break. No offence.'

'None taken. You guys find anything that might be of interest to us?'

'Like I said, all we found was the laptop.'

'Yes,' said Leroy, 'you mentioned the laptop before. We didn't find any laptop. Where was it?'

'We didn't put it there, if that's what you're asking.'

'Come on, I never said that.'

'Relax, just a bit of DHS black humour. You want to know where it was? It was in his closet, inside one of those... what are they called? Duffel bags. You know, like the military use. It was in this bag, which was hanging up inside a suit. So thin, nobody would notice.'

'So that's how my guys managed to miss it.' Well done, Ray, he thought. 'I take it you're taking it?'

'The fact that it was hidden the way it was,' replied Powers, 'tells me that there's something on it that he didn't want found. So yes, we are taking it.'

'But there might be something that -'

'Hold your horses, Sam. Homeland Security will always take priority over general police work, as I'm sure you know. But we have a policy of cooperating with and working with other agencies. So once we've searched it, and are done with it, you can have it. Or we can even email you any relevant files, folders, pictures, whatever.'

Leroy had no choice but to agree. 'Are you coming

back to the station?'

'No point. We're done here. We'll head Downtown and talk to the Latvian. We'll reach out to you Monday about transferring of the evidence; of the M16s and the cartridges. You want to see the place before we seal it?'

Leroy recalled what he saw inside the apartment earlier. 'I'm good.' He pushed himself off the car.

Powers did the same. 'Suit yourself. We'll be in touch; and, thanks again for the lead.'

He and Leroy shook hands.

'No problem,' said Leroy as he got into his car. He watched Powers return to their SUV. Jerry closed the garage door, and joined the other team members who were by now leaving the building. 'Fuck!' he said aloud: he could feel a murder suspect slipping through his fingers. For all the bullshit he had gotten from Powers, he knew that once he had what he wanted, he wouldn't give a rat's ass about the police investigation. In his experience, some agents genuinely worked with the police, wanted to help; others were just concerned with their own work, not giving a shit about the LAPD. It always helped to have a personal contact inside the relevant agency. Leroy had one inside the FBI, which had been invaluable many times. He was kind of hoping he could build up some kind of rapport, some kind of relationship and understanding, which would be an investment for the future, but Powers looked to be a standard asshole.

He reversed off the driveway and onto the street. He turned the wheel to head south, then remembered the message that came through earlier. There was no traffic coming, so before pulling away, he checked his phone screen.

His mood lifted considerably once he had read Stacy's message.

## CHAPTER THIRTY-FOUR

LEROY'S GOOD MOOD was shattered ten minutes into the drive back to the station. His phone rang, not a number he recognised.

'Detective Leroy? Chief Snell.'

*Oh shit.*

'Chief. Yes, it's Leroy here. I wasn't expecting a call from you. Not on a Saturday.'

'It's about this Dempsey case. I'm not in the office. I was meaning to call you last night, but had to go to a civic function. I'm at the Riviera, and there's a line to tee off on the fourteenth, so I have time to speak with you about this case.'

Leroy could visualise where the Chief was. Assuming by the Riviera, he meant the Riviera Country Club, an exclusive golf course in Pacific Palisades.

'Lieutenant Perez has been giving me updates, but I wanted to hear direct from you, and to give you my input.'

That sounded ominous. Leroy gave Snell a rundown on the case so far, including the events of that morning. He finished with, 'To be honest, Chief, I feel that Zhurov is being taken out of our hands.'

After a brief pause, Chief Snell said, 'But you have one other suspect in custody.'

'Yes, that's true, but with all due respect, Chief, that's not the point. If Zhurov and Mitchell are charged with the murders, if Zhurov is spirited away by Homeland Security, then there's a good chance he'll evade the prosecution.'

'If? You said *if.*'

'At this time, the evidence we have is circumstantial at best. We have CCTV evidence of them both using the vehicle in question, but not yet at the time of the incident. We're still working on that, still trawling back on the footage.'

'But Perez said they'd been charged.'

'They've been charged with possession of illegal weapons. That's more of a holding charge while we look further at putting them on the scene at the right time. That's of course, before we found the M16s in his air conditioning.'

'Has the vehicle been checked? Forensically, I mean?'

'I'm waiting to hear from them. I'm expecting to hear Monday; if not, we'll chase them. But again, even if those guys' fingerprints and DNA are all over the vehicle, it doesn't necessarily put them in the car at the scene of the crime, at the day and time.'

'And you're definitely treating it as a murder?'

'Three murders, plus whatever charges we make in respect of the walking wounded. The CCTV clearly shows the vehicle being deliberately driven onto the sidewalk.'

'So what do you propose to do, Detective?'

'Firstly, we're working to establish who was driving the vehicle at the time. The trail seems to begin at the car pound at LAX. We just need to establish where the trail begins.'

'Okay. You said firstly.'

'Yes, that's right, Chief. We're also looking at the victims themselves, on the basis that it was deliberate, and as I said, from the street cameras, it would appear that way. Who was the target? Starting with the three fatalities, Scott Dempsey, Rosa Delgado, and Kenneth Fong, then moving onto the walking wounded, we plan to establish any possible motives anybody would have to kill one of them.'

'You don't need to waste valuable time,' replied the Chief, 'looking at the victims. Two of them are immigrants, so you will not have much data on them. As I explained to you the other day, Detective, the mayor is most concerned about the rising level of street crime in the city, as am I. We are both in agreement that we need a quick result on this, Leroy. Don't waste yours and your team's time on looking for and chasing shadows, don't squander that time looking at the victims. It was a hit and run. You need to focus your efforts on finding the people who were driving the car. Has Lieutenant Perez arranged for more detectives to join your team?'

'I think he's still working on that, sir, but I'm not sure,'

'Many hands make light work, Detective.'

'But the flip side to that, Chief, is that too many cooks, you know?'

Chief Snell sighed loudly. 'Very well' he said, 'but I and the mayor need a quick result on this. Don't fuck around pursuing pointless angles. You need a laser-sharp focus on whoever was driving the vehicle, nothing else, then you'll be able to establish who was actually behind it, the driver, or somebody else. That way you can be sure Scott Dempsey and the other two didn't die in vain. Do you get the picture, Detective?'

'I do, Chief.'

'This is high profile and high priority, so you need to get it right, and get it right speedily.'

'I will, Chief, and enjoy your game,' said Leroy; but the Chief had already hung up.

## CHAPTER THIRTY-FIVE

QUINN WAS STILL working on the car pound cameras when Leroy got back.

'Any luck?' Leroy asked.

Quinn paused the video, leaned back in his chair, and shook his head. 'Nope. Plenty of comings and goings with other cars, but nothing with that Ford.'

'How far back have you reached?'

Quinn pointed to the date and time stamp at the corner of the screen. 'Here.'

'That's about the same time as the hit and run. We're almost there.'

Quinn stood up. 'I need a coffee and a wiz. How did you get on at Zhurov's place?'

'I think we've lost him,' said Leroy, updating him on the events of the morning. 'They found a laptop, in his bedroom closet.'

'No way. I looked through the closet. No way was there

a laptop there. I would have seen it.'

'There were clothes hanging in the closet? Suits, coats?'

'Yeah?'

'According to Powers, hanging inside one of the coats was a laptop.'

'A laptop hanging in a coat.'

'It was in one of those bags the military use.'

'Like a duffel bag?'

'U-huh.'

'Son of a bitch! I never looked inside his coats. Fuck.'

'They've taken it, but Powers said once they've done with it, we can have access to it. Said they can email any files over to us. But I'm not holding my breath. If you'd found it, we would have had first dibs on it.'

Quinn looked at the floor, shaking his head. 'Gee, Sam. I'm sorry.'

'Forget it.' He paused a second to let things sink in. 'I also had a call from the Chief on my way here.'

'Chief Snell? He's working on a weekend?'

'Called me from the golf course. He took pleasure in telling me he was on the thirteenth or fourteenth tee, or something.'

'He wanted an update on a Saturday? I thought the lieutenant was doing that.'

'He wanted an update, but he also wanted to give some directions about how we should handle the investigation.'

'Directions? What kind of directions?'

'Some of what he's said before: it's a high profile case, apparently.'

'Really?'

'I did think of saying why if it's so high profile, have we had no media interest in it? No calls from any TV stations, no calls from the *Times*?'

'No, nothing.'

'Same here. But it's apparently high profile. He also said he wanted a speedy resolution.'

'We all do.'

'I know. But this is the clincher. I told him about our intention to look more closely at the victims, to see if somewhere there was a possible motive for somebody to want to drive a ten ton vehicle at them. And what did he say to that? To use his words, don't fuck around looking at the victims.'

'Jesus.'

'And wait for this: you know I told you last time he kept referring to it as the Dempsey case? This time, he referred to Rosa Delgado and Kenneth Fong as *immigrants*.'

'You're joking!'

'No. He said it was a waste of time and resources looking at backgrounds of the victims as two of them were immigrants and we wouldn't find anything.'

'That's so out of order. Have you told the lieutenant yet?'

'I've not. I got the impression that he doesn't know Snell called, otherwise he'd be calling me to ask what he said.'

'He'll go apeshit. Could he put in a complaint?'

'I guess so, but the higher up the food chain you get, the more difficult it is for that kind of shit to stick. But his basic message was, forget Dempsey; just focus – laser-sharp, he said – on the drivers.'

'So where does that leave us?'

'It leaves us where we were last night. He seems too interested in this case. It's so out of character. I've known him for a few years, and he's never been hands on. Why is he so determined for us not to look into Dempsey's background? And as for the immigrants: fuck that and fuck him. Kenneth Fong had probably lived in this country since before Snell was born. And as for Rosa Delgado: well, somewhere out there, a little boy is never going to see his mother again.'

'So you're still looking at Scott Dempsey?'

'No. You are. You've been on that CCTV all morning. Your head must be done in. If you're staring at the same images for too long, you'll get hypnotised. We'll swap. I want you to check Dempsey out on his social media accounts. Facebook is the best place to start, I guess. That will show contacts, pictures, maybe messages that might be useful to us. Then go onto Twitter, LinkedIn, and so on.'

Quinn nodded and logged onto another workstation. Leroy sat and began to watch the car pound CCTV. A few minutes later, Quinn leaned back. 'Jeez. Look at this, Sam.'

'What is it?' Leroy paused the CCTV and wheeled his chair over to Quinn. It was on Dempsey's Facebook page – a posting by Dempsey's husband, Piers Shipley. It comprised a selfie of the two together, both wearing only shorts. They were on a small boat, and in the background about a hundred yards away it looked like the casino building on Catalina. It looked as if it was Shipley taking the shot, and Dempsey was holding up a large fish, probably a marlin. They were both smiling and had their free arms around each other. The text above the picture was, *I lost my only love today years before his time. My life has changed forever*, followed by two emojis, crying, and a heart split in two. Then, *When I know when my darling Scott is to be laid to rest, I will announce it here.*

There were many messages of condolence, all carrying an emoji, some broken hearted, some crying, some caring.

'Shit,' said Quinn slowly, his hand over his mouth.

'And you said he didn't seem upset,' Leroy said, propelling his chair back to his own desk.

## CHAPTER THIRTY-SIX

IT WAS NOW early Saturday afternoon. Quinn was going through Scott Dempsey's social media accounts, beginning with Facebook. Dempsey seemed to be one of those people who posted an update two or three times daily: where he was, what he was doing, how he was feeling. On his last full day of life he went for a run before breakfast, the traffic was bad on the way into work, he had a fantastic lunch at Wolfgang Puck's, late in the afternoon it was getting chilly for this time of year. Quinn sighed as he went through all the trivia and minutiae of Dempsey's life.

Leroy had sat down to pick up where his partner had left off trawling through the car pound CCTV.

'I need coffee before I start,' he said. 'You want one, Ray?'

'I'm good, thanks, Sam,' Quinn replied, moving his cup around the desk, as if for emphasis.

Leroy wandered out into the corridor, and down to the

staff room. Until the summer, there had been two vending machines from which officers could buy hot and cold drinks and snacks. As a cost cutting exercise, these had been removed, and now officers had to use the filter coffee machine in the staff room. Personally, Leroy missed the convenience of slipping a bill or quarters into the slot, but had to admit the coffee now tasted better. The downside of not having a vending machine, however, meant that they had to bring in their own food. He had already picked up a chicken and mayo burrito on the way

While the coffee machine warmed up, Leroy leaned against the counter and took out his phone. He had not had the opportunity to fully read the message Stacy had sent earlier. The gist of her message was that she also enjoyed the previous evening; it was a pity it had to end early, but she understood the reason why. She suggested continuing their date - if that's what it was – the next day. If he was free, he was welcome to come over to hers around midday, they could go out somewhere in the early afternoon, and she would cook dinner for them both when they got back. Leroy messaged back, saying yes, he was free, and that he couldn't wait to spend tomorrow with her. Message sent, he poured himself a strong cup of coffee and rejoined Quinn.

'Anything yet?' he asked as he sat down next to his partner.

Quinn stretched and took another drink. He shook his head. 'Nah. Plenty of photos of him and his husband in various locations. They were in New York last Christmas.'

'Yeah?'

'Picture of them in front of the Rockefeller tree. Then on vacation in Mexico earlier; even some in Paris.'

'The one in France?'

'Yeah, the French one. GIFs, just general shit. How far back do you want me to go?'

'Keep going. If anybody else is linked in a post, then click on them also. Take a look at their background and postings.'

Quinn carried on while Leroy sat down, took some coffee, and returned to his screen. He rested his chin on his left hand and with his right finger, he pressed the reverse search key and watched the footage, occasionally glancing down at the date and time stamp.

Before long, he had reached the time of the hit and run, and continued backwards. Into the early morning of the hit and run, the view changing from daylight to early morning half-light, to the darkness of the night before.

There was very little activity throughout the night, just the occasional vehicle movement, all sedans, no Ford Territory.

Then, finally, there was the activity he was looking for. It was nine thirty the evening prior to the hit and run, and he saw the Ford reversing into a space. The video was being played in reverse, so in reality it was being driven away.

Leroy took the video a few seconds more, froze it, and zoomed in to the driver and passenger. However, the darkness and point of view preventing him getting to see their faces. Their build, though, suggested Mitchell and Zhurov; however, that was not enough.

'Got it,' he said to Quinn. Nine thirty the evening before.'

'Mitchell and Zhurov?' Quinn asked, looking over at Leroy's screen.

'Possibly, but all I can get here are silhouettes. Nothing like enough for a positive ID. How are you getting on?'

'Just postings. Plenty of friends. There's more than one camera there, though?'

'Several. I'm going to try them.'

Leroy made a note of the exact time on the screen, then switched to one of the other cameras. He found the correct time, but here there was a similar image of the two people, but the same as before. The third camera was even worse: he could barely see the spot in the parking lot. The next video was from one of the two cameras positioned at the gate. One faced into the lot, the other onto Northside

Parkway. He dismissed the camera pointing in the direction of the parkway, and clicked on the footage from the other gate camera. He quickly moved the video onto the correct time. Once there, he slowly advanced the footage, frame by frame, then froze the picture.

He sat back in his chair, arms folded. 'Look at this, Ray.' Once more, Quinn pushed his chair back from his desk and Scott Dempsey's Facebook pages and leaned over to look at Leroy's screen.

'That's them,' Quinn said. 'Isn't it? That's Mitchell and Zhurov.'

'It certainly is,' Leroy said, then added, talking to the two faces on his screen, 'Got you, you bastards.'

'So what now? We have a positive ID.'

'Before you get carried away, breaking out the champagne, we have a positive ID here, of them driving the Territory out of the car pound twelve hours before the hit and run; but it's still circumstantial. It doesn't prove they were driving the vehicle twelve hours later.'

'So we're still screwed.'

'Maybe not. It doesn't prove they were driving the next morning, and it is just circumstantial. But Mitchell doesn't know that.'

'You're going to try and bluff him? Surely his lawyer won't wear that.'

Leroy pushed his chair back a few inches and folded his arms again. 'What I'm thinking,' he said, 'is of course his lawyer's going to say the police are bullshitting you and no way does that put you at the scene of the crime; but it might push him just that tad enough so he's prepared to talk. Assuming it was premeditated, it was done very well: remember Pamela got nothing from the street cameras; everything was planned and carried out exactly so any means of identifying the vehicle was obscured. We just got lucky. You've met Mitchell: not exactly the sharpest tool in the shed. I'm thinking he was acting on orders; paid to do it. We ought to check his bank account, but I'm sure he'll have been paid in cash.'

Quinn nodded. 'That makes sense. What about Zhurov? Mitchell could've been working for him.'

'Possibly. What I'm getting at, is that even the slightest hint that he's been identified - even if the DA's office says no way – he might spill the beans, say who he was working for. If it was Zhurov, then we can charge him, although I suspect we'll have to get in line behind DHS.'

'That's so unfair.'

'What? Them getting first dibs on him? It is, but I can kind of see where they're coming from. Ten assault rifles and God knows how many rounds of ammunition must surely indicate something big being planned. So it has to be higher up the food chain than a homicide. We can still charge him, even though he's being held for a terrorism offence, or something like that.' He checked the time. 'I may go over there later today, or this evening. It would do that lawyer good to be called out at a weekend.' He stretched and rubbed his eyes. 'So, anything useful?'

'Nothing I could pick out as being relevant to us. He liked to travel – *they* liked to travel, I should say. Picture after picture of him and Piers Shipley here, there, and everywhere. They appeared to like fishing. Plenty of shots of them and other guys holding up what they had caught.'

'Kind of my one's bigger than yours?' Leroy grinned.

'I guess.' Quinn flicked through the images to show Leroy what he meant.

Leroy looked at the images as Quinn flicked though them. Then, 'Hold on, Ray. Go back to that last one.'

Quinn did so and Leroy stared at the picture. It was taken at a marina somewhere. Dempsey and his husband, with two other men. All were dressed in summer gear – tee shirts, one with a bright yellow Hawaiian shirt.

'Ray – the one on the left.'

'This one? The one who's dressed like he's Steve McGarrett?'

'Yes. Don't you recognise him?'

'I don't. Do you know him?'

Leroy replied, speaking slowly. 'Ray, that's the

mayor.'

## CHAPTER THIRTY-SEVEN

'THAT MIGHT EXPLAIN,' said Quinn, 'why the Chief is so interested in the case. He's getting his nuts chewed off by the mayor. By the illustrious Mayor James Cryer.'

'It certainly would. Also why he didn't give a shit about Rosa Delgado or Kenneth Fong, or the others in hospital. Why he kept referring to it as the Dempsey case.'

'Didn't you say he told you not to check out Dempsey? To just focus on Mitchell and Zhurov?'

'He did. Now we see why. Ray: just keep going through those postings. Is Cryer tagged into that post?'

Quinn checked. 'He is.'

'Carry on looking at Dempsey's page; go back the last six months. They're more likely to have posted something like that in the summer months. Then do the same with Cryer's. I'm going to set up another interview with Mitchell, at the jail. I guess it'll be this evening. You okay for that?'

'Sure. I've nothing on tonight. And I could use the overtime.'

'You still paying the mortgage as well as your rent?'

'Half. When we bought the place, Holly and I agreed to split the payments fifty-fifty. When I moved out, we put a kind of agreement in place until...'

Leroy spoke before Quinn could finish the sentence. 'I'll reach out to the jail then; and, of course, that little prick McQueen. I'm sure he'll insist on coming along.'

'I'm sure he will. Look, Sam: there's another here with the mayor.'

'Yeah; I think a pattern is forming. Keep looking.'

Leroy needed to call the Assistant Sheriff of the Men's Central Jail. He decided to make the call outside, ostensibly to allow Quinn to concentrate, but really as he wanted to check his phone unobtrusively for any messages from Stacy. There was one, saying she was looking forward to seeing him at noon the next day.

When he returned to his desk ten minutes later, Quinn was nowhere to be seen, but his screen was displaying a picture, three men in dinner jackets. Slowly, he lowered himself onto Quinn's chair and stared at the picture. Momentarily, Quinn returned.

'Men's room,' he said. 'You saw the picture?'

'I did.' Leroy slid himself over to his own chair. 'And whose page was that on?'

Quinn pointed to the name at the top. James Cryer. 'Our mayor,' he said.

Leroy nodded to Quinn and turned his gaze to the photograph. It appeared to have been taken at a formal function, as all three men were wearing dinner jackets, white shirts and black ties. The wall behind them was dark oak panelling. Three men: Scott Dempsey, Mayor Cryer, and Chief of Police Snell.

'What do you want to do, Sam?' Quinn asked. 'Dempsey had friends in high places. Whatever he was up to, Cryer and Snell might also be involved.'

'Yeah. Or he might not have been up to anything; just kept high class company.'

'So do we carry on looking at Dempsey's background, or do as the chief says?'

Leroy exhaled deeply. 'It might just be a coincidence. They belong to the same golf club or something, and that was their annual dinner or something like that. But my gut tells me that if Snell is more or less telling me to keep away from Dempsey, then somebody has something to hide.'

'So we continue looking at Dempsey?'

'I need to run all this past the lieutenant first, get his take on things.'

'What if he says keep away from Dempsey?'

'He'll probably say do what you need to do but make sure I don't know about it; that's his style.'

'So where do we start?'

'I'll talk to Perez Monday morning. I could call him over the weekend, but I don't want to convey any urgency on our part. Then we can decide how we approach Dempsey and the others. I've arranged for us to go see Mitchell at six thirty. Later than I'd have liked, but that was the only time his attorney was available.'

'What do you plan to say to him? It's still kind of circumstantial, doesn't put them at the scene.'

'I know that, and while it would be nice if he took a look at that picture and confessed, that's not going to happen. I'm hoping knowing we have him on video might spook him enough to tell us more than he has already. I'm looking for a motive if he was behind it; or if he was hired, who the person was doing the hiring.'

'What about Zhurov?'

Leroy gave a humourless laugh. 'He's gone already.'

'Gone?'

'The Assistant Sheriff said three guys from DHS showed up an hour ago with a court order and took him away.'

'So we've lost him?'

'Powers, the guy from DHS, told me they'd probably take him into custody, but we'd still be able to talk to him or charge him.'

'You believe that?'

'No way, but I'm not sure what we can do about that. In the meantime, let's focus on Mitchell. And, of course, our mayor and his friends in low places.' He checked the time. 'Let's give it another hour here, then head Downtown. The traffic'll be shit this time of day.'

\*

## CHAPTER THIRTY-EIGHT

LEROY MISJUDGED THE level of traffic, and they arrived at the Central Men's Jail at five fifty, way too early for their interview with Mitchell. There was a food stand across the street, which looked as it was closing, so hurried across before it was too late.  Just a coffee each.  Unlike most other parts of the city, the Downtown area tends to close down early evening once the office workers have left and gone home, and this was all the more so on weekends.

'That's McQueen. That's his lawyer,' said Leroy as they walked back to the jail and saw a silver convertible waiting at a red light. 'Let's avoid any eye contact.'

Built in 1963, the LA County Central Men's Jail is one of the oldest county jails in California. From the outside, it is uncompromisingly grim, with its light grey concrete construction, and narrow slits for windows. For years, there had been talk of demolition, and replacing it with an alternative, but without any action, in spite of a campaign by the *Times*.

They were taken through three barred and gated areas to get to the reception area. To get there, they had to walk along a long corridor, a wall on one side and bars the other. It had been a while since Leroy had been here, and this was his memory of the place. It always reminded him of a dog pound. Then there was the constant smell of stale sweat and urine. When they arrived, McQueen was waiting there.

'I hope this is really necessary, Detective,' said McQueen, fussily looking at his watch. 'On a Saturday evening.'

'Law enforcement is never a nine to five job, sir,' Leroy said. 'Maybe as we're all here early, we could get started. The sooner we begin, et cetera.'

'And maybe we could keep the questioning to a minimum,' McQueen added. 'I have an event to attend afterwards.'

Leroy nodded. 'Then it's just as well Sergei Zhurov was taken away by Homeland Security; otherwise we'd be talking to him as well.'

McQueen said nothing.

They were soon in the interview room with William Mitchell. Leroy was the first to speak. He showed Mitchell and McQueen the still of him and Zhurov driving out of the car pound.

'This was taken a few hours before the hit and run.'

Mitchell looked at McQueen, who discretely nodded.

'I need to talk to my client in private first,' said Mitchell.

'As you wish,' said Leroy. 'We'll be outside.' He and Quinn left McQueen and Mitchell alone. Outside, the warder supervising Mitchell said quietly, 'I've turned the recording off temporarily; I could always accidentally switch it back on again.'

Leroy cast an eye at the blank screen then to Quinn. 'No point,' he said. 'Any conversation that goes on in there is covered by attorney-client privilege. If we listen in and use anything we might hear, then it's going to be inadmissible, anyway.'

The warder shrugged. 'Suit yourself.'

Momentarily, the door opened.

'My client is ready,' McQueen said. Leroy and Quinn followed him inside. McQueen was the first to speak. 'My client wants to talk about a deal.'

Not what Leroy was expecting. It was rare for him to be on the back foot.

'Oh, yes? So your client is confessing?'

'No, he's not confessing or admitting to anything.'

'If that's so,' Leroy asked, sitting down across the table, 'why are we talking about a deal?'

McQueen sat up straight, resting his hands on his attaché case. 'What my client is trying to say is: that without admitting anything – after all, that image only puts my client in a particular location at a particular time. Not at the scene of your accident, or at the time of it. And please note, my client was not driving.'

'So what are you saying?'

McQueen used the same tone that an adult would when explaining something to a child. 'What I am saying, Detective, is that in the interests of justice, and helping the police, my client is prepared to do whatever he can to assist you, and to provide whatever information he can.'

Leroy said nothing.

'After a few seconds, McQueen asked, 'So what do you want to ask, Detective?'

'I was waiting to hear what your client wants in return.'

'In return for his full cooperation, my client would like for said cooperation to be taken into account in any charges the police might make; both in respect of that traffic accident, and the firearm possession.'

'No way,' Leroy countered. 'The traffic accident, as you call it, and the illegal possession of a firearm are two separate matters.'

McQueen sat back and folded his arms. 'That's my client's offer.'

Leroy glanced up at Quinn, who was in the corner of the room, leaning against the wall. 'I'll need to discuss this with my supervisor,' he said, pushing himself off the table.

'You go do that,' said McQueen. 'But no delays, please.'

Resisting the temptation to reply, Leroy led Quinn outside. They stopped in the corridor.

'You going to call Lieutenant Perez, then?' Quinn asked.

Leroy shook his head. 'Nah. Just need time to think. What do you think, Ray?'

'About his offer?'

'Yeah. Should we take it up, or tell him to fuck off?'

Quinn scratched the back of his head. 'What he might tell us, even if insignificant, might push the investigation a bit further on. We're never going to put him at the scene with what we have right now. What does your gut tell you?'

'My gut tells me exactly what you just said. Let's call his bluff.' Leroy pushed himself off the wall and led Quinn back into the interview room. 'Okay, Mitchell. It's a deal.'

'We were paid to drive the car that day,' said Mitchell.

'Who by?'

'Well, Sergei was the one who was actually paid. I was paid out of his share. A grand. He kept the other four as he was the one driving.'

'And who paid Sergei? I'm guessing you're saying you were hired by a third party.'

'Some guy.'

'I'm going to need more than that.'

Mitchell looked over at McQueen, who nodded.

Mitchell took a deep breath and answered Leroy's question.

## CHAPTER THIRTY-NINE

'THIS GUY,' MITCHELL said, 'paid Sergei. Not me.'

'So you just went along for the ride?' asked Leroy.

'He just paid Sergei. That's all I know. They must have talked before because nobody said anything about the job.'

'So who was this guy?' Leroy asked. 'Where did you meet him?'

'His name was Tony,' Mitchell said. 'Tony Chinn.'

'Tony Chinn,' Leroy repeated. He looked up at Quinn, who shrugged. 'Who is he? What does he look like?'

'He's Chinese. Youngish. Younger than me, about the same age as you.' Mitchell looked at Quinn as he spoke. 'Tall mother, at least for a Chinaman. Black hair. That's all I know.'

'And where did he pay Zhurov?'

'Some bar Downtown. It was a Saturday night. Last Saturday night.'

'Which bar?'

Mitchell shook his head. 'Can't remember the name. It was on Spring. Part of it was on top of a roof.'

'So you two just showed up, saw this Tony Chinn guy, then left?'

'We had a drink, then I left. Caught the Red Line home.'

'Okay,' said Leroy quietly. He looked up at Quinn and nodded, satisfied.

'I think he means the Treehouse Rooftop,' Quinn said as they left the jail a while later. 'I'm certain that's on Spring. North Spring.'

'Really?' asked Leroy. 'You know far more about LA's nightspots than I do.'

'That's because your clubbing days are long gone,' grinned Quinn as they got into the car.

'Bite me,' retorted Leroy as they drove off.

'Are we headed to the club?' Quinn asked. It looked as if Leroy was headed back to the station.

'I think so, but it's too early. I was thinking eleven, eleven thirty. You okay for that?'

'Sure. I had no plans.'

'We'll head back for a while; I might try grab some zees. Ray: you have Pamela's number in your cell?'

'I do.'

'You want to text her? Tell her what we've done so far today, and does she want to come with us to the Treehouse later? Tell her I said it's her decision, totally voluntary, and for overtime. If she says yes, tell her to meet us at the station ten, ten thirty. I don't want her to feel she's being kept out of the loop.'

'Sure.' Quinn found her number and sent the message. 'What will the lieutenant say about the overtime?'

'By overtime, I mean she may have to take some personal time to cover it. Or I'll talk to Perez Monday. No, scrub that. I think I'm going to need to reach out to the

Chief in the morning. We might need him to oil the wheels at a high level with DHS if we're going to see Zhurov again. I'll float the concept of overtime past him.'

The detective suite was quiet, unlike the front office, which was busy, the normal Saturday evening business. Leroy and Quinn snuck past the front desk, hoping to avoid getting drawn into anything. In the detective suite, two of the weekend shift were at their desks, one on the phone, the other online.

Lieutenant Perez had left his office unlocked: Leroy announced that he was going to try to snatch some sleep on the couch in the office; after all, he said, he was the only Detective III in the building, and rank had its privileges. Quinn settled for the chair in the staff room. He lay across two armless chairs, and dozed off, only to be woken after thirty minutes by one of the weekend shift.

This was Detective Bruce. Bruce had been with the Department for almost twenty years. He would tell everybody who was interested that he was not interested in promotion, and that was why he was still a Detective II after so long. The other thing about Bruce was that his first name was Wayne, and if he had a dollar for each time somebody went up to him and said, 'I'm Manbat,' he could have retired in comfort years ago.

Bruce made himself a drink, apologised for waking Quinn, then spent the next ten minutes talking to him so that there was no way Quinn could get back to sleep. Instead, he got himself some strong black coffee and returned to his desk.

Leroy emerged from Perez's office an hour later. He had ordered three pizzas for delivery at ten, after which he, Quinn, and Velasquez would head back Downtown.

Velasquez arrived at ten fifteen. She said she had already eaten, so Leroy and Quinn demolished the third pizza between them. After a quick briefing session, they set off. They arrived at the club around eleven fifteen.

The Treehouse Rooftop bar is what it says on the tin: a bar on the roof of a building in LA's Chinatown, on the intersection of Ord and North Spring Streets. In contrast to the traditional construction of the surrounding buildings, it is a modern structure, off-white concrete and blackened glass, rounded at the street corner. They parked in a small shopping centre next door: the centre comprised a 7/11, a liquor store, a launderette, and an empty unit. A red-bricked hotel stood at the other end of the lot. As they got out of the car, Leroy paused and pointed up at the roof-mounted hotel sign.

'That gas station where Mitchell works: I remember it was across the street from that hotel.'

'Small world,' said Quinn. 'Nothing like keeping everything local.'

'You mean worked,' said Velasquez as they walked round to the club.

'What?' Leroy asked.

'You said he *works* at the gas station. Shouldn't that be past tense?'

Leroy got it. 'Worked.'

The entrance to the club was up a small flight of steps on the Ord Street side, leading to a veranda, and the entrance doors. They showed their badges and got past the two bouncers, one of whom recognised Leroy. There was a small line of around half a dozen waiting to get in. Once inside, they took the small flight of stairs up to the roof. The club consisted of a huge dance floor, part of which was in a covered area. The bar was in this covered area. The floor was wooden, large stars projected onto it from the ceiling. Tables and chairs were dotted around the inside area, and outdoor too, with rattan sofas and long low tables in the centre. The indoor dance floor was crammed with twenty somethings dancing. The DJ had a booth across the floor from the bar; loud music was playing: Velasquez shouted into Leroy's ear that it was Joey Negro. Leroy nodded, having no idea what she had said, or what she was talking about.

All they had was a physical description of Tony Chinn, no photograph. They asked at the bar if anybody knew

Chinn, or was he in, but the two staff serving did not. It was just a matter of checking out all those here and hoping he was in tonight.

Leroy ushered his partners outside. Here, while the music was still relatively noisy, at least the air was fresher and it was easier to think. Wires criss-crossed above, pale white light bulbs hanging from the wires. Around the perimeter of the roof was an artificial hedge, neatly trimmed. At one of the tables, chatting to two girls, was a figure who could have fitted the bill.

'That's him, Sam,' said Velasquez discretely.

'Let's go see.' Leroy led them over. The man looked up as they walked over. He was Chinese, muscular, jet black hair.

'Can I help you?' the man asked, not happy at being interrupted.

'Tony Chinn?'

'Who wants to know?'

Leroy held out his badge; the others did likewise. 'Five-0.'

Chinn mouthed, 'Fuck,' and pushed back in his seat.

'You ladies want to powder your noses?' Velasquez asked.

'Yeah, I won't be long,' sneered Chinn as the girls got up and left. Leroy, Quinn and Velasquez sat down at the table.

'You got ID?' Leroy asked.

'What?'

Leroy said nothing, held out his hand.

'What the fuck?' Chinn reached into a back pocket, pulled out a wallet. Tossed a drivers licence over to Leroy, who picked it up and methodically checked it. Velasquez glanced at Quinn.

'You had a goatee then?' Leroy asked, as he returned the licence.

Chinn snatched the licence back. 'What of it?'

Leroy got out his phone. He showed Chinn the mugshots of Mitchell and Zhurov. 'You recognise these?'

'No.'

'You want to look at them first?'

Chinn leaned forward and looked at Mitchell. Then Leroy scrolled over to Zhurov.

'Nope,' Chinn said, leaning back. 'Don't know those guys.'

'You sure?'

'I told you, didn't I? Who are they?'

'This is William Mitchell. He's American. The other is Sergei Zhurov. He's Latvian. We have information that you met them here, this time last week, where you gave Zhurov five thousand dollars.'

'Five grand? Now why would I do that?'

'To kill somebody,' said Velasquez.

'That's bullshit. I don't know what you're talking about, man.'

Quinn asked, 'Did you arrange the vehicle also, and get them to drive it?'

'What vehicle? What the fuck are you talking about?'

Leroy leaned forward and spoke quietly. 'I'm talking about three people who were killed Downtown, not too far from here, the other morning, plus several still in hospital.'

'I told you, I don't know what you're talking about. This is all bullshit.'

Leroy pointed to the picture of Zhurov. 'This is Sergei Zhurov. We have a witness to say that you paid him five thousand dollars in cash for something.'

Velasquez added, 'Or did you just pay him to get the job done, how they did it wasn't your concern?'

'I told you before, I don't know what you're talking about. You got any proof? Or are you here to waste my motherfucking time on account of what somebody told you?'

Leroy said, 'So you're telling me that you have never met these two men, and you never gave this one five grand in cash?'

Chinn sneered at Leroy. 'You catch on quick, don't you? Now, why don't you get your fucking cuffs out, and take me the fuck to whatever hole you come out of, or stop wasting my time and get the fuck out of here?'

Leroy paused a few seconds, then blinked slowly. He put his phone away and stood up. Quinn and Velasquez stood.

'I'll be seeing you again,' Leroy said, locking eyes with Chinn. 'As they say, don't make any plans.' He turned and they all walked out.

As they walked down the stairs to the doors, Velasquez asked Leroy, 'You believe him?'

'Not a word. But he was right: we have no evidence. Only Mitchell's word, which probably won't be enough. Let's let him think he's got the better of us. Monday, I'll arrange surveillance. We'll see where he goes, what he does, and who he talks to.'

'How are we going to do that?' Quinn asked. 'We don't know where he lives.'

'Ray…' Velasquez starred to say.

'I asked for his ID, didn't I?' said Leroy. 'He showed me his driver's licence. I know where he lives.' He looked at the others with a *no applause, please* look on his face. 'Let's get out of here. It's been a long day.'

## CHAPTER FORTY

THE FOLLOWING MORNING, Sunday morning, Leroy woke at nine. He had arranged to arrive at Stacy's house at twelve, and from there they would go out for brunch. After brunch they would hang out somewhere yet to be decided, then she would cook him dinner. This was all something he was looking forward to, so he made sure he set his alarm, as by the time they had got back to the station, cleared everything up, and he had driven home, it was almost two.

He forgo any breakfast, just settling for two cups of strong, black coffee before and after a long shower. He would also normally have walked down to the beach, almost passing his old apartment building, and taken a run either to and from the pier or the marina. Personal fitness was always part of his regime, but today there was a time factor, and secretly he was hoping to get a different type of exercise later.

He left home at eleven and took a comparatively leisurely drive along Santa Monica Boulevard into Hollywood. He arrived at Grace Avenue eleven forty, thought this was far too early, so parked fifty yards down from her house for fifteen minutes, then made the last part of the journey.

He parked on her driveway behind her car when a text message came through. It was Stacy, saying she saw him arrive, and the door was unlocked, and he was to go straight in. He did so, and as he closed the door behind him, she called out that she was in the kitchen. He joined her there. She was at the sink.

'Hey,' she said, turning and drying her hands.

He leaned down and kissed her on the cheek. 'Hey back.' He straightened up. 'You know, it's not a good idea to leave your front door unlocked. Not in this part of town. Not in any part of town.'

Stacy shook her head. 'Sam, what do I do for a living? I know all that; don't fuss. I saw you parking, then unlocked it. Did you shut it behind you? You can't be too careful this part of town,' she grinned.

He held up his hands in mock surrender. 'Okay, point taken. So where shall we go for brunch?'

'I was thinking the Farmer's Market. You know it?'

'On Third and Fairfax? Of course I know it. Ray and I grab something there most weeks.'

'I'll get my stuff and we can head out. Dinner's cooking.'

'I thought I could smell cooking. Nice. What is it?'

'Beef pot roast, slow cooked. That your thing?'

'Absolutely. Best not eat too much for brunch.'

On arrival at the Market, they checked out a few eating places before settling for a patio table at Du-pars. Leroy ordered pancakes with syrup and coffee, Stacy French toast and a herbal tea. They chatted in vague terms about their respective jobs while they ate, inevitably the case of Jordan Washington came up.

'I don't want to bore you about that,' Leroy said.

'You're not. Tell me what you were going to say; I might be able to help.

'Okay,' said Leroy, mopping up some syrup with a piece of pancake. 'I think I've exhausted the angles I've been working on. I thought I'd go back to Trejo himself; his habits, routines, that kind of thing. But the problem is, the trail has long gone cold.'

'Do you have any friends in the Cold Case Unit? Anybody there who owed you a favour?'

Leroy shook his head. 'The problem there is that the Cold Case Unit is now part of Robbery Homicide. If I do reach out to RHD, the case we're working on now might get on their radar.'

'So?'

'Their jurisdiction includes homicides where three or more persons are killed at the same time. This case began with two deaths, with a third dying later. Now three murders, same event. I don't want them muscling in, taking all the credit while we've done all the ground work. I feel we're almost there.'

'Are they likely to want to take the investigation over?'

'I do know they are snowed under at this time. The Chief knows how many people were killed: he ordered regular, personal one-to-one updates, so I guess he's content for us to keep it, although that might change if he feels we're not making enough progress. The other thing is,' he said, looking around to make sure nobody was listening, before realising how stupid that looked, 'we think there might be some connection between one of the victims, the mayor, and the Chief himself.'

'No shit? What kind of connection?'

'Not sure yet. Ray was checking through the victim's social media, and found photographs posted of this victim Chief Snell keeps asking about, together with the mayor and Snell himself. It can't be anything clandestine; otherwise, it wouldn't get posted on Facebook. The thought occurred to me that we might still have it – I mean why Snell hasn't reassigned it to RHD - is because with their resources they might unearth something embarrassing.'

'So you're figuring that's why you're not involving the Cold Case Unit for the Washington boy?'

'You think I'm being stupid?'

'No. I know that law enforcement politics are like. I have an idea. Not today, but one day in the week, why don't we get together and we both look over what you have? Fresh pair of eyes, so to speak. What do you think? Then you can finally get closure on it.'

'I'd appreciate that, yes.'

'I'll check my schedule later, so we can pick the right evening for it.'

Leroy was more than happy with that.

He insisted on picking up the check for their brunch; after all, she was cooking dinner for him. Afterwards, they wandered around the market, taking in several places including Sporte Fashion for Stacy and the Newstand for Leroy.

After they had made two circuits of the market, Leroy asked if she wanted to head over to the Grove, a more contemporary shopping centre adjacent to the historic market.

She shook her head. 'Not really. I don't like it much. I prefer more traditional locations, like here.'

'This has certainly been here a long time; certainly traditional.'

'Have you ever been to the one in Hollywood?'

'I thought this one was the only one.'

'No, there's one up in Hollywood. Not open every day, like here; a few days each month. It's on Selma, between Vine and Cahuenga.'

'That would be useful for you.'

'It is, although I like to come down here once in a while.'

They wandered back to Leroy's car and headed back to Stacy's house, which was filled with the smell of cooking.

'I'm almost hungry again already,' said Leroy.

'Anything I can do?'

'Maybe you could peel the potatoes for the mash. I'll prepare the salad.'

As he began work, Stacy put on some music. He recognised the song, but not the singer.

'Who's that?'

'Diana Krall. I'm kind of into jazz. Especially female artists. I find them relaxing to listen to, especially when I'm here working.'

'So she's your favourite?'

'Possibly. Her or Cassandra Wilson. What kind of music are you into?'

'I'm not especially musical. I guess my tastes are pretty eclectic. If I think it sounds good, I like it. Although,' he laughed, 'I've not added to my CD collection in ages.'

'CD collection?' she laughed. 'Where have you been the last twenty years?'

'What's the song playing on?'

'My Alexa.'

'Streamed?'

'Kind of.'

'You sound like Ray Quinn. He's always saying I need to keep with the times.'

'Have you ever been to Amoeba Music?'

'The big music store on Sunset?'

'That's the one, but it relocated a while back. It's down on the Boulevard now.'

'Convenient for you here.'

'U-huh.'

'Just a minute,' he said. 'If you don't buy CDs, if you stream all your music: why would you need a music store?'

'I like to browse.'

'Without buying?'

'I still like to browse the shelves. It's much more fun than trawling the net. If I see something I like, I'll take a picture of the CD or the vinyl, then come home and find it online and download it. I am thinking of getting a vinyl player, though.'

'Instead of the Alexa?'

'As well as. Sometimes I like to have physical media, like books. I'll take those, thanks.' She took the peeled potatoes from Leroy and put them on the stove.' She turned to Leroy and said, 'Shit!'

'What's up?' he asked, slightly taken aback.

'I forgot the wine. I meant to get some at the market.'

'I'll go get a bottle. I should have brought some, anyway. Where's the nearest place?'

'You're best going to the Whitly Market. It's a few blocks up Franklin, corner of Highland.'

'I think I know it. There's a Starbucks there, isn't there? Opposite the church. I'll go now.'

It was a three minute drive along Franklin Avenue to the market, on the intersection with Highland Avenue. Turn left and you were on Hollywood Boulevard; turn right and you were at the Hollywood Bowl. Leroy could remember him and Quinn pinning down a suspect at gunpoint in this very parking lot a while back.

He also remembered the store from a previous visit. In the centre of the aisle were life-sized cut-outs of Elvis, Zac Efron, a young John Wayne, and a female whose face seemed familiar, but not the name, all surrounding a display of beers, chips and candy. Two Japanese teenagers were attempting to take selfies standing next to Zac Efron squealing and giggling. Leroy hurried around them and headed for the wine shelves. Stacy had said they be eating beef pot roast, so it had to be a red. He chose a bottle of Fog Mountain, paid, and hurried back to the car. His phone rang as he climbed in. He took the call.

The smell of cooking was even more appetising when he got back to Stacy's. He took the wine into the kitchen, where she was beginning to lay the table.

'What's up?' she asked, looking at the expression on his face. 'What's happened?'

'I was just getting back into the car,' he explained, 'when I had a call from the Assistant Sheriff at the Central

Men's Jail. Our suspect, one of our suspects for the hit and run killings, was in there waiting for his arraignment Monday. The AS said Mitchell was murdered last night.'

Stacy put down the cutlery. 'No shit. When? What happened?'

'Well, he made it crystal clear that this was a courtesy call, and that two detectives from Central Division had already launched a murder investigation. "No need for you to attend, Detective" were his words, and that if I needed any more information, I should liaise with the appropriate division.'

'Warning you off?'

'Got it in one.'

'So what are you going to do?'

'I'm going to open this wine. But tomorrow morning, I'm going to be speaking, either by phone, or face-to-face with the lead detective. James, I think the name was.'

'That'll be Jo James. Jo as in Josephine. I know her. She won't give you any bullshit, Sam.'

'That's good to know. Then I'll need to call the Chief, give him an update and see if he can punch his weight with DHS.'

'For the other suspect?'

'Yes. I can see what might happen. One suspect is dead, the other had disappeared into another agency's void; therefore, case closed. No fucking way.'

'How was he killed?'

'I don't know. he wouldn't say; just to reach out to James.'

Stacy gave a huge sigh. 'Nothing ever goes to plan, does it? Here, open the wine. Let it breathe for a while. The roast won't be long.'

Leroy helped Stacy bring the mashed potatoes and salad to the table, and poured the wine. Then his phone rang again.

'Who's that now?' he sighed.

'Maybe it's Jo James.'

Leroy listened to the caller for half a minute, then said,

'Hold on for a second, would you, Ed?' He put his hand over the speaker and looked at Stacy.

'Was it her?' she asked.

'No,' Leroy said. 'It's Ed Ellis, the Watch Commander from West Valley station. It's my partner; one of my partners, Ray Quinn. He's been arrested.'

CHAPTER FORTY-ONE

'YOU HAVE TO go to him, Sam.'

'I know, but...' Leroy gestured to the table, all prepared for a meal.

'It doesn't matter about that. You're his supervisor. What happened?'

'According to Ed, he was in a bar up in Reseda. What the hell he was doing up there, I have no idea, but he got into a brawl. Correction: he started a brawl.'

'And he was arrested?'

'Not exactly. Fortunately for him. The two uniforms took him to the station, handed him in to be booked, but the Watch Commander - Ed – recognised him. Ed owes me a favour from a few years back. He has a son, who's probably around thirty by now. He was caught in Culver City Park one night with some other guy's dick in his mouth. He was taken to our station, but I recognised him and intervened. Called Ed to come pick him up.

Professional courtesy, you'd call it. Ed said he owed me one; looks like he's just collected on the debt. He said Ray's in an interview room, waiting for me.'

'What's his problem? Has he done this before?'

'Never. On a scale of out of character things to do, one to ten, this is an eleven. He and his wife split up a while back. I kind of feel a tad guilty as I caught her leaving a motel room with another guy, but didn't say anything. Not to him anyway; I just let her know that I knew, subtle-like, but it didn't make any difference.'

'You can't feel like that; nothing for you to feel guilty about.'

'I know, but... Anyway, they split, he's moved out, and isn't taking it too well.'

'Kids?'

'No, no kids. Look: I'd better go.' He pointed to the pot roast. 'All this: I could come back later.'

'You won't have time, Sam. Let's take a rain check. I have some prep for tomorrow I need to get done. Wait until we get together over that cold case of yours.'

'That's a promise. Thanks. I'd better head up there.'

'Let me know how you get on.'

He leaned down and kissed her. 'You got it.'

He left Stacy's house, walked down the drive to his car. As he began to reverse onto the street, he saw Stacy hurrying over. He stopped, and wound down the window. She was holding a clear plastic box.

'Here,' she said. 'Some pot roast and mashed potato. No salad, sorry.'

'You don't need to do that, but thanks.' He took the box.

'Otherwise, you're not going to eat anything, or you'll stop off for some crap from a street food truck.'

Leroy laughed. She was right. 'Thanks. Call you later.' He left the food on the passenger seat, and continued reversing. As he straightened up to head down Grace Avenue, he looked over and saw Stacy disappearing into her house. 'Damn you, Ray,' he muttered as he pulled away.

From Grace Avenue, he made a right onto Franklin. As he turned onto Highland Avenue, he passed the store where he had bought the wine not so long ago, and reflected it was lucky he had not drunk any of the Fog Mountain. He joined the 101 at the Hollywood Bowl, and headed up the freeway to Reseda. A short drive up Reseda Boulevard took Leroy to Vanowen Street, where the West Valley station was situated.

He parked on the street, and walked inside. He waited in line for five minutes, and eventually asked for Ellis. He waited another two minutes, then Ellis appeared. He was just as Leroy had remembered, only a little older and greyer. Ellis showed him in to one of the interview rooms.

They shook hands. 'Thanks for this, Ed.'

'I didn't get you at a bad time, did I?'

'You did, to be honest, but that's not your fault. I appreciate you calling me. How you doing?'

'Six months off retirement, so I'm doing good.'

'No shit, six months. Where does the time go? Where is he?'

'He's in the next room.'

'What happened, Ed?'

'The old story. He was in a bar two blocks from here. He had been there at least an hour. Had downed half a bottle of whiskey. He wanted another; the bartender said no, he'd had enough. Best to get along. Although there was no way he could have driven home. Then he started to get aggressive, shouting at the bartender. A regular decided to intervene, tried to calm him down, suggested he went home. Your boy lashed out, then the fight started. The bartender called 911; a black and white was only a block away. He was brought in here.'

'What about the other guy? The regular?'

'Once they'd pulled Quinn off him, he calmed down. A couple of witnesses there said it was Quinn doing the fighting, the other fella was just trying to get him to behave. He was the one causing the trouble. What's his problem?'

'Long story. Has he been booked?'

Ellis shook his head. 'As soon as they got him in here, I recognised him. I threw him next door and called you. He's had three cups of black coffee.'

'Are you planning on doing anything? What about the bartender? The other guy at the bar?'

'Not as far as I know. Sam, you did me a big favour back then, and I said I owed you one. This is the one. Just get him the fuck out of my station, and out of my division.'

'I will. And I'm sorry you had to deal with this. And I want to thank you again.'

'No problem. He's in here.' Ellis led Leroy to the adjacent room and opened the door. Quinn looked up. He was sitting at the table, nursing a white plastic cup. He looked to be dressed in the same clothes as he had worn the evening before, and he had clearly not shaved since the morning before.

'You can leave now,' Ellis said. He looked at Leroy. 'All yours, Sam,' he said quietly.

'Get up,' Leroy said. 'Let's go.'

Quinn stood and followed Leroy. Leroy walked briskly out of the station and down to his car. Quinn was six feet behind him.

'Where are we going?' he called out.

Leroy paused and turned round. 'I'm taking you home, where do you think?'

'I have my own car. I don't need you to take me home like I'm some naughty kid.' Quinn started to walk the other way. He held his hands up as he shouted at Leroy. 'Just leave me alone!'

Leroy looked around to make sure nobody was watching. He stepped over to Quinn and grabbed his arm. They were standing next to Leroy's car. 'I'm not going to say it again. Just get in the fucking car.' He opened the door and manhandled Quinn into the passenger seat. Fortunately he had already put Stacy's pot roast on the back seat. Quinn slumped into the seat.

'Buckle up,' Leroy ordered; once Quinn had complied, Leroy pulled away. Neither spoke for the next ten minutes.

'I'm sorry, Sam,' Quinn said quietly.

'You stink like a saloon,' Leroy said. 'How much have you had?'

Quinn shrugged.

'Where are we going?'

'I'm taking you home.'

'Home? Or where I'm staying?'

'Where you're staying.'

Eventually they got to Quinn's apartment. Leroy got the key off of Quinn and let them both in. He half laid, half dropped Quinn onto the couch, then went into Quinn's kitchen. He found a jar of instant coffee and put the kettle on the stove. He took over two mugs of very strong black coffee. 'Here, drink these,' he said, before sitting down across from him. He watched while Quinn finished the first cup.

Leroy stood up. 'Finish the other. Then take a shower and get something to eat. Look: you were working yesterday. Don't come in till Tuesday.'

Quinn looked up at him. 'But what about Chinn and -?'

'Pamela and I will deal with that tomorrow. If anything important happens I'll reach out to you. Don't worry; I won't keep you out of the loop. But you need to get your shit together. You're fucking lucky Ellis called me instead of charging you. It's only because he owed me a favour that you're not in a cell and looking for another job. We've been partners for a long time, Ray; I'd hate for it to end like this.'

Quinn sat on the couch, holding his second cup of coffee. He said nothing as Leroy let himself out. Leroy sat in his car, outside his partner's building, for at least a minute. Then he whispered, 'Damn you, Holly,' started the ignition, and drove away.

## CHAPTER FORTY-TWO

MONDAY MORNING, AND Leroy had almost arrived at the station when Chief Snell called.

The Chief was, in fact, returning Leroy's call from the previous evening. On his way back home after depositing Quinn on his couch, Leroy decided that, after all, he would speak to Snell then and not leave it until Monday morning. As it turned out, all he got was the Chief's voicemail. He left a brief message that he had called to give an update on the Dempsey case, as the Chief continually referred to the investigation. He added that a lot had happened concerning the investigation over the weekend: that might whet the Chief's appetite, he figured, and should prompt a speedy call-back. There was much about the case that Leroy wished to discuss with Snell.

'You left a message on my voicemail, Detective,' Snell said. 'You have more to report? You said something about developments over the weekend.'

'Yes sir. A lot has happened since we last spoke.' Leroy than ran through with the Chief the identification on the video of Mitchell and Zhurov and their arrest; Zhurov's being taken into custody by Homeland Security; their connection with Tony Chinn; and finally, Mitchell's murder in the jail. When he had finished the update, there was silence at the other end of the line: Chief Snell had a lot to assimilate.

Snell finally spoke; slowly, as if he was thinking as he spoke. 'William Mitchell, killed in the jail. What do you know about it?'

'Only what the Assistant Sheriff told me yesterday.'

'Are we involved yet?'

'Oh, yes. The investigation is already under way. It's being headed by Detective James, from Central. I'm going to be reaching out to her this morning.'

'We don't know how, when, by whom?'

'I don't know any of those things, Chief. The Sheriff wouldn't provide me with much, only to refer to Detective James.'

'Do you feel it's connected to your case?'

'It's one hell of a coincidence if it's not, Chief. A few hours after he divulged who paid him and Zhurov to kill Dempsey and the others, he is killed himself.'

'I agree. Liaise, then with Detective James, and include that in your next update. I may speak to her myself to get the details first hand. Now, the second man, the Russian. What is his name?'

'Zhurov, Chief, Sergei Zhurov. He's Latvian. We had him in custody, but on account of the large number of M16s we found at his house, we were obligated to call Homeland Security.'

'I dread to think what he had planned with them. Yes, it is their jurisdiction; but he is the only surviving suspect you have, apart from Chinn, whom the dead one says paid them.'

'That's my problem, Chief, and where I need your help. If we are going to get access to Zhurov, I think it needs to be from somebody above my pay grade, or even that of Lieutenant Perez or Captain Walker.'

'You're asking me to?'

'I'm thinking, if a request came from the lieutenant, or even the captain, there would still be hoops to jump through, protocols to follow; but if it came from your level, sir, that should speed things up no end.'

Snell sighed. 'Very well, Detective. I'll speak to DHS on your behalf. You also said you wanted to discuss the man who allegedly paid Mitchell and Zhurov.'

'Yes, Chief. As I reported, we spoke to him Saturday night. He denies all knowledge of anything. At this time, it's a matter or Mitchell's word against his, so I want to begin carrying a few days' surveillance on him; see where he goes, who he sees, what he does.'

'And you want to discuss manpower for that?'

'Yes, Chief, in a nutshell.'

'I recall, Detective, that I offered you extra officers for your use, but Lieutenant Perez said you declined the offer.'

That was an interesting reveal, which caught Leroy by surprise.

'At that time, I didn't feel it was necessary, sir, but now we find we need surveillance on Tony Chinn, which means we do in fact need extra officers. We didn't before, and I was trying to support the lieutenant around his budget.' That should go down well.

'We all have to work within budgets, Detective; it's a matter of allocating resources in a cost-effective and efficient manner.'

'Yes, Chief.'

Snell paused. 'Let's wind this up. I will talk to Captain Walker about additional support for the next few days. I'm guessing you need this as soon as possible?'

'Preferably, Chief.'

'Very well. I don't need to stress that, especially with the extra resources we are throwing at this investigation, that it needs to be wrapped up without any further delay.'

'You don't need to, sir, and we're all working to that

end.'

Snell hung up, ending the call. By now, Leroy was in a space in the station parking lot. He walked into the station, pausing briefly to chat with one of the officers from the K-9 Division, who was taking a cigarette break.

He grabbed a coffee and headed for his desk. Velasquez was already there.

'Don't you sleep?' he asked. 'I thought I was early.'

'Never on the job, Sam. Never on the job. I've not seen Ray yet.'

Leroy wondered if she was fishing, but just answered her question.

'No. He was here with me all day Saturday, so I told him not to come in till tomorrow. But,' he added as he sat down, 'I spoke to Chief Snell on the way in. We're being given some extra manpower, seconded for the surveillance on Tony Chinn.'

'That may be what the lieutenant wanted to speak with you about. He was around here five minutes ago, asking if you were in.'

'Was he? I'll go see him.'

'Anything you want me to start on? I was just doing housekeeping on here.'

'That might depend on what he has to say. Be right back.'

Lieutenant Perez was sitting at his desk, looking to and from his computer screen and some papers on his desk. Probably working on a spreadsheet, Leroy thought.

'Lieutenant?' he said.

'Come in, Sam. You've spoken to Chief Snell?'

'Yes, just come off the phone from him.'

'You'll be pleased to know that I've arranged some extra manpower for you. You have the use of Detectives Perry and Harrington, until Wednesday. So you need to make the best use of them as you can.'

'I will, Lieutenant, but two won't be enough.'

'What? Why not?'

'But if it's for surveillance, we need more than two.'

'Surveillance?'

'Didn't the Chief tell you? Hasn't he just called you?'

'He called me half an hour ago. Said you left him a voicemail last night and did I know what it was about. We came to the conclusion that you had relented about more personnel and so I pulled Perry and Harrington. Now you're talking about surveillance.'

Leroy explained about Tony Chinn. Now he understood how the relief officers were available so soon after his conversation with the Chief.

Perez grimaced. 'Okay. There aren't any more detectives to spare, but I'll have a word with Double-R and see if you can borrow some of his team.'

Leroy nodded. 'Thanks.'

'By the way, Sam,' Perez added on his way out, 'I know you and the Chief are getting nice and cosy, but you will remember the chain of command, won't you?'

'I will, of course, but I needed his input with regard to the witness DHS took.'

'Run that by me again?'

Leroy stepped back into the office and told Perez about Zhurov and about Mitchell's murder.

'My God, Sam,' Perez said. 'This seems to never end. Who's dealing with the murder of the witness? Please tell me you haven't taken it on board.'

'No, it's gone to Central. I'm going to reach out to the lead detective later to find out what I can. We'll have to have some kind of liaison, but they are keeping the case.'

Perez nodded. 'Good. Let's keep it that way. I'll let you get on, and keep me up to date. I'm sure Snell will be calling me at some stage.'

'Sure thing. By the way, Lieutenant, Ray won't be in today. He was working here with me all day Saturday, so I told him to take today off. It would save on the overtime costs.'

'So, let me get this straight: I'm providing relief officers at the same time as you're giving one of your team a day off?'

'I was just thinking of the costs. Your spreadsheet, you know.'

'Bullshit. Is he okay?'

'He's okay. He'll be back tomorrow.' With that, Leroy left the office before Perez could ask any more questions.

When he got back to his desk, he could see Velasquez talking to two other detectives. These were Dwight Perry and Frances Harrington. Detectives II and I respectively, Leroy had known them both for a while, and was quite happy they had been seconded. Perry was another officer acquaintance who had been with the Department for many years; in fact, he had taken retirement the previous year, and had returned under the DROP scheme. He knew Harrington less, but had heard good things about her.

'Good to have you guys on board,' Leroy said as they shook hands.

'Surveillance job, is it then?' Perry asked.

'Yes. I've just come from the lieutenant, and we're also going to have some support from Double-R's team. Not sure who that's going to be, yet.' As he spoke, two uniformed officers appeared; again, two who Leroy knew to a degree: Alicia Thorne, and Rose Rolston. Thorne was an Officer II with several years' experience, and Rolston an Officer I, a relatively new recruit.

'Detective Leroy?' said Thorne as they approached. 'We come with Supervisor Rosenberg's complements.'

'Good to have you on board,' Leroy said. 'Let's get a briefing started. See you in the conference room in ten.'

Leroy spent the ten minutes preparing what the others would need, and headed to the conference room. In the centre of the room was a long table, big enough for around twenty. Velasquez and the other four were sitting, waiting.

His team.

## CHAPTER FORTY-THREE

THERE WAS A jug of coffee on a table at the side of the room. Leroy went over and filled himself a white plastic cup. He returned to the end of the table and opened up his laptop. An image of a drivers licence appeared on the screen.

'This,' he said as he pointed to the screen, 'is Tony Chinn. Anthony Chinn as it says here. He is the subject of our surveillance. As you know, we are investigating the murder by auto of three people, and attempted murder of four others, still in hospital. We've identified the two men who were in the vehicle at the time, and taken them into custody. They were due to be arraigned this morning. However, one of the suspects is now in the custody of Homeland Security, and the other was being held in the Central Men's Jail, but was killed over the weekend.'

Frances Harrington whistled and looked around at the others.

'What's the connection with Homeland Security?' Officer Thorne asked.

'We found a shitload of assault rifles and ammo hidden in his air conditioning,' Velasquez explained. Thorne opened her mouth and uttered a silent *wow*.

'That's why Homeland Security has him,' Leroy said, wanting the conversation to keep on track. 'At the moment we don't even know where he is, but I've asked Chief Snell to reach out to his counterpart at DHS to give us access to him.'

'Even more important now your other suspect is no longer alive,' Thorne commented.

'But,' Leroy said, 'Ray Quinn and I were able to speak with him Saturday evening, not long before he died, and he was able to tell us that he and Sergei Zhurov were paid to carry out the hit and run. Paid by Tony Chinn.'

'Do we know who they were aiming for?' Detective Harrington asked. 'You said there were three murder victims.'

'He didn't know. He said Zhurov was the one being paid; he wasn't party to the conversation. Zhurov will know that.'

'We did get to speak to Chinn Saturday night,' Velasquez said to the others. 'Of course, he denied everything.'

'That's right,' said Leroy. 'So at the moment it's his word against that of the late William Mitchell. Certainly until we get to talk to Zhurov. Which is where you guys come in. I don't believe Chinn's denials for one second, so for the next few days, I need to know what he does, where he goes, who he talks to. Twenty-four seven, open all hours, we never close. So, Dwight and Frances: you two want to start? Head over to his address. I don't know if he'll be in; you'll just have to watch and wait. Alicia and Rose will relieve you at two. Obviously they'll be out of uniform.'

There was a short buzz of amusement at Leroy's joke.

'And obviously follow him if he goes anywhere?'

Harrington asked.

'You got it. Plenty of photographs. If you see him with anybody, take some shots and send them to my cell. I want to identify anybody he sees as soon as possible.'

He turned to Velasquez. 'Pamela, while they're out in the field – Ray was looking at Scott Dempsey's social media accounts. He got as far as a picture on Facebook of Dempsey with the mayor. You want to pick up where he left off?'

Velasquez nodded in agreement; Perry said, 'With the mayor. So the victim had friends in low places. Is that why there are so many of us working on one investigation?'

Leroy said, 'Let's just say that people above my pay grade are keen for this case to come to a satisfactory and speedy conclusion.'

There was a few moments' silence as they all digested what Leroy had said. Velasquez broke the ice.

'Where will you be, Sam?'

'I'm going to be talking to the lead detective over at Central about the Mitchell murder. Either face to face or virtual. Although we're not taking that case, I just want to get more information about what happened and what they're doing. It could impact on what we're doing.'

'Where is Mr Quinn, by the way?' Perry asked.

Not a question Leroy wanted. 'He's at home. He was working on this case till the early hours of Sunday morning. But I've got him online for some other stuff which he doesn't need to do here. He's back here in the morning. Any questions, anyone?'

Nobody had.

'Dwight and Frances: when you get relieved by Alicia and Rose, grab yourselves some lunch and come back here. You can be useful with the social media checks. Let's get started. I'll send you all this copy of Chinn's licence. He hasn't changed much. He's tall – six feet easily – and he's lost the little goatee. I've had the address on the licence confirmed through his social security details.

Centennial Street: outskirts of Chinatown, just across the 110.'

The meeting broke up and everybody gathered their notes and left to start their assignments. Leroy asked Velasquez to hold on. When they were alone in the room, Leroy spoke.

'I didn't want to say anything in front of the others, but when Ray was looking at Dempsey's social media, he found some photographs of Dempsey and the mayor.'

'You said. So he was friends with the mayor.'

'Some of the pictures were of Dempsey, Shipley, the mayor… and the Chief.'

'Chief Snell? What does that mean?'

'It may have something to do with the fact that he has said several times not to waste time and resources looking at Dempsey, but to focus on the drivers.'

'But I thought you wanted me to…'

'I do, but I'd sooner the others, particularly Perry and Harrington don't know about it. Perry has a big mouth, and you know what this place is like for gossip and Chinese whispers.' He paused a second. 'Bad choice of words, but you see where I'm coming from.'

'What do you want me to do if I do find the Chief there?'

'Just note it as usual, but keep it quiet. Once I've done with Detective James, we'll review things.'

'You going to see him – her – now?'

'Her. Yes. I'm going to call her. I'm hoping we can keep it to a telephone conversation, or a video call. I don't really have the time for another drive Downtown.'

'And Ray really is coming in tomorrow?'

'Definitely. I told him the Saturday work would be overtime - and if he hadn't gone to see Mitchell, we wouldn't know about Chinn - and you know what the lieutenant's like about overtime costs.'

'What about the vehicle? Have forensic come back yet?'

'I'd forgotten about that. They called me when I was on

my way in, just before the Chief called. There were prints on the door, steering wheel, and mirror. All Zhukov's: well, they had to be, didn't they? And a few of Mitchell's the passenger side. And while there was no physical evidence, the damage to the front of the car - the bumper, the grille – was consistent with impact with a body, or bodies. It had been valeted as you would expect for a hire car, but just leaving some prints.'

'So a dead and?'

'Kind of. But the prints do show Zhurov and Mitchell were inside. But it's still all very tenuous and circumstantial. That's why it's so important to get a result with Chinn.'

'Sure. I'll make a start, pick up where Ray left off.'

'And I'll go talk to Detective James, and find out what I can about how the only one of our suspects in our custody gets himself killed in jail.'

## CHAPTER FORTY-FOUR

DETECTIVE JO JAMES was in court that morning.

'I should be done by eleven. You want to meet here? To be honest, I would like to talk to you also, but I would prefer to have the conversation face to face, away from all this.'

That suited Leroy fine. He would have preferred over the phone, either voice or video; however, if she wanted to see him face to face, then he would rather not go to the court house. There was the danger of bumping into Stacy there, and he wanted to avoid any clash between work and his personal life.

'Where do you want to meet?' he asked.

'You know FIGat7th? There's a coffee stand the same level as the Target store. Meet you there, say eleven thirty. Good for you?'

That was good for Leroy. He said he would see her there eleven thirty. He just had enough time to clear up a few things here then take a trip Downtown.

FIGat7th is an open-air shopping mall located at the intersection of South Figueroa and Seventh Streets, in the Financial District of Downtown Los Angeles. Situated between two office skyscrapers, the 777 Tower and Ernst & Young Plaza, it primarily caters to office workers, who would be arriving in hoards at midday. So an eleven thirty meeting would be just right.

Leroy parked in the adjacent Eighth Street parking structure and walked round to the meeting point. He saw the deep red coffee stand and, leaning against a walled flowerbed, was a figure which had to be Detective James. Tall and thin, mixed race, shoulder-length dark hair. She wore a light grey pant suit, and a light blue silk scarf around her neck. A black bag was over her shoulder. She pushed herself off the wall as Leroy approached.

'Detective Leroy?' she asked.

'Detective James?' he responded.

They shook hands.

'It's Jo.'

'Sam.'

'Let me get you a coffee. I've not had to drive across the city to get here.'

'Don't mind if I do. Americano.'

She bought an Americano for Leroy and a latte for herself. 'Let's sit over here,' she said, pointing to a seat. 'It's discrete and out of the way.'

They walked over to the seat and sat down. James took a mouthful of her latte and spoke first.

'You wanted to know about the killing of William Mitchell? I'm guessing you're also interested in why I insisted on talking to you face to face about it; here, away from everybody else.'

'That's a yes on both counts.' Leroy sipped his scalding hot Americano.

She nodded. 'Okay, let's start with Mitchell himself. He was being held in the Central Men's Jail. He was due in court this morning – firearms violations, I understand.'

'Kind of. Yes, firearms violations are really holding charges. They are genuine: when we searched his place, we found the handgun on a bedside closet. We checked, and it had been reported stolen a while ago. All he could say was that he bought it from some guy somewhere, at some time.' Leroy went on to relate the story of the hit and run investigation. She nodded as she listened.

When Leroy was done, she said, 'So what you're telling me, you have fuck all evidence putting him at the scene.'

'That's exactly what I'm telling you. My vibe is, that the Latvian, Sergei Zhurov, was the main man and Mitchell was there as back-up.'

And the Asian – Mitchell said he paid Zhu…?'

'Zhurov. Yes. We spoke to Chinn Saturday night and he of course denies everything. We have his word against Mitchell's, and Mitchell is no longer around: the DA wouldn't touch it with a ten-foot pole. So my team has Chinn under surveillance for the next two days.'

'Just two days?'

'For now. The cost.'

James shook her head and blew into her latte. 'The cost. Don't even talk to me about cost control. So you spoke to Mitchell before he went to the jail?'

'No, we visited him Saturday evening. That's when he told us about Chinn.'

'You went to the jail?'

'We did. Didn't you know that?'

'No. The sheriff must have forgotten to mention that.'

'You feel as well as I do that his murder is in connection with our visit?'

'One son of a bitch of a coincidence otherwise. Who knew you were going to visit?'

'We arranged it with the Assistant Sheriff.'

'With how much notice?'

'Two hours, maybe three. What are you thinking?'

'I'm just thinking whether whoever killed him, killed him to stop him talking to you guys.'

'If that's the case, they were too late.'

'And revenge for talking to you is unlikely. It would be very high risk to kill somebody in the jail; not worth the risk if you'd already spoken to him.'

'Unless,' said Leroy, 'there was something he didn't tell us, and the killer wanted to stop him talking further.'

'There are a few possibilities.'

'How did it happen?' Leroy asked.

'Broken neck. It looks as if somebody got him in a headlock, twisted, then… *click*.'

Leroy grimaced. 'Nasty. Mitchell was a big guy; whoever did it must have been at least the same size, and muscular.'

James nodded. 'That's what we're going to focus on. To be honest, we haven't gotten very far. We only got the call yesterday morning. We've had one visit to the jail, saw the body, checked out the scene, spoke to the Assistant Sheriff. I had to go to court this morning; once we're done here, I'm meeting up with my partner and we're headed back there.'

'Yeah,' Leroy mused, 'I would've been in court this morning also, if things had gone to plan. Do me a favour, would you, Jo: keep me in the loop on this one? It might be relevant to our investigation.'

She nodded. 'No problem.'

'The other matter you wanted to talk to me about,' Leroy said.

'Yeah,' she said, taking another mouthful of latte. 'Nothing concrete here; more a vibe I'm getting. Something about Mitchell, and I'm guessing about your case. Is there anything unusual about it?'

'Apart from having diddly squat evidence, one dead suspect, and one suspect whisked away by Homeland Security?'

She laughed. 'What I mean is, we were called in yesterday morning, and since then I've had two calls from Chief Snell, *personally*, asking about progress.'

'Well, well.' Leroy finished his Americano in one final

mouthful. 'Another coincidence. I've been getting the same treatment.'

'Why is he so interested?'

'One of the victims of the hit and run was a guy called Scott Dempsey. There were two other victims, a Mexican woman and a seventy-seven-year-old Asian.' He paused a second. 'Another coincidence: two unrelated Asians. Anyways, Snell was only interested in Dempsey; he couldn't give a shit about the others. Even kept referring to the investigation as the Dempsey case. Even told me not to waste time looking at Dempsey's background, but to just focus on Mitchell and Zhurov.'

'No way? What did you do?'

'We carried on looking at Dempsey's background, of course. One of my partners was checking Dempsey's Facebook account, and what did he find? Photographs of a fishing trip. Dempsey, his partner, the mayor, and Snell himself.'

'You're kidding me.'

'That's what my partner said, more or less.'

'What are you planning on doing?'

'I figure, either they're all friends, or members of some club; I'm still figuring that one out.'

'But at the best, Snell is pulling strings here.'

'He is. Or worse, there's something he doesn't want us to find out. We're just gathering the information - I wouldn't even call it evidence yet – and see where that takes us. Keep all this to yourself, won't you?'

'Oh, absolutely.' She checked her watch. 'Listen, I need to get out of here now. I appreciate you coming over, and for what you told me.'

'Likewise. And for the coffee. Let's keep in touch.'

Detective James tossed her empty paper cup into the paper recycling bin adjacent to their bench and left. Leroy remained on the bench and watched while she walked out of view. He wondered if she had walked from the courthouse, which was some distance, or parked nearby. He mulled over what she had told him. What she had told him about the manner of William Mitchell's death: given Mitchell's size and the manner of his killing, then only a certain build of person would be physically capable of breaking Mitchell's neck. It would just be a matter of identifying which inmates fitted that description. Or warders? Another thought passed through his head. Once the Assistant Sheriff had arranged his and Quinn's visit, he would have to have told at least some of his staff. What if…? Maybe he was being too fanciful; in any case, this was not his investigation. He really couldn't care less who killed Mitchell, unless it had some impact on his own investigation. In any case, he and James would be keeping in touch; maybe he could run that theory by her when they next spoke.

He decided before he went back, he would check in on how Perry and Harrington were doing. They had two more hours before they would be relieved, but Leroy was not going to wait for that. He called Perry, a fellow detective he disliked.

'Dwight. How are you guys getting on? You found Chinn's place, then?'

'We found it, but we're not there as we speak.'

'Has he gone out or something?'

'He has. Your boy has gone out for either a late breakfast or an early lunch. If this was the weekend, I'd call it brunch.'

'So where are you? Where's he?'

'He's sitting at a patio table at Mr Churro's on Olvera. We're across the street. And he's not alone: he's breakfasting or lunching with a young lady.'

'Have you taken any pictures?'

'Sam, we have a whole album here.'

'Send me what you have of them eating. I need to know who he's meeting.'

'On their way, Sam. Enjoy.'

After a few moments, Leroy's phone pinged as the photographs arrived. There were six in total. From slightly different viewpoints, they were all images of Tony Chinn sitting at a patio table in the sun with a young lady. Leroy selected one of the photographs. Using two fingers, he enlarged the picture to get a better view of who Chinn was with. Leroy had stood up as he waited for the photographs to arrive. Now he sat down again as he recognised who Tony Chinn was with.

## CHAPTER FORTY-FIVE

NOW IT ALL fell into place.

It took Leroy a few seconds to realise who the woman was with whom Tony Chinn was having brunch. He had met her before.

It was Sandra Fong, the daughter of Kenneth Fong, one of the victims.

He leapt off the bench and hurried back to the car. On the way back, he first called Perry.

'Dwight – whatever you do, stay with them. If they separate, one of you go with him; the other with her.'

'But we only have one car.'

'I'm on my way over there. I'm not far away. I'm at FIGat7th. I'm getting Pamela over as well.'

'You got it, Sam.'

As he reached the parking garage, he called Velasquez.

'Pamela, you need to get yourself over to Olvera Street. Perry and Harrington are on Chinn. He's having brunch there – with Sandra Fong.'

'Sandra Fong? As in Kenneth Fong, one of the victims?'

'Yes, and by all accounts getting very cosy with Tony Chinn over coffee and pancakes.'

'I'll head over now. What about Ray?'

'I'll call him on my way over. You just get here. Red light it, but switch the siren off when you get near. I don't want them spooked.'

With a scream of brakes, Leroy pulled out of his parking space, down the ramp to street level, and onto Figueroa Street, which he took north-east as far as East Temple, which he took, red-lighting with no siren, until he made a left onto North Alameda Street. On his way along Figueroa, he called Quinn.

'Ray, where are you? What are you doing?'

'Just taking some personal time, like you told me. Why?'

'Get your pants on and get your ass up to Olvera Street. Shit; I forgot, we left your car up at Reseda.'

'No, I got a cab up there first thing this morning, and got it back. Why? What's going on? I'm in the car now.'

'We had Chinn under surveillance. As we speak, he's enjoying a very cosy brunch with none other than Sandra Fong on Olvera Street, a few yards from where we caught Mitchell, if you believe in coincidences.'

'Sandra Fong? She's the daughter of…'

'Exactly. You know what I think? I think while we were fucking around thinking Dempsey was the target and Fong and Rosa Delgado were collateral damage, all the time it was Fong who was the target. Why else would you be getting cosy with the man who paid to kill your father?'

'I'm on my way, Sam. I can't red-light my way; this is my own car.'

'All right; get there as soon as you can. I'm here now. I'm going to park on Alameda, across from the station.'

A few minutes later, he pulled up and parked, much to the irritation of a truck driver who was behind him. As he hurried round to Olvera Street, he called Perry.

'Are they still there?'

'They are. Second cup of coffee. Looks like they're in no hurry.'

'Where are you?'

'Outside the clothing store the other side of the street. Don't worry: they can't see us, there's a souvenir kiosk between us. If they leave, we have a view of the café, so they can't go anywhere without us seeing.'

'Be with you in half a minute; I'm at the monument now.'

As Leroy turned the corner, it occurred to him that this was where they had arrested Mitchell the other day. He never expected to be back at the same spot so soon. Now he could see the other side of the street, and the restaurant where Tony Chinn and Sandra Fong were eating, sitting on a patio table. Staying close to the buildings this side of the street, he walked up to where Perry and Harrington were waiting for him.

Then it all went wrong. He saw Sandra Fong look up. She sat back and said something to Chinn, who swung round. Both stood up, wildly looking around. Then they both made to leave hurriedly. He began to run in the other direction, she the opposite way. At that moment, Perry and Harrington appeared on the street.

'Sam!' Harrington called out.

'Get after him!' Leroy called out. 'I'll take her.'

Perry and Harrington took off after Chinn; meanwhile, Fong had made it to the other end of the street. Leroy turned to follow, then realised she was armed. She swung round and fired a shot at him.

'LAPD! Get down!' Leroy called out to the passers-by. Fortunately, for that time of the day, the street was not that busy. The half dozen or more pedestrians either hit the deck or ran to the buildings for cover, screaming.

Leroy had drawn his own weapon. Fong was just walking down the street, backwards, pointing her gun at Leroy, who also had her covered.

'Sandra: there's no way out,' Leroy called out. 'Put the gun down on the ground.'

Fong backed away. She looked over at a couple of tourists who were standing cowering at the corner. She pointed at one of them - a young man - and beckoned for him to go over to her.

'No!' Leroy called out, but it was too late. He had already stepped over to her. She had grabbed him by the collar and was dragging him across the square. His girlfriend was also screaming.

Fong put her gun to his head. 'Get me a car!' she called out.

'Sandra,' Leroy said, slowly walking towards her. 'Put the gun down and let's talk.'

'Sandra,' another voice called out. Leroy turned round in the direction of the voice. It was Tony Chinn, handcuffed and being held by both arms by Harrington and Perry. 'It's over, Sandra.'

'Fuck you,' she yelled. 'Get me a car! Now!'

As if to make a point, she fired into the air. Two other passers-by who were hiding in a doorway, and the hostage's girlfriend, screamed. The young man she was holding was in tears.

'I told you; I'll fire,' Fong shouted. 'I want a car. I'll count to ten.'

'Sandra. Listen. There's no way...'

'One.

'Two.

'Three.'

'Sandra, put the gun down. Let the boy go. This has nothing to do -'

'Four.

'Five.

'Six.'

As she reached seven, another shot rang out. Leroy flinched at what he thought had happened. The boy she was holding fell forward onto his hands and knees. His girlfriend, still at the side of the street, began to scream his name loudly.

Sandra Fong slumped to the ground, her weapon clattering onto the concrete.

He heard running down the street. Velasquez appeared on the scene and came to a halt at Perry, Harrington and Chinn.

Leroy looked around.

Standing perfectly still on the edge of the piazza, legs apart, gun still pointing at where Sandra Fong had stood, was Ray Quinn.

## CHAPTER FORTY-SIX

TONY CHINN LOOKED across the table at Leroy and Quinn. He had a look of contempt on his face as Leroy read him his rights.

'Let the record show that Mr Chinn waived his right to an attorney,' Leroy said, for the benefit of the recording. 'That means,' he added, addressing Chinn, 'that when you get to court, an attorney will be appointed for you.'

There was no reaction from Chinn.

'Now,' Leroy said, looking Chinn in the eyes, 'you and Sandra Fong.'

'I don't know who you're talking about, man.'

'Why did you pay William Mitchell and Sergei Zhurov to kill Kenneth Fong? He was the target, wasn't he? I'm guessing you know he was her father.'

Chinn stared into space for a minute, then, 'I want a deal.'

'Excuse me?' Leroy said. 'I don't think you know how

this works. You go to court, you get found guilty of conspiracy to commit murder, then you go to prison. Say goodbye to daylight, Tony.'

'The Golden Dragons.'

Leroy and Quinn looked to each other. Leroy looked up at the camera. 'I know who the Golden Dragons are. What about them?'

The Golden Dragons were one of the many gangs operating in Los Angeles. They were formed in the seventies; formed by a group of Asian men to protect themselves and their communities from Latino gangs and other Asian gangs. They were known to operate in Chinatown and the San Gabriel Valley. Their income was derived from Asian-American communities, and from prostitution and brothels, money laundering and narcotics. They were also involved in street-level crime, such as robberies, homicide, and car theft. Their reach also extended to the coast, bringing them into contact with Leroy's Division.

'He was one of the original ones,' Chinn began, 'back in the day.'

'You telling me Kenneth Fong founded the gang?'

Chinn nodded. 'He was one of the originals. Now he was the only one left.'

'Go on.'

'When he died, Sandra was to take control of the gang. But the old bastard just wouldn't die. The others: well, they'd all gone. But he was left.' Chinn laughed. 'Talk about outstaying your welcome.'

'So you're telling me Sandra Fong got you to pay some guys to kill her old man?'

'He wasn't really her father. Back in the day her old lady was fucking one of the other Dragons. Got pregnant by him. The old man thought Sandra was his. Sandra knew otherwise; her old lady told her years ago. So she had no problem arranging for him to get offed.'

'What is she to you? Your girlfriend?'

'We'd spend some time in the sack; nothing special.'

Leroy leaned back and sent a text message.

'What is it?' Chinn asked.

'Nothing. So where did you get Mitchell and Zhurov?'

'No idea. She set up the meeting with the Russian. She wanted to keep plenty of distance between her and them.'

'He's Latvian, not Russian.'

'Whatever.'

'And the MO? Who decided they would run Fong down?'

'They did, the… Latvian. I just paid him to get the job done, how he did it was up to him.'

'You know they took out two others with her old man?' Quinn said. 'Plus injured some.'

Chinn shrugged. 'So? I just paid him to get the job done. It's not my fault there was collateral damage.'

'Collateral damage?' said Leroy angrily. 'Because of your collateral damage, a little boy has to grow up an orphan, motherfucker. There was no reason for her to die.'

'Sam…' Quinn said.

Leroy nodded and put his hand up to Quinn. 'Did you know Zhurov was into other shit?' he asked Chinn.

'What other shit?'

'A pile of M16s in his apartment? Was that something you Dragons had planned?'

'I don't know anything about that. She was the one who knew Zhurov. Ask her. Oh no; I forgot: you can't. Now what about my deal?'

Leroy leaned forward. 'There'll be many more things we need to ask you, Tony. So will the Feds. Just don't bother buying any sun block for a while. Like, for the rest of your life.'

## CHAPTER FORTY-SEVEN

FOR EVERY POLICE station building, somewhere within a two-block radius, there will be a bar, used almost exclusively by the men and women from the Division. Martha's was no exception. Situated on Iowa Avenue, between Colby and Butler, Martha's had been an established watering hole since the early eighties. Martha herself, the granddaughter of an émigré from Germany between the two World Wars, had retired to Palm Springs seven years back and the bar was now run by her son Kenny. Since Martha had left, nothing had changed: Kenny had retained his mother's name for the bar, the food was just as bad, and the same clientele visited.

That evening, Lieutenant Perez was in the chair. He passed a beer to Leroy, to Quinn, and to Velasquez.

'Cheers,' they said in unison, raising their bottles. Leroy took a sip then his phone rang.

'Chief Snell,' he mouthed to Perez, then went to a

quieter part of the bar to take the call.

'Congratulations on a good result, Detective,' the Chief said.

'Thank you, sir.'

'As I told you, it paid to focus on the two drivers, and not on Scott Dempsey. He was just in the wrong place at the wrong time. Very unfortunate.'

*Very unfortunate?*

'Yes, Chief. Collateral damage, you might say. Are there any developments regarding Sergei Zhurov? You said you would reach out to your counterpart at Homeland Security.'

There was a moment's silence, then Snell cleared his throat.

'Yes, I did discuss him with DHS. However, realistically there isn't much chance of him being returned to you. No chance, to be honest. If my understanding is correct, the evidence you had against him and the other man was very thin, and it's unlikely the District Attorney would have gone ahead and pressed charges. However, they remain very interested in that little cache of weapons you discovered. In the air-conditioning, as I understand it. And that's all credit to you, Detective. They are seeking to uncover whether Sergei Zhurov was working on his own, or whether he was part of a ring. So, watch this space, as they say.'

Disappointed, although not surprised, Leroy said, 'I understand. I appreciate your call, Chief.'

'There is one more matter on which I need to congratulate you.'

'There is?'

'The murder of your witness William Mitchell. I understand from Detective James in Central that you tipped her off that the Golden Dragons gang was involved. With that knowledge in mind, she was able to work with the Sheriff at the jail and have Mitchell's killer arrested.'

'That is good news, sir.'

'Yes, the Sheriff's Department had been conducting its

own investigation, and as soon as James made them aware of the gang involvement, they confronted their main suspect, who confessed.'

'Glad to be of help. One of the inmates, I guess?'

'No, one of the guards, who was a member of the gang. So, thanks to you once more, another case is closed. She doesn't even need to involve Gangs and Narcotics Division.'

'Thank you, sir.'

'Next time you're passing this way, drop in and say hello. We could have lunch together.'

'Thank you, Chief. I'd like that,' Leroy said, grimacing. 'Thank you for your call.'

Leroy walked back to the others. He passed by Quinn, who was on a pinball machine. Quinn looked over at his partner.

'Are we okay, Sam?' he asked.

Leroy looked Quinn in the eyes. 'We're getting there, Ray.'

'I have my counselling appointment in the morning,' Quinn said. This is something that all officers have to undergo, after shooting somebody, then it is two weeks before they can return to the field.

Leroy nodded. 'Yes. Then two weeks before you return.'

'It'll give me a chance to get my shit together.'

'I know,' said Leroy, touching his partner's arm.

'How was the Chief?' Perez asked, when Leroy had rejoined the group.

'As you'd expect. You knew he was going to call, didn't you?'

Perez admitted it. 'Did he tell you about Mitchell's killer? Once you texted James about the Dragons, it was plain sailing all the way for her.'

'Yes, he told me.'

'What is it, then?'

'Something he said about Zhurov. He said DHS won't be returning him to us – but then, you knew that, didn't you? He also said that they were trying to discover whether he was working alone, or as part of a larger group.'

'Like a terrorist cell?'

'Yeah. It got me to thinking, how many more of them there are out there.'

Perez took a mouthful of his beer. 'That's a tad too deep for tonight, Sam.'

Leroy nodded and took a mouthful of beer. Velasquez wandered over to him.

'Congratulations, Sam.'

'Congratulations to you. You contributed to the result.'

'And thank you. I've learned a lot in my short time on your team.'

'Glad to have you aboard.'

'Sam,' she asked, 'what about the Chief and Dempsey and the mayor? Is there something going on there? And what about the Golden Dragons?'

Leroy shrugged. 'That's GND's area, nothing to do with us. And as far as the Chief and Dempsey, and the mayor - you know what, Pamela? I've no idea. And to be honest with you, tonight I'm too tired to even care. All I want to do is finish off the paperwork, go get drunk, have a life for a day or so, then get back on rotation for the next case. Same goes for you and Ray. I may get the urge to go back to that, kind of off the reservation later, but there is an old case I'm looking at right now. When that's over, I'll see.'

'Let me know if you do,' Velasquez said.

'Sure.' Leroy finished his drink and accepted another from the lieutenant. He was looking forward to tomorrow. He had the usual mountain of paperwork to finish off; then in the evening, he would be seeing Stacy, who promised to go through the Jordan Washington file with him. This would be the last attempt to solve it. After tomorrow, if there were no avenues to follow, he would finally tell Jasmine that he had done all he could. Then that would be over.

But first, there was one more thing he had to do.

## CHAPTER FORTY-EIGHT

ROSA DELGADO WAS laid to rest at the Calvary Cemetery.

Ironically, just three blocks from where she lived. Ironically also, in contrast to the sombre mood of the occasion, the sun was blazing. The temperature reading on Leroy's dashboard was eighty-six degrees, higher than normal for that time of year.

Leroy and Stacy sat in his car, parked on the roadway, a discreet fifty yards away from the graveside. In silence, they watched the small party gathered around the grave. All in all, there were six people there: a priest, a man, a couple, and the woman Leroy recognised as Isabella. She was wearing a black dress and hat, with a matching veil. With Isabella, holding her hand and wearing a black suit, white shirt and black tie, was a little boy.

'That must be her son,' Stacy said quietly.

'Pedro,' said Leroy. 'Yes, it must be.'

'Poor little boy,' she said sadly. 'Do you think his

father's there?'

'Who knows? One of them could be.'

'Didn't you tell me Rosa hadn't seen the father in years?'

'Isabella told me that; but she might have reached out to him to tell him about Rosa. You never know.'

'Did you ever call Social Services?'

'About the boy? No, I haven't yet. He seemed safe with Isabella, and with the investigation, it wasn't a priority.'

'And now the investigation is over?'

He looked over to her.

'Look at the two of them. Do you think I should?'

'Strictly speaking, yes; but didn't you say she was family?'

'Not exactly, but as close as. I think she said the father was last seen in Oaxaca.'

'That's in the south, isn't it?'

'I checked. It's south of Mexico City, closer to Acapulco. My intention is to give it a week or so, then call in on them. See how they're doing. Take a view then.'

'Mm,' Stacy agreed. 'But Sam, do me a favour: don't give her your cell number and tell her to contact you if she needs anything, will you? You shouldn't have done that with Jasmine Washington: there are people paid to do that.'

'I know, I know. But there's no reason why I can't check up on them every so often, is there?'

'Of course not. But remember, you're not a social worker. If you see a need, make a referral to the relevant agency.'

Leroy nodded. He knew she was right.

'Look,' she said, 'things are winding up.'

'Looks that way.'

Led by the priest, the mourners were walking away from the graveside. The couple hugged Isabella and the single man, then knelt to embrace Pedro before returning to a car which was parked further along the road. The single man walked with the priest towards the cemetery building. Still holding hands, Isabella and Pedro lingered at the side of the grave; then she led him away.

As Leroy and Stacy watched them leave, they paused a second and Pedro turned round and took one last look. Not at his mother's grave, but at Leroy's car. Leroy felt a lump in his throat. Then the woman and the boy were out of view.

Leroy waited a minute then took a deep breath and got out of the car. Alone, he walked across the grass to the grave. Two diggers approached: Leroy said, 'Give me a minute, will you?' They nodded and waited under a tree an unobtrusive distance away.

Leroy stood in front of the headstone. It was brand new and clean, looking out of place amongst the older, weather-beaten stones.

'No reason,' he said quietly, then crouched and laid the single pink rose he had been carrying at the foot of the stone. He stood, took one step back and looked at the stone one last time.

Then he turned and walked back to his car, where Stacy was waiting for him.


THE END

INTRODUCING LAPD DETECTIVE
SAM LEROY...

# LAST TO DIE

Los Angeles, late September, and the hot Santa Ana winds are blowing, covering the city with a thin layer of dust from the Mojave and Sonoran deserts.

That night, there are three mysterious, unexplained deaths.

The official view is that they are all unrelated. The victims had no connection, and all died in different parts of the city.

However, Police Detective Sam Leroy has other ideas, and begins to widen the investigation. But he meets resistance from the most unexpected quarter, and when his life and that of his loved ones are threatened, he faces a choice: back off, or do what he knows he must do…

SAM LEROY RETURNS IN…

# WRONG TIME TO DIE

**'I don't think I've ever seen so much blood.'**
When LAPD Detective Sam Leroy is called to a murder scene, even he is taken aback by the ferocity and savagery of the crime.

Furthermore, there seems to be no motive, which means no obvious suspects.

Believing the two victims themselves hold the key to their own murder, Leroy begins his investigations there, and before long the trail leads him to the island of Catalina, where a terrible secret has remained undiscovered for almost thirty years…

SAM LEROY IS BACK IN
# NO PLACE TO DIE

**A severed head is found beneath the Hollywood Sign.**

Fresh from wrapping his previous case, LAPD Detective Sam Leroy is called to the scene. Now he is tasked with identifying the victim and finding the rest of him.

Not necessarily in that order.

Following up on the few leads they have, Leroy and his partner, Detective Ray Quinn, find themselves unravelling a complex puzzle, one which began two thousand miles from home, and which involves sex, extortion, and ultimately murder.

While Leroy follows the trail, he is feeling himself coming to the end of a relationship, and may possibly be making decisions he might later regret.

## SAM LEROY IS BACK IN
# ANOTHER WAY TO DIE

Seven years ago, LAPD Detective Sam Leroy shot and killed Harlan Cordell, and breathed a sigh of relief that the reign of the infamous Pentagram Killer was over.

But now, the killings have begun again. The police believe they are dealing with some fanatical copycat, but these new murders share a small detail with those before, a detail only the police and the killer would know.

How can today's killer know the intimate details of seven years ago?

Or, as he fears, did Leroy kill the wrong man, leaving the real Pentagram Killer to wait and resume his grisly trade on an unsuspecting city?

# READY TO DIE

**The FIFTH Sam Leroy thriller!**

**In the middle of the night, a woman reports her husband missing. Soon after, his body is found by the side of Mulholland Drive, killed by a single bullet through the head.**

When an adult movie executive is found shot, execution-style, LAPD Detective Sam Leroy and his partner Ray Quinn take on an investigation with minimal clues and no obvious suspects. Statistically, if a murder is not solved within forty-eight hours, it is likely to remain unsolved, and so they are in a race against time to find the killers.

Meanwhile, both men are each facing life-changing events, all of which conspire to make this case all the more challenging…

ALSO BY PHILIP COX

# THE VALUE OF NOTHING

A WET AUTUMN NIGHT
Newspaper reporter Jack Richardson lends his coat
and car to a friend

AN ACCIDENT
Within thirty minutes, Jack's car lies in flames

The crash seems suspicious, and Jack wonders if it
was an accident, or murder.

But if it was murder,
Who was the intended victim?

# THE ANGEL

Investigative reporter Jack Richardson is assigned to a story involving sleaze and a prominent Member of Parliament.

During the investigation, Jack receives a call relating to an old case, one involving the murder of a twenty-year-old girl, suggesting that the case might not be as closed as everybody thinks.

Torn between his assigned story, and one where there might have been a terrible miscarriage of justice, Jack must make a choice.

His decision leads him into a dark place he never knew existed, and which puts him in great personal danger…

# THE COYOTE

London newspaper reporter Jack Richardson is working on a story when he receives the news that his brother-in-law has been found dead in his car.

Having reservations about the verdict of suicide he starts to probe the circumstances, and finds similarities between his brother-in-law's death and the story he is working on, both connected to a chain of events which began three years earlier, and over a thousand miles away…

# THE TRAIL

**Tower Bridge, London**

It is two in the morning, and a young student is seen diving off the bridge into the dark, icy waters below. When his body is recovered from the river, it is found to contain high levels of the drug Ecstasy.

The dead student shared a house with the niece of investigative newspaper reporter Jack Richardson, who decides to retrace the student's last few days to establish the true story behind his death.

However, as Jack follows this trail, he encounters dark forces, and a perilous outcome for both himself and his niece…
#followthetrail

ALSO BY PHILIP COX

# AFTER THE RAIN

Young, wealthy, handsome - Adam Williams is sitting in a bar in a small town in Florida.

Nobody has seen him since.

With the local police unable to trace Adam, his brother Craig and a workmate, Ben Rook, fly out to find him.

However, nothing could have prepared them for the bizarre cat-and-mouse game into which they are drawn as they seek to pick up Adam's trail and discover what happened to him that night.

# DARK EYES OF LONDON

When Tom Raymond receives a call from his ex-wife asking to meet him, he is both surprised and intrigued – maybe she wants a reconciliation?

However, his world is turned upside down when she falls under a tube train on her way to meet him.

Refusing to accept that Lisa jumped, Tom sets out to investigate what happened to her that evening.

Soon, he finds he must get to the truth before some very dangerous people get to him…

# SHE'S NOT COMING HOME

EVERY MORNING
At 8.30 Ruth Gibbons kisses her husband and son goodbye, and goes to work.

EVERY EVENING
At 5pm she finishes work, texts her husband leaving now, and begins her walk home.

EVERY NIGHT
At 5.40 she arrives home, kisses her husband and son, and has dinner with her family.

EXCEPT TONIGHT

# SHOULD HAVE LOOKED AWAY

It began on a Sunday. An ordinary Sunday, and a family trip to the mall.

Will Carter takes his five-year old daughter to the bathroom, and there he is witness to a fatal assault on an innocent stranger.

Over the next few days, Will tries to put the experience behind him, but when he sees one of the killers outside his home, he becomes more and more involved, soon passing the point of no return.

Becoming drawn deeper and deeper into something he does not understand, Will feels increasingly out of his depth and is soon asking where this is going and was the victim as innocent as he first thought…

Printed in Great Britain
by Amazon

21491948R00161